FULL DEATH REHEARSAL

"We were just practicin'," wailed Mavis, "for the play. Just foolin' around. I swear I never dreamed this was gonna happen."

"And Gil sat in the ducking stool?"

Mavis gave a gigantic sniff. "He was saying my lines. Jus' jokin'. Hopped in the stool, and the next thing happened was that big ol' shovel came right down on his head. . . ."

MORE MYSTERIES FROM THE
BERKLEY PUBLISHING GROUP...

DOG LOVERS' MYSTERIES STARRING HOLLY WINTER: With her Alaskan malamute Rowdy, Holly dogs the trails of dangerous criminals. "A gifted and original writer." —Carolyn G. Hart

by Susan Conant

A NEW LEASH ON DEATH	A BITE OF DEATH
DEAD AND DOGGONE	PAWS BEFORE DYING

DOG LOVERS' MYSTERIES STARRING JACKIE WALSH: She's starting a new life with her son and an ex–police dog named Jake... teaching film classes and solving crimes!

by Melissa Cleary

A TAIL OF TWO MURDERS	FIRST PEDIGREE MURDER	THE MALTESE PUPPY
DOG COLLAR CRIME	SKULL AND DOG BONES	MURDER MOST BEASTLY
HOUNDED TO DEATH	DEAD AND BURIED	OLD DOGS

SAMANTHA HOLT MYSTERIES: Dogs, cats, and crooks are all part of a day's work for this veterinary technician... "Delightful!" –Melissa Cleary

by Karen Ann Wilson

EIGHT DOG FLYING	COPY CAT CRIMES
BEWARE SLEEPING DOGS	CIRCLE OF WOLVES

CHARLOTTE GRAHAM MYSTERIES: She's an actress with a flair for dramatics—and an eye for detection. "You'll get hooked on Charlotte Graham!"
—*Rave Reviews*

by Stefanie Matteson

MURDER AT THE SPA	MURDER AT THE FALLS
MURDER AT TEATIME	MURDER ON HIGH
MURDER ON THE CLIFF	MURDER AMONG THE ANGELS
MURDER ON THE SILK ROAD	MURDER UNDER THE PALMS

PEACHES DANN MYSTERIES: Peaches has never had a very good memory. But she's learned to cope with it over the years... Fortunately, though, when it comes to murder, this absentminded amateur sleuth doesn't forgive and forget!

by Elizabeth Daniels Squire

WHO KILLED WHAT'S-HER-NAME?	REMEMBER THE ALIBI
MEMORY CAN BE MURDER	WHOSE DEATH IS IT, ANYWAY?

HEMLOCK FALLS MYSTERIES: The Quilliam sisters combine their culinary and business skills to run an inn in upstate New York. But when it comes to murder, their talent for detection takes over...

by Claudia Bishop

A TASTE FOR MURDER	A DASH OF DEATH
A PINCH OF POISON	MURDER WELL-DONE

A TASTE F·O·R MURDER

Claudia Bishop

BERKLEY PRIME CRIME, NEW YORK

A TASTE FOR MURDER

A Berkley Prime Crime Book / published by arrangement with the author

PRINTING HISTORY
Berkley Prime Crime edition / September 1994

The Penguin Putnam Inc. World Wide Web site address is http://www.penguinputnam.com

ISBN: 0-425-14350-3

Berkley Prime Crime Books are published by The Berkley Publishing Group, a member of Penguin Putnam Inc., 200 Madison Avenue, New York, NY 10016.
The name BERKLEY PRIME CRIME and the BERKLEY PRIME CRIME design are trademarks belonging to Berkley Publishing Corporation.

PRINTED IN THE UNITED STATES OF AMERICA

10 9 8 7 6 5

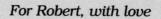

For Robert, with love

ACKNOWLEDGMENTS

This novel was supported by my good friends Nancy Kress, Miriam Monfredo, and Patricia Trunzo. My sister Whit supplied information on menus, recipes, and culinary technique. She is a far better cook than my interpretation would suggest.

The Cast of Characters

The Inn at Hemlock Falls
the staff
Sarah Quilliam—the owner
Margaret Quilliam—her sister, the chef
John Raintree—the manager
Doreen Muxworthy—head housekeeper
Peter Williams—assistant manager
Frank Torelli—a *sous* chef
Bjorn Hjalsted—a *sous* chef
Kathleen Kiddermeister—a waitress
Julie Offenbach—a waitress
Dina Muir—the receptionist
Nate—the bartender
Mike—the groundskeeper
(Also part-time waitresses, bartenders, and housemaids)
the guests
Amelia Hallenbeck—a widow
Mavis Collinwood—her companion
Keith Baumer—a bachelor
Edward Lancashire—a bachelor
The Reverend Willy Max—an evangelist

Members of the Chamber of Commerce
Elmer Henry—the mayor
Gil Gilmeister—a car dealer
Tom Peterson—his business partner
Christopher Croh—a bar owner
Nadine Gilmeister—Gil's wife
Harvey Bozzel—advertising agency owner
Howie Murchison—town justice and local lawyer
Mark Anthony Jefferson—a banker
Esther West—dress shop owner
Marge Schmidt—diner owner
Betty Hall—Marge's partner
Ralph Lorenzo—newspaper publisher
Norm Pasquale—high school band director
The Right Reverend Dookie Shuttleworth—a minister
Harland Peterson—farmer, and president of the Agway
   cooperative
Freddie Bellini—a mortician
Miriam Doncaster—a librarian

The Sheriff's Department
Myles McHale—the sheriff
Dave Kiddermeister—a deputy

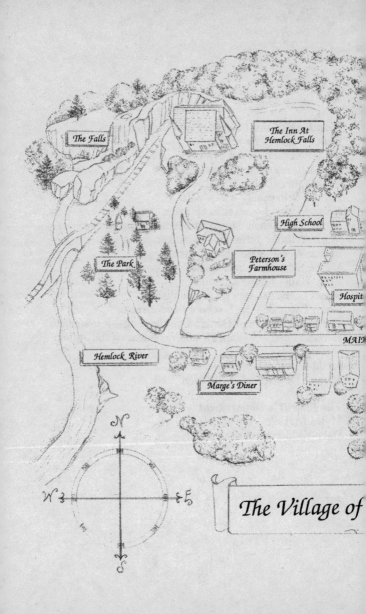

The Falls

The Inn At
Hemlock Falls

High School

The Park

Peterson's
Farmhouse

Hospit

MAI

Hemlock River

Marge's Diner

N

W   E

The Village of

Football Field

Paramount Paint

ROUTE 96

TO ITHACA

Quik Freeze

Peterson's Transport

City Hall

STREET

Hemlock Falls Gazette

Trailer Park

Wal-Mart

Hemlock Falls

The Marriott Hotel

A TASTE
F · O · R
MURDER

CHAPTER 1

Elmer Henry, mayor of Hemlock Falls, swallowed the last spoonful of zabaglione, disposed of the crystallized mint leaf with a loud crunch, and burped in satisfaction. He whacked the Hemlock Falls Chamber of Commerce official gavel and rose to his feet. This familiar signal jerked Sarah Quilliam out of a daydream involving rum punch, Caribbean beaches, and a lifeguard. She grabbed her notebook, scrawled "HFCOC Minutes," and tried to look attentive.

Elmer looked down the length of the banquet table with a somewhat bovine expression of pleasure. Twenty of the twenty-four members of the Chamber looked placidly back. The imminence of the annual celebration of Hemlock History Days brought the members out in force. The corps of regulars—Quill, the mayor, Marge Schmidt, Tom Peterson, and Gilbert Gilmeister among them—were swelled considerably; like Easter, Hemlock History Days offered unbelievers a chance to hedge their bets.

Oblivious to the command of the gavel, Marge Schmidt and Betty Hall held a *sotto voce* conversation concerning their mutually expressed preference to die rather than consume one more bite of suspect foreign substances such as the Italian pudding just served them. Quill rejected various witty rejoinders in defense of her sister's cooking and opted for a dignified silence.

Elmer rapped the gavel with increasingly louder thwacks

1

until Marge and Betty shut up and settled into their seats. "This meeting is called to order," Elmer said. He nodded to Dookie Shuttleworth, minister of the Hemlock Word of God Reform Church.

Dookie was thin, rather shabbily dressed, and had a gentle, bemused expression; under stress, input frequently vanished altogether from Dookie's hard drive, a circumstance wholly unrelated to his vocation and met with tolerance by his parishioners. He wiped his napkin firmly across his mouth and stood up for the invocation. "Lord, bless this gathering of our weekly session, and all its members." He paused, looked thoughtful, and suppressed a belch. "Most especially, the management of the Hemlock Falls Inn, Meg and Sarah Quilliam, for this fine repast."

Quill smiled and murmured an acknowledgment, which Dookie ignored in his earnest pursuit of the Lord's attention. "Lord, if you see fit, please send us fine weather and generous folks for the celebration of Hemlock Falls History Days next week. May these men and women seek you out, Lord, particularly in Your house here at Hemlock Falls. When the collection plate is passed, may they open their hearts and more, in Your service. As you know, Lord, the church checking account . . ."

Elmer Henry cleared his throat.

Dookie concluded hastily, "All these things we ask in Jesus' name. Amen."

"Amen," echoed the assembled members.

"Hadn't you ought to ask the good Lord for blessings on our stummicks so we don't end up in the hospital after eatin' this pudding?" Marge Schmidt demanded. A principal in the only other restaurant in town, Marge's German heritage was evident in her fair hair, ruddy complexion, and blue eyes. The protuberance of those eyes, the double chin, and the belligerence were all her own.

Quill straightened in indignation.

Marge continued blandly, "Made with raw eggs, this stuff. What d'ya call it? Zabyig-something."

"Zabaglione," said Quill. She pushed back her mass of red hair with one slim hand and said mendaciously, "It's one of Meg's eggless varieties."

"It's made with raw eggs everywheres else," said Marge. "You won't find raw eggs in good old American food. Strictly against the New York State Department of Health instructions. Din't you and your sister get that notice they sent out last week? Got one down to the diner if you need a copy."

"Salmonella," interjected Marge's companion and business partner, Betty Hall. "All of us in the restaurant business got that notice. Maybe that sister of yours can't read."

Quill reflected that nobody, including the patrons of the Hemlock Hometown Diner (Family Food! And Fast!), got along with Marge and Betty, and a response would invite acrimony. The first law of successful innkeeping was to maintain neutrality, if not outright peace. "I can't imagine anyone getting sick on Hemlock Falls cooking, Marge," she said diplomatically. "Yours *or* ours."

Marge rocked back in her chair, to the potential danger of the oak. "Me, either. No, ma'am. But that's something different from bein' in violation of the American law with weird Italian food. Betty and me stick to pizza. And this-here pudding is a clear violation of the law. Right, Sheriff McHale?"

Myles McHale nodded expressionlessly and dropped a wink in Quill's direction. He was looking especially heroic this afternoon, and Quill made a mental note to ask him if he'd ever been a lifeguard. With that chest, it was certainly likely.

Myles said, "Why don't I just go ahead and arrest both Meg and Quill, Marge? Been wanting to do it anyhow. Locking Quill up may be the only way I'll get her to marry me. And I'd have Meg's cooking all to myself."

"Ha, ha." Marge adjusted her blue nylon bowling jacket with a sniff and subsided, muttering, "Eggless, my ass."

"Let's get to the agenda," Elmer said. "First off, Quill, will you read the minutes from the last meeting?"

"Shall I move to dispense with everything but the agenda for today?" Quill asked. She hadn't translated her scrawled shorthand and wasn't at all sure she could read last week's notes out loud.

"She can't do that," said Marge. "She's the secretary. The secretary can't move not to read the minutes."

"Then I'll so move," said Myles.

"Let's just get to the agenda for today," said Elmer. "History Days is less than seventy-two hours away, unless everyone's forgotten. What's the status as of last week, Quill?"

Quill squinted at her notes. "Booths. Four *P*'s," she read uncertainly.

There was an expectant silence.

Four *P*'s. Quill tugged at her lower lip. Four *P*'s . . . "Parade. Play. Parking . . ." She tugged harder. "Promotion!" She smiled triumphantly. "We need a report on the status of the booths, on the parade, and on the rehearsals for the play. . . ."

Elmer deciphered the remaining *P* with no trouble; Quill had been Chamber secretary for five years. Promotion was adman Harvey Bozzel's job. "So the first thing is the booths. How many we got registered, Howie?"

Howie Murchison, local attorney and justice of the peace, paged methodically through a manila folder drawn from his briefcase. "One hundred and twenty-two, as of yesterday." He peered deliberately at Quill over his wire-rimmed glasses. "I'll go slowly so you can get the information *into* the minutes. Twenty-three home-crafts. Sixteen jewelry. Fifty-eight assorted pottery and painting. Six food. Seven habadashery, that is to say, T-shirts, straw hats, and other clothing items. Eleven miscellaneous, such as used books, something referred to as 'collectibles,' and Gil's display of the new line of Buicks. Forty-three percent of the registration fees have been prepaid for a total of six hundred and fifty-nine dollars and forty-six cents."

Quill scrawled: 101. 23 ditz. 16 ? ? ? ? $659, 46 is 47%. Then, after a moment's thought: Re. NYS memo: Meg.

"And the parade report?" Elmer turned to Norm Pasquale, principal of the high school.

Norm bounced to his feet. "The varsity band's been rehearsing all week. They sound just terrific. The Four-H club has fourteen kids on horses signed up to ride. We've got eight floats, down one from last year because Chet's Hardware went out of business after the Wal-Mart moved in." He sat down.

Elmer nodded matter-of-factly. "I told Chet he'd never get a dollar and a half a pound for roofing nails. What about the play, Esther? Rehearsals going okay there?"

Esther West owned the only dress shop (West's Best) in

Hemlock Falls. She was director of the re-creation of the Hemlock Falls seventeenth century witch trial, *The Trial of Goody Martin*, a popular feature of History Days. She frowned and adjusted the bodice of her floral print dress, then patted a stiff auburn curl into place over her ear. "I do believe that the Clarissa's sickening for flu."

A murmur of dismay greeted this statement.

"Who's playing Clarissa Martin this year?" asked Quill.

"Julie Offenbach, Craig's girl."

"Oh, my." Quill knew her. A wannabe Winona Ryder, Julie spent the summers between high-school semesters waitressing at the Inn. "She'll be crushed."

"You got that right!" hooted Gil Gilmeister. Even Quill, a relative newcomer to Hemlock Falls, knew Gil had been a star quarterback for the high school twenty years before; like Rabbit Angstrom, he'd gone into that quintessential small-town American business—car sales. Unlike his fictional counterpart, he was filled by more *Sturm* than *Angst*, with a boisterous enthusiasm for Buicks, Marge Schmidt, and town activities not unrelated to his days on the football field. "Go-o-o-o *Clarissa!*" he shouted now, thumping a ham-sized fist on the table.. "Splat! Splat! Splat!"

The witch trial dramatized the real seventeenth-century Clarissa's death by pressing. Most pre-Colonial American villages burned, hanged, or drowned their witches, and Hemlockians were inordinately proud of their ancestors' unique style of execution—Hemlock Falls witches had been pressed to death. Although any large flat surface would have done, Hemlock Falls citizens of bygone days dropped a barn door on the condemned, then piled stones on the door until the victim succumbed to hemorrhaging, suffocation, or a myocardial infarction. Julie, as Clarissa Martin, would be replaced by a hooded dummy at the critical moment, but there was a wonderful bit of histrionics as "Clarissa" was driven off to await her fate. Julie had rehearsed with enormous relish for weeks.

"Doesn't Julie have an understudy or something?" asked Betty Hall. "No?" She jerked her head at her partner. "Marge here. She could do it. She's a real quick study. Memorizes the specials at the diner every night, just like that." She snapped her fingers.

Elmer, perhaps thinking of the size of the barn door required to squash a dummy of Marge-like proportions, not to mention the creation of a new, more elephantine dummy to replace the one traditionally used for years, said sharply, "Budget," which puzzled everyone but Quill, whose thoughts had been running along the same lines but in a much less practical way.

"Marge'd be terrific," said Gil Gilmeister earnestly. Since almost everyone at the table—with the possible exception of Dookie Shuttleworth—knew that Marge and Gil had been a hot item for several years, Gil's support was discounted without any discussion. "Although," Esther whispered to Quill, "if Nadine Gilmeister could get herself out of those Syracuse malls long enough to do right by the poor man so he didn't have to spend his nights over to the diner, maybe more people would listen to him." Elmer rapped the gavel loudly, and Esther jerked to attention.

"What do you want to do then, Esther? Appoint an understudy?"

"It should be somebody stageworthy. Somebody with presence. And good-looking. The execution is the highlight of *The Trial of Goody Martin*. It's what everyone comes to see." Esther's eyes glinted behind her elaborately designed glasses. "When the actors pile the stones on the barn door, the audience should be moved to enthusiasm as Clarissa's blood spews out. Most years, as you've observed, the tourists join in."

"Well, they'll more likely laugh if fat ol' Marge is supposed to be under there," said Harland Peterson, the president of the farmer's co-op. A large, weatherbeaten man, Harland drove the sledge that carried "Clarissa Martin" from the pavilion stage to the site of the execution. "No offense, Marge," he said, in hasty response to her outraged grunt. "Now, the ducking stool—that's gonna be just fine. That ol' tractor of mine'll lift you into that pond, no problem. But we get a dummy your size under that barn door, it's gonna stick out a mile. What about Quill, there? She'd be great."

Harvey (The Ad Agency That Adds Value!) Bozzel cleared his throat. "I'd have to agree." His tanned cheeks creased in a golf-pro grin. "Try this one on, folks. 'Quill fills the bill.' "

Quill, who so far had managed to avert Harvey's advertising plans for the Inn (No Whine, Just Fine Wine When You

Dine!), said feebly, "I don't really think . . ."

"I'm not sure that Julie's vomiting is going to continue through next week," said Esther thoughtfully, "but you never know. And of course, the costume is black, and just shows everything."

Myles said, "I move to nominate Sarah Quilliam as understudy for Julie Offenbach."

Quill glared at him.

"I second," said Harland Peterson.

"All in favor?" said Elmer, sweeping the assembly with a glance. "Against?" He registered Marge's, Betty's, and Gil's upraised hands without a blink. "Carried. Quill takes Julie's place as Clarissa Martin, if necessary."

Quill experienced a strong desire to bang her head against the solid edge of the banquet table. This was followed by an even stronger desire to bang Myles McHale's head against the banquet table, since he'd started the whole mess in the first place. She took a deep breath and was preparing to argue, when the Hemlock Inn's business manager, John Raintree, appeared at the door to the Banquet Room.

"Yo, John!" said Gil. "Mighty glad to see you. Sorry I missed our meeting last night. I figured you and Tom could handle any stuff that needed to be decided anyways, and I had some things come up at home."

Esther looked significantly at Quill and mouthed, "Nadine!" Then more audibly, "Poor Gil."

"No problem, Gil," said John easily, "but I won't be able to get the audit to you until next week."

"That's okay with you, innit, Mark?" Gil wiped a handkerchief over his sweaty neck. "It's not gonna hold up the loan or anything?"

Mark Anthony Jefferson, vice-president of the Hemlock Falls Savings and Loan, tightened his lips. "Why don't we discuss this later, Gil? Your partner should be present anyway, and John's on Quill's time, now."

"Oh, I don't mind," said Quill. "John's moonlighting has never interfered with our business." She looked hopefully at him. "Do you need me, John?"

"Yep."

Quill sprang out of her chair with relief. "I'll be right there.

Would you all excuse me? Esther, could you take over the minutes? I'd appreciate it."

Quill made her way swiftly into the hall and closed the door behind her. "Just in the nick of time. I was about to be forced into taking Julie Offenbach's star turn. I have no desire to be dunked and squashed in front of two hundred gawking tourists." She frowned at his glum expression. "Any problems?"

John claimed three-quarters Onondaga blood, whose heritage gave him skin the color of a bronze medallion and hair as thickly black as charred toast. He had an erratic, whimsical sense of humor that Quill found very un-Indian. Not, Quill thought, that she knew all that much about Indians, John in particular. He'd been with them less than a year, and for the first time, the Inn was showing a profit. Despite the money he made between his job at the Inn and his small accounting business, John lived modestly, driving an old car, wearing carefully cleaned suits that were years out of date. He refused to touch alcohol, for reasons tacitly understood between them, and never discussed his personal life. He nodded. "Guest complaint. And one of the waitresses called in sick for the three to eleven shift. Doreen's on vacation this week; otherwise she could pinch-hit. So that means we're short two staff for the dinner trade."

"Did you try the backup list?"

John nodded Yes to the phone calls and No to the results. "Exam week for summer session," he said briefly.

"Damn." Most of the summer season help came from nearby Cornell University. "All right. I'll take the shift myself. Unless Meg's short-handed in the kitchen?"

"Not so far."

"And the guest complaint?" She swallowed nervously. "No digestive problems or anything like that? Meg had Caesar salad on the menu for lunch, and she just refuses to omit the raw egg."

"Not food poisoning, no. But we'd better comply with the raw egg ban, Quill. We're liable to a fine if we don't."

"I know." Quill bit her thumb. "*You* tell Meg, will you, John? I mean, I should take care of this guest problem."

"Tell your sister she can't use raw eggs anymore? Not me, Quill. No way. I'd walk three miles over hot coals for you, shave my head bald for you, but I will not tell your sister how to cook."

"John," said Quill, with far more decisiveness than she felt, "you can't be afraid of my sister. She's all of five feet two and a hundred pounds, dripping wet. That makes her a *third* your size, probably."

"You're half again as tall as she is, and *you're* afraid of your sister."

"Then you're fired."

"You can't fire me. I quit."

They grinned at each other.

"I'll flip you for it," said Quill.

John pulled a nickel from his pocket and sent it spinning with a quick snap of his thumb. "Call it."

"Heads."

"Tails." John caught the coin and showed her an Indian-head nickel, tail-up. "My lucky coin. Came to me from my grandfather, the Chief. I told you about the Chief before. You want to keep this in your pocket while you tell her no more raw eggs?"

"I'll take care of the guest first. Is it a him or a her?"

"Her."

"Perennial?" This was house code for the retired couples who flooded the Inn in the spring, disappeared in autumn, and reappeared with the early crocus. In general, Quill liked them. They tended to be good guests, rarely, if ever, stiffing the management, and except for a universal disinclination to tip the help more than ten percent, treated the support staff well. This was in marked contrast to traveling businessmen who left used condoms rolled under the beds—which sent Doreen, their obsessive-compulsive housekeeper, into fits— or businesswomen demanding big-city amenities like valet services, a gym, and pool boys.

"It's an older woman," said John. He paused reflectively. "Kind of mean."

"I'm good with mean." She glanced at her watch; fifteen minutes before the start of the afternoon shift. She'd just make it if John's complainer didn't have a real problem. "The wine shipment's due at four. The bill of lading is . . . um . . . somewhere on my desk."

"I'll find it. My grandfather, the Chief . . ."

"Was a tracker," Quill finished for him. "I'd like to meet your grandfather. I'd like to meet your grandmother, too, as a matter of fact—" She stopped, aware that the flippant conversation was heading into dangerous waters. John's quiet, lonely existence was his business. "Never mind. Where is she?"

"Lobby." He grinned, teeth white in his dark face. "Good luck."

Quill took the steps up to the lobby with a practiced smile firmly in place. She and Meg had bought the twenty-seven-room Inn two years before with the combined proceeds of her last art show and Meg's early and wholly unexpected widowhood. Driving through Central New York on a short vacation, Meg and Quill had come upon the Inn unexpectedly. They came back. Shouldered between the granite ridges left by glaciers, on land too thin for farming, Inn and village were fragrant in spring, lush in summer, brilliant with color in the fall. Even the winters weren't too bad, for those tolerant of heavy snowfall, and Hemlockians resigned themselves to a partial dependence on tourists in search of peak season vacations. The Inn had always attracted travelers; as a commercial property, it proved easy to sell and less easy to manage. It had passed from hand to hand over the years. New owners bought and sold with depressing regularity, most defeated by the difficulty of targeting exactly the right customer market. The relationships among longtime residents of Hemlock Falls were so labyrinthine, it was a year before Quill realized that Marge Schmidt and Tom Peterson, Gil Gilmeister's partner, had owned the Inn some years before. Marge had made a stab at modernizing. She installed wall-to-wall Astro-turf indoors ("Wears good," said Marge some months after Quill removed it. "Whattaya, stupid?") and plywood trolls in the garden.

The reception-lobby was all that remained of the original eighteenth-century Inn, and the low ceilings and leaded windows had a lot to do with Quill's final decision to buy it. Guests were in search of an authentic historical experience, as long as it was accompanied by heated towel racks, outstanding mattresses, and her sister's terrific food. If they could restore the Inn with the right degree of twentieth-century luxury, people would come in busloads.

Quill had stripped layers of paint and wallpaper from the plaster-and-lathe walls, replaced vinyl-backed draperies with simple valances of Scottish lace, and tore up the Astro-turf carpeting. The sisters had refinished the floors and wainscoting to a honeyed pine, and landscaped the grounds.

The leaded windows in the lobby framed a view of the long sweep of lawn and gardens to the lip of Hemlock Gorge. Creamy wool rugs, overwoven in florals of peach, celadon, taupe, and sky blue, lightened the effect of the low ceiling. Two massive Japanese urns flanked the reception desk where Dina Muir checked guests in. Mike, the groundskeeper, filled the urns every other morning with flowers from the Inn's extensive perennial gardens. As usual this early in July, they held Queen Elizabeth roses, Oriental lilies of gold, peach, and white, and spars of purple heather.

The lobby was welcoming and peaceful. Quill smiled at Dina, the daytime receptionist, and raised an inquiring eyebrow. Dina made an expressive face, and jerked her head slightly in the direction of the fireplace.

An elderly woman with a fierce frown sat on the pale leather couch in front of the cobblestone hearth. A woman at least thirty years her junior stood behind the chair. The younger one had a submissive, tentative air for all the world like that anachronism, the companion. Quill's painter's eye registered almost automatically the lush figure behind the modestly buttoned shirtwaist. She could have used a little makeup, Quill thought, besides the slash of red lipstick she allowed herself. Something in the attitude of the two women made her revise that thought; the elder one clearly dominated her attendant and just as clearly disapproved of excess.

"I'm Sarah Quilliam," she said, her hand extended in welcome.

"I'm Mavis Collinwood?" said the younger woman in a southern drawl that seemed to question it. Her brown hair was lacquered like a Chinese table and back-combed into a tightly restrained knot. "Mrs. Hallenbeck doesn't shake hands," Mavis, in a voice both assured and respectful. "Her arthritis is a little painful this time of year."

Only the glaucous clouding of Mrs. Hallenbeck's blue eyes and the gnarled hands told Quill that she must be over eighty. Her skin was smooth, shadowed by a fine net of wrinkles at eye and mouth. She sat rigidly upright, chin high to avoid the sagging of throat and jowl. Her figure was slim rather than gaunt, and Quill took in the expensive watch and the elegant Chanel suit.

Mrs. Hallenbeck fixed Quill with a basilisk glare. "I wish to speak to the owner."

"You are," said Quill cheerfully. "What can I do for you?"

"Our reservations were not in order." The old lady was clearly displeased.

"I'm very sorry," said Quill, going to the ledger. "You weren't recorded in the book? I'll arrange a room for you immediately."

"We were in the book. I had requested the third-floor suite. The one overlooking the gorge, with that marvelous balcony that makes you feel as though you were flying." She paused, and the clouded blue eyes teared up a little. "My husband and I stayed here, years ago. I am retracing our days together."

Quill's look expressed sympathy.

"That girl of yours. She put us into two rooms on the second floor. It overlooks the back lawn. It is not a suite. It is not what I require. I demanded to see the owner, and John Raintree said that these arrangements had been made and could not be changed."

"Let me see what we can do." Quill checked the booking: *Hallenbeck, Amelia, and Collinwood, Mavis.* The reservation had been made three months ago, by one of the gilt-edged travel agencies in South Carolina. Paid for in advance with an American Express Gold card. There it was: *Requested Suite 312–314.* And just as clearly marked in John's handwriting were their current rooms: *Confirmed 101 and 104.* "Did Mr. Raintree say anything at all about why the rooms were booked this way? He's a wonderful help to us, Mrs. Hallenbeck, and rarely makes mistakes. It's not like him to make a change like this without a reason."

"He did not say one word." The tones were decisive. If she'd had a whip, she would have cracked it.

Quill suppressed a grin. "I'm certain that no one's in three-fourteen. Shall we go up and see if it's suitable for you?"

Mrs. Hallenbeck nodded regally. The three of them went up the stairs. Any notion that John may have booked them into first-floor rooms due to Mrs. Hallenbeck's arthritis was quickly dispelled; she took the steps with a lot less effort than Mavis Collinwood, who began to breathe heavily at the second-floor landing. Quill unlocked the door to the suite and stepped aside to let them enter.

Quill loved all twenty-seven rooms at the Inn, but 314 was one of her favorites. A white Adams-style fireplace domi-nated the wall opposite the balcony. The carpeting was crisp navy-blue. The couch and occasional chairs were covered in blue-and-yellow chintz, the colors of Provence. French doors opened out onto a white-painted iron balcony cantilevered over the lip of Hemlock Gorge, giving 314 a panoramic view of the Falls.

Quill stepped out and watched the cascade of water over granite. Bird calls came from the pines and joined the water's rush. Sweet smells from the gardens and the hemlock groves mingled with the daffodil-scent of fresh water. Mrs. Hallenbeck followed Quill onto the balcony, her chin jutting imperiously. She inhaled. "Dogwood," she stated precisely, "and one of the scented roses."

"Scented Cloud," said Quill. "It's a lovely rose, too. We grow it out back."

"This," Mrs. Hallenbeck said, "is what I asked for. I will walk in the hemlock glade after dinner."

"I'm sorry about the confusion, Mrs. Hallenbeck." Quill drew her inside the suite. "I'll see that your luggage is brought up here. Would you like some tea? I can have it brought to you, or you can have it in the dining room."

"An English tea? I believe your brochure described an English tea."

"Yes. A traditional high tea, with scones, Devonshire cream, and watercress sandwiches."

"Perhaps there will be no charge for that, since I have been seriously inconvenienced."

Quill, slightly taken aback, swallowed a laugh. "I'll be sure that there isn't."

"Then we shall be down after Mavis unpacks us." She

nodded dismissal. Quill meekly took the hint, and went back to the Chamber meeting. She took the stairs slowly, not, she told herself, because she wasn't anxious to get back to the meeting, but because it was a beautiful July day, the Inn was booked solid for the week of History Days, and a relaxed country environment was one of the many reasons she'd left her career as an artist to move to Central New York.

"There you are," said Esther West, as Quill stepped into the lobby. "We're taking a bit of a break before we go back and vote."

"Somebody else volunteered to take Julie Offenbach's place?" Quill said with hope. "I've got a couple of ideas for you, Esther. What about Miriam Doncaster? You know, the librarian. She's a heck of a swimmer. I couldn't swim to the side of the pond as gracefully as she could after being dunked in the ducking stool."

"No. Everyone agrees you'd be the best Clarissa. Marge wants us to vote on whether or not the monthly Chamber meetings should be held at the Hemlock Home Diner instead of here."

"Oh," said Quill.

"But we all decided to take a bio break before we voted, and anyhow, Myles and Howie both thought that you'd probably want to be there for the discussion part."

"You bet I would," said Quill. "That monthly Chamber lunch is a good piece of business. John'll have my guts for garters if I lose it. Maybe I'd better have him sit in." An increasingly noisy argument from the lobby succeeded in drawing her attention. "Excuse me a second, Esther. Dina seems to need help."

Dina, one of the Cornell Hotel School graduate students on whom the Inn depended for much of its staff, was scowling ferociously at a middle-aged man at the counter. An elegantly dressed man in his thirties stood behind him, watching with interest.

"Can I give you a hand here, Dina?"

"I've been trying to tell this guy that we're booked for the week. He said the Marriott called and made reservations for him this morning." She scowled even harder. "Then he said well maybe the Marriott forgot to call, but that places 'like this' always hold back a room in case of emergencies, and he wants it."

"Keith Baumer," said the middle-aged man. He extended his hand. Quill took it. He grinned and wiggled his fingers suggestively in her palm. "You the manager, or what?"

Quill freed herself. "I'm really sorry, Mr. Baumer, but Dina's right, of course. We're booked for the week."

"Come on, kiddo, I need some help here. I've got a sales convention at the Marriott, and the bastards overbooked. I hear this is the only decent place to get a room. I know you guys; you're always holding something in reserve. Whyn't you check the reservations book yourself? I'm here for the week. I don't mind paying top dollar." He grinned and edged closer to her.

Quill took two steps back, hit the counter, and repeated, "I'm sorry, Mr. Baumer. We simply don't have a room available." The phone shrilled twice, and Dina picked it up as Quill continued, "We'll be happy to call a few nearby places for you—"

"Quill?" said Dina.

"—but I'm afraid you're going to have a rough time if you want to stay close to your sales meeting. This is the height of the tourist season . . ."

"Quill!" Dina tugged at her sleeve. "We just got a cancellation. Couple that was booked for the week for their honeymoon, Mr. and Mrs. Sands. Only it's Mrs. Sands that just called, and she said they had a fight at the wedding and the whole thing's *off*! Isn't that sad?"

"There," said Baumer. "Not that I believe that phony phone call for one little minute. What? Ya got a button down there?"

Quill counted to ten. "Would you check him in please, Dina? Enjoy your stay with us, Mr. Baumer."

He cocked his head, swept a look from her ankles to her chin, gave her a thumbs-up sign of approval, then leered at Dina. "Okay, dolly. You take American Express Traveller's Cheques?"

Quill looked longingly at the Japanese urn nearest Baumer's thick neck.

"Too heavy," said the man who'd been waiting behind Baumer. "Now, that replica of the Han funeral horse on the coffee table? Just the right size for a good whack."

Quill choked back a laugh. "Are you here to check in?

Let me help you over here." He was, thought Quill, one of the best-looking men she'd ever seen, with thick black hair attractively sprinkled with gray. He wore a beautifully tailored sports coat.

"Quill," Esther called, "we're going back to vote now."

"I don't mind waiting for young Dina, there," he said. "I'm Edward Lancashire, by the way."

"We're looking forward to having you at the Inn, Mr. Lancashire."

"You go ahead to your vote. I'll be just fine."

Quill went back to the conference room and sat down, a little breathless.

"Who was *that*?" hissed Esther. "The second one, I mean. The first one sounded horrible."

"The first one *was* horrible. Speaking of horrible, where's Marge?"

"In the kitchen." Quill froze. Esther looked at her watch. "This darn meeting's got to get over soon; I've got way too much to do on the costumes."

"The kitchen? Marge is in Meg's kitchen?"

"She was headed that way."

"Oh, God," said Quill. "I'll be right back."

Quill pushed open the kitchen door to silence, which meant one of two things: either Meg had discovered Marge among her recipe books and had killed her, or nobody was there.

The flagstone floor was clean and polished. The cobblestone fireplace in the corner, where Meg had a Maine grill to do her lobsters, crackled quietly behind the Thermo Glass doors that kept the heat from the rest of the kitchen. Meg's precious copper bowls and pans hung undisturbed in shiny rows from the pot hanger. No sign of either Marge or for that matter, her sister. Quill pulled at her lower lip, went to Meg's recipe cabinet, pulled out the lowest drawer, and flipped through the zs. *Zuppa d'Inglese*, zucchini, zarda, zabaglione. She edged the zabaglione card carefully out of the file. Was that a greasy thumbprint? It was. But was it Marge's or Meg's? And if it were Marge's, did that mean she was going to place a phone call to the Board of Health? She read the recipe gloomily. There it was in Meg's elegant script: four raw eggs per serving. She closed the file drawer and marched determinedly back to the conference room.

It was empty, except for Myles.

"Where'd they all go?" Quill demanded. "Did they vote on whether or not to move the meetings to Marge's diner?"

"Since neither you nor Marge were here, Howie voted to table. Esther asked for an adjournment because she's still sewing costumes. I waited for you to see what you wanted to do tonight. Would you like to go to supper? Can you get away about eight-thirty?"

"Myles, can you take a fingerprint from a recipe card?"

"Yes, Quill," Myles said patiently. "Do you want to go to supper? I thought I'd make a stir-fry at my place."

"Where was Marge, when I wasn't here?"

"I don't know. She came back in here grinning and said she had to make a phone call. Why?"

Quill gazed at him thoughtfully. Myles had strong views on law and order. He had an annoying tendency to spout phrases like "due process" and "probable cause." Those gray eyes would get even icier if she asked him to arrest Marge for snooping. That strong jaw would set like an antilock brake at the merest suggestion of a phone tap on the Hemlock Home Diner. There was no way he'd test a recipe card for fingerprints without uncomfortable questions regarding the existence of an eggless zabaglione.

She decided to answer his first question, and solve the Marge problem herself. "Why don't you come by the kitchen for dinner about eleven, after we close? You made dinner last night. It's my turn."

"Fine." He kissed her on the temple. Quill wasn't fooled for a minute. This was a man who'd lock her in stir the instant she whacked Marge up the side of the head with Meg's skillet.

Halfway out the door, Myles turned to look at her. "You sure nothing's wrong? You're not coming down with anything, are you?" His eyes narrowed. "Wait. I know that look. You're fulminating."

"No," said Quill absently. "One of the waitresses is, though." She gasped and glanced at her watch. "The second shift! It's after three o'clock! Damn!" She sprinted past him and ran down the hall.

CHAPTER 2

Quill dashed through the lobby to the locker room at the back of the kitchen. The fresh odor of Meg's private stock of coffee filled the air, but there was no sign of her sister, just two assistants scrubbing pots at the triple sink. Quill grabbed a clean uniform and looked at her watch: three-ten. No time to go to her own quarters and change into more comfortable shoes. She changed her silk blouse and challis skirt for a freshly laundered uniform and swung into the dining room. Three tables were already occupied for tea. John stood at the opposite end, carefully polishing the silver tea urn.

"John, where's Meg?"

"Supervising the fish delivery in the back. Red fish in lime for the special tonight."

"I think Marge Schmidt went through the recipe file and found we use raw eggs in the zabaglione."

"Yeah?"

"Yeah. Thing is, I told her Meg had an eggless version."

"Even Marge isn't going to believe in eggless zabaglione." He thought for a moment. "Dookie Shuttleworth might."

"Did you see Marge in the kitchen?"

"No. That what's-her-name—Mavis Collinwood—went through on her way out back." He rubbed harder at the tea urn, his lips tight. "Said she wanted to explore."

"Don't you think we ought to do something?"

"Like what?"

Quill wrapped a strand of hair around her finger and pulled on it.

"I don't know," she confessed. She let the curl spring back. "Why did you book Mrs. Hallenbeck on the second floor when she'd asked for the best suite in the house three months in advance?"

John rubbed at a spot on the handle and didn't reply.

"And she's not mean," Quill continued. "Rather sweet, as a matter of fact. In terrific shape for her age. She's a little bossy, but God, at that age, that's allowed."

John shook his head. "Move them both to the first floor."

"Why?"

"Bad feeling."

"Oh." John's bad feelings were not to be taken lightly. "About what exactly? Isn't her credit good? She's paying for both of them. Should I check with American Express? I *hate* doing that."

John shrugged. "It's not money."

"What then, John?"

"Remember the guy from IBM?"

Quill took a deep breath. "Of course I remember the guy from IBM. Who around here doesn't?"

"Had a bad feeling about that, too."

"He was drunk. And high on coke. He fell over that balcony into the gorge by accident. I can't see Mrs. Hallenbeck stoned on a gallon of Rusty Nails smuggled into her room in a Thermos bottle, which is what that guy did."

"You're the boss." Quill knew that attitude: polite, courteous retreat. He looked at the open archway. "More guests. I'll seat them."

Quill's intention to grab a quick look at the script for Clarissa's speech, probe John for the real reason behind his discomfort with the widow and her companion, and finally, talk to Meg about the raw egg ban and the threat posed by Marge, got lost in the rush of the next six hours. The tea trade was followed by the Early Birds, patrons who took advantage of reduced-cost meals before seven o'clock, then the regular evening trade, and finally, at ten o'clock, a few late diners, Mrs. Hallenbeck and Mavis among them.

They ordered a dinner as enormous as their tea had been. Mavis requested a single glass of the house white, which she sipped all through the meal, and Mrs. Hallenbeck no liquor at all. On one of her trips to the kitchen, Quill hissed to John in passing, "They're both sober as judges."

Just after ten-thirty, Quill stopped to take a rapid survey of the tables. Mrs. Hallenbeck and Mavis were at table two by the big windows that overlooked the gardens. The man in his fifties at table seven was Keith Baumer, who'd said he was part of the overflow crowd from the sales convention at the Marriott on Route 15. Baumer slumped over the menu, smoking a cigarette and flicking the ashes onto the rug. Table twelve held another sole diner—the dark, good-looking Edward Lancashire. After careful deliberation, he'd ordered some of the specialties that had made Meg's reputation: Caesar salad, Steak Tartare, Game Hen à la Quilliam. He finished his Caesar salad with a thoughtful expression, writing briefly in a notebook by his plate. Quill hesitated, alarmed. He looked awfully well-dressed to be a Department of Health inspector, who tended to be weedy, with thin lips and polyester sports coats. The suit on the guy seated at twelve was an Armani. Could Department of Health inspectors afford Armani?

Quill went to Baumer to take his order, one eye mistrust-fully on table twelve.

"Quill," Baumer purred, reaching up to lift her name tag away from her breast pocket. He let it fall back with a smirk. "Let me guess. The hair. Hair that red and curly has gotta be the reason. Looks soft, though, not prickly like porcupine quills."

Quill moved the ashtray nearer his cigarette with a pointed thump. She was tired. Her feet hurt. If Edward Lancashire *was* from the Department of Health, the Inn could be in trouble. She had Marge to fence with and Clarissa's stupid speech to memorize. It'd be another three hours before she could even think of going to bed. If this turkey pushed it, he was going to find out just how prickly she could be. She'd admired Mrs. Hallenbeck's beady stare. She tried it. Baumer jumped a little in his chair. She said politely, "Are you ready to order, sir? I can recommend the Red Fish in Lime, or the Ginger Soy Tenderloin. Either is delicious."

Baumer dropped the menu onto the table, knocking his knife and fork onto the floor. Quill bent over to pick them up. He slipped his hand past her knee up her thigh. She disengaged with the ease of long practice, took the place setting from table six, and laid fresh silverware next to his plate.

Baumer closed the leather-covered menu with an exaggerated pursing of his lips. "Hemlock Inn," he mused. He looked arch. Quill braced herself, then lip-synched silently with him, "Sure I can trust the chef?"

"We're named for the Hemlock Groves, Mr. Baumer, not the poisonous herb. You must have noticed the trees when driving in. A lot of our guests like to walk the path to the foot of the gorge at this time of year. The hemlocks are in full bloom."

She deflected the invitation to join him in a walk after dinner, with gritted teeth, and took his order for the New York strip, medium, no veg, extra sour cream and butter on the baked potato. She cheered up. That meal and the two Manhattans preceding it forecast a short life of waitress-harassing. She crossed the mauve carpeting toward the kitchen, and stopped at the Hallenbeck table. Mavis had teased her hair into a big bubble. The scent of hairspray fought with the perfume of the scarlet lilies in the middle of the table. "How is everything, Mavis, Mrs. Hallenbeck? Are you comfortable? Was your dinner all right?"

"It's just lovely here," said Mavis, "and the room is wonderful. The food! Why, it's just the best I've ever had."

"I am having hot water and lemon after my meal," pronounced Mrs. Hallenbeck. "It's a habit I acquired while traveling abroad with my husband." She lifted her chin. "We prefer England. Although this place is quite English, for an American restaurant." She paused and fixed Quill with a modified version of The Glare. "I assume there is no charge for the hot water?"

"No," said Quill. Then as she reflected on the probability of Mrs. Hallenbeck's next question, "Just for the meal itself."

"Mavis," said Mrs. Hallenbeck disapprovingly, "had the tournedos. Quite the most expensive thing on the menu."

Mavis blushed, and Quill said curiously, "Have you and Mavis been together very long, Mrs. Hallenbeck?"

"Mavis is my companion. We are both impoverished widows." She waved a gnarled hand at Quill. The third finger of her left hand held a diamond the size of an ice rink. "We are companions in loss, on an adventure. I assume that we are eligible for a senior citizen's discount?"

Quill ignored the latter half of this statement and said warmly, "I hope you both find adventure. You're going to stay for the whole week of Hemlock's History Days? Admission is free."

"We will consider it," said Mrs. Hallenbeck regally. She sat up straighter, if that were possible, and said, "Move, please. You are blocking my view of the entrance." Quill stepped sideways. "Mavis! I recognize that person. What is her name?"

Quill turned around and groaned. Marge Schmidt stumped in. She'd exchanged her blue bowling jacket for a pink one, which did nothing to soften her resemblance to an animated tank. Marge's turret eyes swung in their direction.

"Marge!" squealed Mavis. "Coo-ee!" She waved energetically.

"Mavis!" Marge bellowed. She marched up to the table. "So you made it okay!" Mavis got up. The two women embraced. Mavis squealed again. Marge thumped her back with bluff good humor.

"This is a friend of yours, Mavis?" said Mrs. Hallenbeck sternly. "She is dressed abominably. She is too fat."

Quill warmed to Mrs. Hallenbeck.

"You remember Marge Schmidt, Amelia. She ran the Northeast region for a couple of years before she quit to come home here. She runs a restaurant now."

"Northeast region of what?" said Quill.

"Brought that D.O.H. order for you, Quill," Marge said loudly. " 'Bout the salmonella? You din't eat the Italian puddin', did you, Mave?"

"No, not yet," said Mavis, sounding alarmed.

"Nasty," said Marge with satisfaction. "Very nasty."

"Marge," said Quill, "dammit . . ."

"This food is bad?" said Mrs. Hallenbeck. "I don't believe we should pay for a meal if the food is bad."

"Here!" Marge rummaged in the pocket of her bowling jacket and thrust a creased paper at Quill.

Quill took it and said, "Marge, we are well aware . . ."

Marge grabbed it back. "I'll read it to you." Her lips moved and she muttered, "Shipment of beef tainted with E. coli, that ain't it. Here! Wait!" She took a deep breath, preparatory to another bellow.

Quill grabbed the memo, scanned it, and translated the governmentese which boiled down to John's statement of that afternoon: no more raw egg. "Now look, Marge . . ."

"I am ready to go up, Mavis." Mrs. Hallenbeck rapped the tabletop imperatively. "This person is loud. I am tired."

"Now you got the memo, you got no excuse, Quill," said Marge.

"MAVIS!" said Mrs. Hallenbeck loudly.

"All right, all right," Mavis replied, flustered. "Marge. I cain't take time to talk to you now, but I'll see you soon, you hear?"

"Right." Marge nodded ponderously. "We got old times to talk about."

"Northeast manager of what?" said Quill, hoping to divert Marge's attention from further bellicose thunderings about salmonella.

"You got some more damn fools wantin' to eat here," said Marge. "C'mon, Mave, I'll walk out with you."

Quill turned a distracted glance to the maitre d' station. Tom Peterson was waiting there patiently. John was nowhere in sight.

" 'Lo, Tom," said Marge as she walked by. "Stay away from the Italian puddin'." Marge disappeared in the direction of the front door. Mavis supported the miffed Mrs. Hallenbeck up the stairs. Quill wondered if she'd actually serve time if she gave Marge a fat lip.

"I should have made reservations," said Tom Peterson. "Is the kitchen still open?"

"Oh, sure, Tom." Quill picked up a menu. "How many in your party?"

"Just one other. He's looking at the mural in the men's room. He'll be out in a moment."

Quill took another menu. "Would you like to sit near the window?" Tom followed her to the table next to Edward Lancashire. The Petersons had lived in Hemlock Falls for close to three hundred years, their fortunes fluctuating with the business competency of each generation. A shrewd nineteenth-century Peterson had boosted the family fortune for some considerable period of time through investments in railroads. Tom, whose pale eyes and attenuated frame were a diluted version of his richer ancestor, had stuck with the transportation business after his brief excursion into the hotel with Marge; Gil's Buick partnership was part of Tom's larger trucking firm.

Quill seated Tom, then banged into the kitchen with Baumer's order in one hand. "Hey!" she said to her sister. "I quit."

Meg stood at the Aga. She'd inherited their father's rich dark hair and gray eyes, along with his volatile Welsh temper. Quill was an expert at reading her sister's moods; Meg's hair stood on end, which meant that the cooking was going well.

"The sauces are really behaving," said Meg, ignoring the familiar imperative. "I think it's the weather. I wasn't sure about the dessert for the Chamber lunch, though. Damn mint leaves kept wilting. Got the sugar syrup too hot, I guess."

"The food was great. The meeting was kind of a pain in the rear."

Meg raised an eyebrow in question.

"Myles nominated guess who to be squashed artistically under a barn door. Under the current circumstances, that's a consummation to be wished for devoutly. Probably because of the consummation devoutly wished for by the jerk at table seven."

"Uh-oh," said Meg. She grinned, shook her head, and skillfully ladled three perfect brandied orange slices over a crisply browned game hen. "Don't tell me you got hooked into playing Clarissa this year."

"Julie Offenbach is sick," said Quill gloomily. She sighed and consulted her order pad. "We've got one more order. One medium-rare New York marinated in fungicide. No veg. Double cholesterol on the potato. Table seven."

"Mr. Baumer?"

"Yes indeedy. He almost forced me to break my number one rule."

"I thought the number one rule was don't hit the help."

"That's number two. Number one is don't piss off the patrons." Quill flopped into the rocking chair by the fireplace. "It's been a long day. I've still got to pay bills and go over the accounting with John before I go to bed. And my feet hurt." She glanced at her sister, wondering how and when to bring up the raw egg ban.

Meg, indifferent to the business side of the Inn, sniffed appreciatively at the copper pot filled with orange sauce on the stove. Her brown hair was shoved back from her forehead by a bright yellow sweatband. She liked to be comfortable when she cooked, and wore her usual chef's gear—a tattered Duke University sweatshirt, leggings, and a well-worn pair of sneakers. She looked at her sister's elegant feet. "It's those shoes, kiddo. Handmade Italian leather is the worst possible thing for your disposition. Want to borrow a pair of sneakers?"

"I want to borrow a life." Quill pushed the rocker in motion and closed her eyes. "Preferably on a beach somewhere. In the Caribbean. With a gorgeous twenty-year-old lifeguard and an endless supply of rum punch."

"Umm. I've heard *that* song before. And what about Myles? Face it. You love it here." Meg piped potato rosettes around the base of the bird, added two rings of spiced apple to the brandied orange slices, and presented the platter. "Ta dah! For table twelve. Bless his little heart. Ordered *all* my specialties, including game hen stuffed with The Sausage that made us famous."

Quill got up and took the platter. "Meg. About table twelve . . ."

Meg placed a silver dome over the bird. "You said he was cute."

"Very cute. The sort that could take us both away from all this."

"Rich? Single? Got a yacht?"

"No, the sort that could take us away from all this because I think he might be from the D.O.H."

Meg scowled. "What are you saying?"

"I'm not sure. But he was scribbling notes. And he ordered the Caesar salad and the Steak Tartare"—Quill took a deep breath—"and I wouldn't put it past Marge Schmidt and her creepy pal to have called them after that memo about the salmonella came out. She showed up here with the memo not ten minutes ago. Although I don't see how he could have gotten here so fast. Meg, you'll have to stop with the raw eggs. Just temporarily."

Meg slammed down her wooden spoon, marched to the swinging doors to the dining room, pushed them open, and peered through. She looked back at her sister. "That's an Armani, or I'm a short-order cook. People from the D.O.H. wear polyester."

"Yes, but is he taking notes?"

Meg peered out the door again. "How should I know? He's holding the Merlot by the stem. He's swirling the wine. He's inhaling it." She shrieked suddenly. "Quill! He's taking notes!"

"I *told* you he was taking notes." She looked over Meg's head into the dining room. "Oh, damn. There's Tom Peterson ready to order. Where's John!"

Meg let the doors close and said tensely, "*L'Aperitif*! You know, 'The Magazine to Read Before You Dine.' "

"I know *L'Aperitif*, Meg." Quill patted her sister's shoulder soothingly. "Forget it. I'll just go out and get Peterson set up."

Meg tore her sweatband from her hair and wound it around both hands. "I'm going to scream."

"Meg . . ."

"It's been eighteen months since we were last reviewed, Quill. Oh, God. And that managing editor hates me. She hates me. You know what they said in that article?"

"They love you, Meg. You're the only three-star . . ."

"My tournedos were dry! That's what they said. That I overcook my beef!" She grabbed the game hen out of Quill's hands, stamped to the stove, and ladled more brandied orange juice over the hen, drenching the potatoes. "There! That'll teach the sons of bitches to call my cooking dry!"

"Meg!" Quill grabbed the platter back. "You have absolutely no proof that this guy's a food critic."

"Well, you thought he was from the Department of Health! In an Armani suit!" She shoved Quill toward the dining room. "You go out there. You find out what kind of review he's going to give me. If he dares even *hint* that that bird is dry, I'll personally shove the rest of his bloody meal down his bloody throat!"

Table twelve faced the window overlooking the gorge. Edward Lancashire's eyes crinkled at the corners when he smiled. They crinkled as Quill set the game hen in front of him. "Looks great."

"Thank you."

He looked around the dining room. Quill noticed his wedding ring, and discarded the possibility of a nice flirtation with Meg. "Not bad for a Thursday night," he said. "You must do pretty well."

"We do. Is there anything else I can get for you, Mr. Lancashire?"

He forked a piece of the game hen. His eyes widened. "This is terrific. That's tarragon. Maybe a touch of Italian parsley? And mint. Excellent." He swallowed, and waved his fork at the chair opposite. "Dining room closes at ten-thirty, doesn't it? It's past that now. Have a seat."

"The owners don't care for the help fraternizing with guests." He looked up, his eyes shrewd. She smiled. "What? Do I have a sign that says 'Owner-Manager'?"

"No. But there's a bronze plaque in the front that reads 'Your hosts, Sarah and Margaret Quilliam.' And your name tag says 'Quill'."

"I might be their impoverished cousin from Des Moines, living on the bounty of relatives, pinch-hitting as manager and eking out a bare existence as a waitress."

"The uniform doesn't fit," he continued unperturbed, "and a woman wearing a three-hundred-dollar pair of shoes wouldn't voluntarily wear a dress that was too big across the hips and too tight across—" He stopped, as Quill frowned indignantly. "Sorry. You had enough of that this afternoon." He nodded towards Baumer, happily swigging down a final Manhattan. "Besides, I saw your show in New York a few years ago. Your picture was on the poster."

"Oh. That."

"Yes. You aren't painting anymore?"

"Some," she said, deliberately vague. "I don't have much time during the season. Are you staying with us long?"

"Depends on the food." He smiled, and Quill's heart gave an excited thump. He was asking enough questions to qualify as a food critic. Although he was awfully thin. Quill worried about the skinny part. But Meg was skinny, and she was the greatest chef in the state.

"Then you're not here for History Days?" He raised an interrogative eyebrow. "Hemlock Falls' biggest tourist attraction. Featuring Central New York's only three-star gourmet restaurant. Among other attractions."

He laughed a little. "Other attractions?"

"Craft booths and everybody in town dressed up like the Empress Josephine and Napoleonic soldiers. It's the wrong century of course, but the Ladies Auxiliary decided a long time ago that Empire costumes are prettier than Colonial." She cleared her throat a little self-consciously. "I may be prejudiced, but I think the reputation of the Inn has a lot to do with History Days' success. We're booked a year in advance for the whole week. We were even written up in the *Times* last year in the Sunday travel section. Maybe you saw it?" She leaned forward anxiously. "How's the sausage stuffing in the game hen?"

"Fine."

"Just fine?" she said worriedly. "It's my sister's recipe, you know. Margaret Quilliam. *L'Aperitif* wrote an article about her when we opened up two years ago. Maybe you saw that, too. 'Engorged at the Gorge'? Meg received Central New York's only three-star rating. Some people think it's time she was given a four. She's terrific, don't you think?"

"I'm not much of a gourmet," he said apologetically, "tastes great to me."

Quill calmed down. She'd pushed him too far. "Anything you need, just ask us."

"Coffee would be nice."

"Coffee. I'll have it here in a minute. Freshly brewed, of course."

Quill signaled to Kathleen Kiddermeister, who was clearing the Hallenbeck table, to take the Peterson order, and swept back into the kitchen. Meg sat nervously in the rocker, her feet up, smoking a forbidden cigarette. She jumped up and demanded, "Well?"

"It's *L'Aperitif*."

Meg turned pale.

"He registered as Edward Lancashire. I've never seen an Edward Lancashire byline in *L'Aperitif*. Probably a pseudonym."

"Now? Now!? The week of History Days. Oh, God."

"Meg! I'm not positively sure it's *L'Aperitif* . . ."

"Oh, God."

" . . . but we are overdue for a review."

"Oh, God."

"And he's asking *very* gourmet-type questions. He wants coffee. I'll make sure the whipped-cream is fresh . . . and the cinnamon sticks . . . fill the bowl of cinnamon sticks."

"Why not the week after next? Oh, God."

"I'll tell Kathleen to make sure the orange juice is fresh-squeezed tomorrow morning. What's the room service breakfast?"

"Blueberry muffins. It's July, remember? Oh, God."

"Take a deep breath."

Meg took a deep breath and let it out in a long sigh.

Quill patted her back. "We've survived Health Department notices, cranky widows, horny businessmen, drunks, even that kitchen fire last year—and the quality of your cooking's *never* dropped! Right?"

"Right."

"So!" Quill smiled affectionately at her. "What could happen that the two of us can't handle? You, the cooking genius. Me, the business genius."

John Raintree came through the door. He looked at Quill, his face grim. "That woman that checked in with the widow? The one with the stiff hair?"

"Yes, John. Mavis Collinwood. I moved both of them to three-fourteen."

"I've called the police. She's gone over the edge of the balcony in three-fourteen. To the gorge."

CHAPTER 3

"I just don't have the littlest idea what happened!" Mavis slumped plaintively on the yellow-and-blue couch in front of the fireplace in Suite 314.

Mavis had been found dangling over the lip of the gorge, like a baby in a stork's beak. Her patent leather belt had caught on one of the joists which fixed the balcony to the side of the building. Mrs. Hallenbeck, with great presence of mind, had taken a sheet from one of the beds, wrapped it around Mavis' stomach, then tied the other end to the handle of the French door. Mavis' wildly swinging hands had scratched her cheek.

The volunteer firemen found Mavis' predicament hilarious. Herbie Minstead and his crew winched Mavis off the balcony with the fire truck ladder, and shaking their heads, left for the Croh Bar and a restorative glass of beer at Quill's expense. Myles and two of his uniformed officers were exploring the balcony. Mrs. Hallenbeck sat upright and disapproving by the open French doors. Meg jigged from one foot to the other in a corner with John Raintree. Doc Bishop, the young internist who treated most of Hemlock Falls, bent over Mavis. Clearly suppressing his amusement, he straightened up and wiped a bit of blood off his surgical gloves with one of the expensive peach towels from the bathroom.

"Is she going to be all right?" asked Quill.

"Scrapes and bruises; that's about it. No evidence of oxygen deprivation. She wasn't high enough." He grinned. Quill looked at him in exasperation; his expression sobered. "Sorry, Quill. It could have been a real tragedy. If her belt hadn't caught onto the joist like it did, she could have gone into the river, but it *is* ten feet deep there. She would have floated like a cork down to the sluiceway and been able to climb out."

Quill dropped to her knees beside Mavis. Her knees were scraped and bloody, the torn pantyhose gritty with concrete dust from the balcony. Her cheeks were scratched, her makeup smeared, and her expression furious.

"Can you talk about it?" asked Quill gently.

"I done *tol'* you," Mavis snapped, her Southern accent deepening to incomprehensibility. "I went out for some fresh air. I leaned against that old railing. Next thang I knew, I *pitched* into the air."

"You eat too much," said Mrs. Hallenbeck, and whether this was referring to Mavis' expensive dinner or her general size, Quill wasn't too sure. Mavis gave her employer a furious glare.

"And then Mrs. Hallenbeck came out and tied you to the balcony with a sheet."

"I like to *choked*, she tied that sheet so tight."

"You may have saved her life, Mrs. Hallenbeck," said Quill, stretching the truth in pursuit of making everyone feel better. "You were very brave. Very quick thinking."

Mrs. Hallenbeck lifted her chin and smiled complacently. "I have often been complimented on my presence of mind."

"I can *swim*," Mavis muttered. "I told her just to lemme *go!*"

There was more to Mavis, Quill decided, than had previously met the eye.

Quill wondered if she should send John downstairs for a brandy for everyone. They all looked as though they needed it.

Myles prowled in from the balcony and drew Andy Bishop to one side. He shook hands with Doc Bishop, then came over and sat next to Mavis. "You had just the glass of white wine for dinner, Mrs. Collinwood?"

"I am not in the habit of overindulgence, Sheriff."

"Huh!" said Mrs. Hallenbeck. "She's forty pounds overweight if she's ten, and *that* is a result of overindulgence. At, I may add, my expense." She lifted her chin again and fixed Myles with The Glare. Quill, admiring, noticed he was totally unaffected. "I believe, Sheriff, that we need to discuss the negligence in this case. I may have to call my lawyer in the morning."

Quill glanced at John and raised both eyebrows. He nodded with quick understanding, then moved unobtrusively around the room. Just one small Thermos bottle filled with Rusty Nails, thought Quill, preferably a large one.

"You were in the bathroom, Mrs. Hallenbeck?" asked Myles.

Mrs. Hallenbeck nodded. "That is correct. I was brushing my teeth. I heard a rumbling sound, then a squall like a scalded cat. I rushed from the bathroom to the balcony. Poor Mavis was swaying over the gorge. I tugged at her to help her back onto what was left of the balcony. I myself was beginning to slip." She closed her eyes momentarily, her face pale. "If *I* had slipped! Sometimes I think that God has taken a personal interest in me, Sheriff, and as you see, I did not. Well, I quickly saw that I was far too frail to pull that great creature up myself . . ."

"Not quick enough," Mavis muttered. "I was out there *hours*."

" . . . so I stripped the sheet from that bed, tied it around her waist, and called the front desk."

"A tragedy averted," said Andy Bishop, solemn now; he had finished repacking his little black bag, and may have been regretting his earlier lightheartedness. He scribbled for a moment on his prescription pad, tore off two sheets, and held out the prescription and a small box of pills to Mavis. "I'm giving you both some Valium. These are samples to take until you can get to the pharmacy tomorrow. You're going to be stiff tomorrow, Mrs. Collinwood. And so will you, Mrs. Hallenbeck, after those exertions."

"I never take drugs," said Mrs. Hallenbeck, "nor do my employees."

Mavis tucked the samples into her purse and said, "Thank you, Doctor. I believe I will take advantage of your kind offer."

Andy Bishop picked up his bag. "I'll leave you ladies now. Stop by my office, Mrs. Collinwood, if you feel the need." He gave Quill a brief hug, nodded to Myles, and walked to the door opening onto the hallway.

"Doctor!" commanded Mrs. Hallenbeck. "You will send your bill to Ms. Quilliam. This entire affair is the responsibility of the Inn."

Quill glanced quickly at John. He nodded reluctantly. "Of course, Andy," she said. "I'm so sorry this happened, Mavis."

Myles, who had been leaning against the mantel with a thoughtful expression, said, "Sarah, maybe you and John could move Mrs. Hallenbeck and Mrs. Collinwood to a different room."

"Why?" Quill asked. "Myles, the Inn is booked to the gills in two days for History Week. There isn't any place we can put them but here, after Sunday."

"I'm going to seal off the room until the investigation is completed."

"Maybe they'll be gone by then," said John, surprisingly ungracious. "Come on, Sarah. Mrs. Hallenbeck, we'll take you down to two-fourteen. I'll see that your luggage is packed up and brought down."

"Where we began," said Mrs. Hallenbeck. "I am assuming the rest of our stay will be free of charge. And we do intend, Mr. Raintree, to stay the entire week."

Quill, distracted, watched them go. "Myles—how long is this going to take? And what kind of investigation? I'll have to have the insurance company in to look at it, of course, but it's just the balcony, for Pete's sake."

"I want to show you something."

Quill looked at her watch; after midnight. She yawned suddenly. "Can't we do this in the morning, Myles?"

"Now."

Quill followed him out to the balcony. The July night was soft, the moon a silvery half crescent over the Falls. The northwest edge of the balcony gaped, bent and broken, just as it had when she'd looked at it before.

"Look at this." Using his handkerchief to protect the wrought-iron surface, Myles gently rocked one of the posts free from the edge of the concrete.

Quill peered at it in the half-light from the suite behind them. "The mortar's all crumbled away," she said. "What do you think the insurance company's going to want me to do? Should I call the architect?"

"Look at it, Quill."

She reached out to touch the mortar. Myles caught her hand gently and moved it aside. "It's *eaten* away," she said.

"My guess is acid. Do you have any here?"

"Sulfuric," said Quill, suddenly wide-awake. "Doreen insists that a solution of sulfuric acid and water is the only thing that gets the mold off the concrete. She uses it once every six months."

Myles crumbled a few bits of mortar in his handkerchief and sniffed it. "Undiluted, is my guess. It's been poured around these five posts here. How much have you got on hand?"

Quill's thoughts scattered, then regrouped. She stood up slowly. "A fifty-gallon drum, at least. John orders it in bulk. It doesn't decay or lose its potency or anything." She stared at him. "But *who*? And *why*?"

"Who has access to it?"

"It's in the storeroom. We lock it at night, but during the day—anyone, I guess."

"I'll send someone down to check it. What did those two do today?"

"They checked in about noon. Mavis went for a walk. Mrs. Hallenbeck stayed in her room until tea-time. They both came down for tea at four o'clock. They ate a huge one. Then Mrs. Hallenbeck went up to her room for a nap, I think. That was about five o'clock. I guess Mavis went with her. They came back down to dinner about nine-thirty. They'd changed clothes after washing up, I guess."

"How many guests did you have for tea?"

"Four tables. Two tables were people passing through on their way to Syracuse. The fourth table was a guest that checked in about two o'clock, Keith Baumer. He—"

"Wait a minute." Myles wrote in his notebook. "And after nine-thirty? Who was at the Inn?"

"The regular kitchen staff. Meg, me, John, Kathleen Kiddermeister. We were short a waitress, which is why I was waiting tables. Other than the guests, just Tom Peterson and some customer of his, I think. They came in around ten-thirty. Oh! And Marge showed up."

"And the guests?"

Quill ran over the roster of the guests. "Excluding Hallenbeck and Collinwood—we've just got six others. There's a family in three twenty-six and three twenty-seven. An orthodontist, his wife, and two kids taking a tour of the Finger Lakes Region. They're due to check out tomorrow, and they were hiking all day today. And—oh, Myles! The most awful thing! We think the food critic for *L'Aperitif* is here incognito. He's calling himself Edward Lancashire. Meg's fit to be tied. But that last one—" Quill broke off.

"What about the last one?"

"The most disgusting human being. Keith Baumer. Eyes like sweaty little hands. Ugh."

"Do any of the guests smoke?"

"Keith Baumer does. He's a sloppy smoker. Why?"

Myles reached into his shirt pocket and took out a plastic evidence bag. It contained a matchbook.

"That's one of ours," said Quill.

"Notice how it's folded?"

Quill examined it through the clear plastic. The cover had been folded over three times, exposing the matches. The book was full.

"Have you seen a matchbook folded like this before?"

Quill shook her head. "Is it a clue?"

"Beats me."

"This doesn't make any sense, Myles."

"Not at the moment it doesn't." He rubbed the back of his neck. "Why don't you get some sleep? It's been a long day. I want to go back to the station and think about this a little bit."

"You think this was just a stupid prank?"

"Beats . . ."

" . . . me," Quill finished for him.

"I'll do some background checks. On all of them. I want to get the state lab boys in here tomorrow to run some tests on the balcony." He put his arm around Quill, and she burrowed gratefully into his chest. He smelled faintly of aftershave and clean male sweat. "I don't want to think about this any more tonight. I want to think about the way you smell. I like the way you smell."

"Quill." Myles tipped her head back. The moonlight shone into her eyes, and his face was a dark shadow behind it. "There's a third option."

"Yippee," said Quill, thinking delightfully lewd thoughts.

"Malice."

"Malice?"

"Someone could be out to put you and Meg out of business."

CHAPTER 4

Quill snatched a few hours sleep, dreaming of Mavis bobbing along the duck pond like a fat cork, Mrs. Hallenbeck yelling, "No charge for the swim!" and Marge Schmidt nailing a "For Sale" sign to the Inn's front door.

She overslept the alarm and woke groggily to sunshine, birdsong, and a distinct feeling of unease.

She threw open the bedroom windows and looked crossly at the scene below. French lavender grew directly under her windows. Mike, the groundskeeper, grew them as annuals; they were a lot of trouble, but worth it, he said, for the scent. Quill inhaled, held her breath, then let it out sharply. She ran vigorously in place for a few minutes. Neither lavender nor exercise cleared her brain enough to make sense of Myles's offhand comment of the night before.

Had Marge Schmidt and Betty Hall advanced from verbal slings and arrows to outright war? The more she thought about it, the madder she got at Myles, who had no business second-guessing without facts. Intuition, thought Quill virtuously, was a rotten character trait in a sheriff. How often had he lectured her about leaping to conclusions? Now here he was, driving her bats with supposition.

Harvey Bozzel had left the new brochure copy for the Inn's advertising campaign with her a week ago. Quill went into her small living room and pulled it out of the desk. She'd already blue-penciled Harvey's tag line extolling the Inn's customer service: "No Whine, Just Fine Wine When You Dine." But his description of Meg's cooking wasn't too bad.

Meg's art was at its peak with the breads, terrines, pâtés, and *charcuterie* of Country French cooking; for the past year, she'd been making increasingly successful forays into French haute cuisine, perhaps as a reaction to *L'Aperitif*'s first review. "Quilliam's coarsely ground sausages are exceptional," *L'Aperitif* had commented in the review that awarded her the coveted three stars. "A celestial blend of local pork, freshly picked herbs, and the crumbs of her excellent peasant breads. Her efforts at the more sophisticated levels of classic French cooking are reliable."

The local pork came from Hogg's Heaven, a pig farm three miles upwind of Hemlock Falls. The herbs came from the gardens maintained by Mike the groundskeeper. The breads were made by a series of apprentice *sous* chefs under Meg's supervision. Meg herself was rebuilding the ramparts of "reliable" into "exceptional."

The ad copy described all this in prose only slightly less purple than the lavender below her window. Quill scowled furiously at the copy, then stuffed it back into the desk. Who would want to put such a great cook out of business? She glanced at the clock. It was obviously running fast; it couldn't be past eight already. She dressed hastily and went downstairs.

Her mood was not improved after an encounter with Keith Baumer at table eight, who stopped her rush to the kitchen with a smarmy suggestion involving the length of her skirt (short) and a repulsive summation of his ideal wake-up call.

Quill held onto her temper. The Cornell Hotel School offered a night course in Customer Relations, and Quill had dutifully attended CR 101 and CR 102. "I'm sure you'll agree your suggestions are inappropriate, Mr. Baumer," she said. "May I take your food order, please?" She kept a prudent distance from his sweaty hands, then stalked self-consciously into the kitchen.

Meg, humming an off-key version of "The Gambler," was folding shiitake mushrooms into an omelette with one hand and stirring a béarnaise sauce with the other. She looked up as her sister came into the room. "Lancashire's ordered the works. French omelette in a bird's nest of cr-r-r-isply fried potatoes, and of course, The Sausage."

"I didn't see him in the dining room."

"How could you miss him? Those good looks fly across the room." She switched to an equally off-key rendition of "Some Enchanted Evening."

"That's because I was contemplating unique *Tortures of the World*. You can order a videotape from Time-Life Books, I think."

"Not Baumer again."

"Baumer. Had a suggestion having to do with short-skirted uniforms and appropriate poses for waitresses over the right table height."

"Ugh!" shrieked Meg. "That foul, grungy pig!" She took the saucepan off the Aga and regarded it thoughtfully for a moment. "What'd he order?"

Quill looked at the slip. "Stuffed tomatoes, scrambled eggs, bacon."

John came softly into the kitchen carrying a room service order. "Two orders of Eggs Benedict, grilled grapefruit with brown sugar, blueberries with whipped cream, German pancakes, and two orders of Smithfield ham."

"That doesn't sound like the orthodontist," said Quill with trepidation.

"Mrs. Hallenbeck." John's tone was curt. "Is all this on the house?"

"For now."

"That's a forty-dollar breakfast," said John.

"I know." She explained briefly what Myles had discovered the previous evening. "We'll wait until the lab results are in, but we don't know anything yet. If it's vandalism, we're responsible."

"I think you should talk to them about keeping costs within reason."

Quill grimaced.

"I'll talk to them, then," said John insistently. "We can't afford this kind of cash drain, Quill."

"John, if we *are* liable for this accident, it's just going to annoy them to insist that they watch it."

"I warned you about those two when they checked in."

"Yes, you did," Quill admitted.

"Did you check the supply of sulfuric acid?"

"No, I don't have any idea of what was there before. Doreen might, but she's not back from vacation until this afternoon."

"I saw her out here yesterday. Mavis Collinwood, I mean. She passed right by the storeroom."

"John, you think *they* staged the accident? Come on! We can afford this, can't we? You said last week this is the first year we're going to show a profit."

"Maybe," he said gloomily. "If you don't keep buying food and drink for the whole town. I can't wait to get the bill from the Croh Bar. Half those guys on the volunteer firemen should be in A.A."

"They may have saved Mavis' life," said Quill. "Meg! What are you doing to that tomato?"

"The one for salesman-creep Baumer?" Meg gleefully shook baking soda into the chopped parsley, sausage, and onion dressing that composed the usual stuffing.

"No." Quill took the orange box from Meg's hand and replaced it in the cupboard.

"Yes!" said Meg. Her face reddened, always a sign of rising temper. Then her hair seemed to flatten, which indicated it had risen. Quill could never figure how she accomplished the trick with her hair. Meg retrieved the baking soda and sprinkled a bit more on the tomato.

"Why don't we suggest that they curb the spending, at least until we establish the cause of the accident?" said John.

"Okay, okay, okay." Quill lifted her hands in a gesture of defeat. "I'll do it."

"When?"

"In a bit. I've got to memorize that stupid speech for *The Trial of Goody Martin*. The dress rehearsal's this afternoon at the duck pond."

"No time like the present," said John. "They're waiting for you in two-fourteen. I said you'd be along to speak to them. Kathleen will bring their breakfast up."

Quill sighed. "Okay. Okay. I'm going. See this? It's Quill, going to do her duty."

Meg was singing " . . . when I am dead and gone, dear,

sing no sad songs for me" to her omelette as Quill left the kitchen.

It was shaping up to be a hell of a week.

Two-fourteen and two-sixteen were two separate bedrooms connected by an interior door. Quill didn't particularly like the decor, having given way to a brief infatuation with grape-and-ivy chintz for the bedspreads and drapes.

Mrs. Hallenbeck opened the door to her knock, dressed in a red double-knit suit that screamed "designer." Quill's painter's eye recoiled from the clash with the purple and green.

"I very much dislike this room," said Mrs. Hallenbeck, by way of greeting.

"So do I," said Quill frankly. "You must have a nice sense of color, Mrs. Hallenbeck. Would you like to move to the rooms below? They're a little more soothing to the eye."

"Perhaps that would settle Mavis down," Mrs. Hallenbeck admitted.

"Coo-ee!" Mavis waved at her from the bed. Quill, momentarily speechless, didn't respond at first.

"Dr. Bishop's Valium samples seemed to have loosened Mavis' more obvious inhibitions," said Mrs. Hallenbeck dryly. Mavis' generous breasts spilled over the top of a lacy nightgown. Her makeup had been applied with a lavish hand. Her hair, released from its tight bun, spilled over her shoulders. Chewing gum with enthusiasm, she waved again, and said, "This is just so *lovely*!"

"Please sit down, Ms. Quilliam." Mrs. Hallenbeck sat stiffly, though with elegance, at the tea table fronting the windows. "I take it you have come to discuss a settlement with us. I am prepared to listen to any reasonable offer."

Quill sat in the chair opposite and took a deep breath.

"Where's that breakfast?" caroled Mavis. "I swear, I could eat a hog whole."

Quill took a second deep breath. A double knock on the door acted as a brief reprieve. She opened it, took the tray from Kathleen Kiddermeister, and set it on the tea table. Mrs. Hallenbeck examined the tray with disdain. Mavis hauled herself out of bed with a whoop, parked the wad of chewing gum on the bedpost, and settled herself at the table. She and Mrs. Hallenbeck had a brief, sharp discussion over who had ordered the grapefruit. Mrs. Hallenbeck won and took the blueberries mounded with whipped cream.

"Would you care for coffee?" asked Mrs. Hallenbeck, after a moment's more-or-less silent chewing. "It's quite decent. I discovered yesterday that one has to insist on the chef's private stock, or else you are served a brew that is quite ordinary."

Quill pinched her own knee hard. She was awake. She was part-owner of this Inn. She was in charge. She had to talk to the widows with the direct yet tactful charm that had never failed her, and convince the widows that costs should be kept down for all their sakes.

"It looks as though sulfuric acid was poured on the mortar around the balcony," she blurted. "The sheriff has sent samples off for tests to confirm it."

The widows stopped eating. Mavis looked at Mrs. Hallenbeck, her mouth open. Mrs. Hallenbeck looked out the window. Her mouth was firmly closed.

"Tests?" said Mrs. Hallenbeck. "Who in the *world* would want to make that balcony unsafe?"

"I don't know," said Quill carefully. "But until we do, I thought you might want to . . . to . . . be as careful about your expenses as you have been in the past."

"Vandals!" said Mavis. "My God. Are we safe in our beds here, Amelia?"

"You seemed to think so when you talked me into coming here, Mavis," said Mrs. Hallenbeck tartly.

"I thought you and your husband had been here before," said Quill.

"Yes, of course. Mavis reminded me of it when we were planning our trip this summer. She did *not*, however, tell me that we would be fair game for malicious tricks."

"I don't know how this happened," said Quill. "But until we know who will have to pay for the repairs to the balcony, we won't know who will be responsible for your hotel bill. We are delighted to have you as guests, of course, but you must understand that we're running a business."

Mavis broke into shrill laughter that stopped as suddenly as it started. Mrs. Hallenbeck shot her a venomous glance, then nodded benignly at Quill. "We will be happy to accommodate you, Sarah." She picked up Mavis' plate of Eggs Benedict and the Smithfield ham. "You may return these to the kitchen and remove them from our room service charge. Mavis does not require that much for breakfast."

"I certainly do!" said Mavis. She snatched the plates back. "I'm sure Miss Quill and the sheriff don't want us to starve while we are waitin' to hear what's what." She picked up a slice of ham in her fingers and rapidly chewed it.

Quill murmured her goodbyes and left them to it.

Going downstairs to her office, Quill had a moment's feeling of control. She fervently hoped it was not illusory. It lasted through the staff meeting (all the waitresses showed up for work) and the business meeting with John (the Inn was booked solid for History Days). She even found time for a quick glance at Clarissa Martin's two big speeches, one before being ducked in the duck pond, the other as she was sentenced to being pressed to death. The feelings of competency even lasted through the lunch trade and Meg's excited report that Edward Lancashire had *come to the kitchen* to compliment her on the omelette. This was offset somewhat by Quill's receipt of a customer-satisfaction card, unsigned, that complained bitterly about the baking soda in the scrambled eggs. Quill, looking ahead to the month's receipts, decided to let it go.

She lost the glow at the Chamber meeting that afternoon. Since the Chamber budget allowed only for a once-a-month lunch in the conference room, supernumerary sessions were held in the Inn's Lounge. Quill donated coffee and soft drinks at these sessions, and she came into the lounge early to make sure of the preparations.

Esther bustled in behind her, clipboard in hand. "Julie Offenbach is sicker than a *dog*," reported Esther in glum satisfaction, "so you'll just have to rehearse with us, Quill."

"Has Andy Bishop seen her?" asked Quill, with slowly extinguishing hope. "They've got all kinds of miracle drugs these days."

"It's just *flu*!" said Esther. "She'll be maybe better by Wednesday. First performance is day after tomorrow, so there you are. You'll do *fine*, Quill."

"Oh, dear," said Quill. "Esther, I'm just not good at this kind of thing."

"But you're so pretty!" Esther said unenviously. "It's for the good of the Town, you know. You have been practicing, dear, haven't you?"

"You bet," said Quill firmly, "I'll just take a minute to . . . to look at it one more time." She escaped into the hallway, only to be swept back into the Lounge by an ebullient Mayor Henry and Gil Gilmeister. Marge Schmidt and Mavis Collinwood were right on their heels, and Marge yelled, "You got that part memorized, Mave?"

Quill turned around. Mavis, in a modest print dress much like the one from the day before, shrieked, "It's just *adorable.* I'm going to love it!"

Quill studied her for a moment. The effect of the Valium had carried over into the afternoon. The big patent-leather belt was cinched two notches tighter. The top of the print dress was unbuttoned. Her hair was loose, and the makeup laid on with a trowel.

"Goings-on!" sniffed a dire voice at Quill's elbow. "Dressed like the scarlet woman of big cities. Detroit, for instance."

"Oh, hi, Doreen!" Quill gave the housekeeper a hug. "So glad you're back from vacation. Did you have a good time?"

Doreen's beady brown eyes bored into hers. "Praise be that I went when I did, Miz Quill. Praise be, for I found the Lord."

Nobody knew how old Doreen was. Meg guessed late fifties, Myles late forties, with a hard life behind her. She'd shown up truculent and bellicose at the Inn's back door one January afternoon, and Quill had hired her on a temporary basis. That was two years ago. Except for a tendency to fierce, short-lived enthusiasms, Doreen was the most loyal, hardest-working employee they had. There was no one at the Inn Quill liked or trusted more. Except, Quill thought, for John Raintree and Meg.

"In Boca Raton? At your nephew's?"

Doreen nodded. "Just in time, too."

"For what?"

Doreen folded her arms, leaned against the wall, and paused dramatically. Quill braced herself. Doreen had run afoul of Quill's erratically enforced guest-courtesy standards before. Cigarette dangling, skinny, and a frequent victim of the Hemlock Hall of Beauty's experiments in permanent waves, Doreen had profanely terrorized more than one unsuspecting visitor. Checkout was a favorite arena: "You inspect that sumabitch's goddam suitcase for towels and ashtrays? I'm missin' towels and ashtrays." Quill had a brief, happy vision of a kindlier, Christianized Doreen accosting visitors with reassuring Bible verses instead of fiercely wielded mops.

"Just in time for what, Doreen?"

"Day of Judgment is at hand," said Doreen darkly. "Those who have not been brought howling in repentance to the throne of the Lord will be damned in the Pit forever."

Quill found the regret in her voice spurious, given the glee in her eye.

"Now, Doreen—" began Quill.

"People!" Esther waved her hands imperiously in the air. "Dress rehearsal, people! Just one day to the Real Thing. Chop, chop!"

"—I'd like to discuss this religion thing with you—"

"Quill!" Esther cried. "Come on! We can't do without our star!"

"—but not right now," Quill finished hastily.

"What's that old bat Esther want with you?" asked Doreen suspiciously.

"Julie Offenbach's got the flu."

"So you're gonna be Clarissa?" She shook her head. "You ain't never been in a play in your life. I better pray for you."

"Pray for rain instead. A thunderstorm, even. I don't want to do this, Doreen."

"You'll be fine." Doreen gave her hand a rough, affectionate squeeze. "You can do anything you set your mind to. But I'll pray for a disaster, if you want." Her face lit up. "One to demonstrate His power."

"Great. After the rooms are done, though."

Esther, thorough as always, had left a stack of scripts by the coffee table in the Lounge, and Quill thumbed glumly through a copy as the Chamber members settled into their seats. Myles walked into the room and Quill greeted him with a swift, intimate smile.

"Everyone seated!" Esther said. "Clarissa? Are you ready?"

Quill waved the script feebly at Esther, and settled across the table from Myles and Gil Gilmeister. "Any results from the lab yet, Myles?" she asked hopefully.

He shook his head. "Not until Monday or Tuesday. It's not exactly a priority problem."

"Maybe it was just a prank," said Quill, "or an accident. Doreen was gone on vacation and one of the temporaries could have spilled it."

"Full strength?" said Myles. "I doubt it."

"Accident," said Quill stubbornly. "Maybe you should just drop the investigation."

"We need to get to the bottom of it," Myles said. "You've got to be tougher than that, Quill."

"I'll say." Gil, his attention drawn by the latter part of this comment, leaned back in his chair and took an overlarge bite of the beignets Meg had set out with the coffee. Sugar dribbled down his chin. He licked it off reflectively. "You got to be tough all over. That darn Mark Anthony Jefferson at the bank? Well, I had to get tough with him this morning. Wants to call in that loan I got right this minute." He looked at Myles. "He can't do that can he, Sheriff? I mean, it's gotta be against some law or other. I've been paying on the note right along."

"Can't help you there, Gil."

"Well, it's not right," Gil said again. "I have to find some cash somewhere. Thing is, people just aren't buying cars. Got any rich widows here at the Inn, Quill? One that might want to invest in one of the best little businesses in Hemlock Falls?"

"Sorry, Gil. It's been a tough year for everyone. But things are getting better, don't you think? Business looks great for us for the rest of the summer."

Gil gave her a cheerful smile. "You might be right. Now, I'll tell you who's got money. Marge Schmidt. That diner business is all cash, if you know what I mean, and she's not paying half the taxes I have to. 'Course, she doesn't have my expenses, either."

Quill, who knew how frequently Gil's wife, Nadine, went to Syracuse with Gil's charge cards, murmured sympathetically.

"Where *is* Marge, anyway?" asked Gil. "She's supposed to have my judge's costume with her."

"Right here!" boomed Marge. "And guess who I have with me!" She stumped into the Lounge towing Mavis behind her. "Everybody? I wanna introduce you to an old pal of mine, Mavis Collinwood. Mavis, this is the cast of the play I was telling you about. That's Gil Gilmeister." She winked at the car salesman and waved heartily. "Gil's the judge in the play. Next to him is Myles McHale, our sheriff. He's here 'cause of the traffic control and on account of we use some equipment that's gotta be safe. Then there's Howie Murchison, Tom Peterson, Mayor Elmer Henry. They're all witnesses to the witch, and say the things she's done. And Reverend Shuttleworth plays the minister who condemns the witch. Esther's our director. And Norm Pasquale directs the high-school band. You know, they play that Funeral March as the witch is dragged off in the sledge." Marge paused for breath.

Mavis waved at the crowd, and spoke in a low voice to Marge.

"Hah? That there's Betty Hall. She's my business partner. No *way* she could play the part."

Betty, unclear as to the nature of the discussion, clearly heard an insult implicit in Marge's dismissal of her, and said, "What the hell?"

"No," Marge said, again in response to a question from Mavis, "Clarissa's usually played by some girl from the high school. Miss Sarah poison-your-guts Quilliam's supposed to play it this year." She gestured in Quill's direction.

"Marge!" said Esther. "For heaven's sake! This is a *private* rehearsal. As director, I must insist that your guest wait outside while we finish."

"You've met before?" said Betty icily.

"Met before?" said Mavis breathlessly. "Why, we worked together for this age!"

"Doggone good dogs," said Marge cryptically.

"*Doggone* good dogs," responded Mavis, and both women went off into gusts of laughter.

"The fast-food chain," said Tom Peterson. "It's out of Syracuse. You wouldn't know this, Quill, but they do quite a bit of recruiting from the high school." He blinked his pale eyes slowly—rather, Quill thought, like a lizard in the sun.

"Yeah," said Norm Pasquale. "Hot dogs and paint are the

only jobs our graduates get unless they go to college. It's not like the old days, when all the kids went back to the farm."

"So what's your point, Marge?" said Elmer impatiently.

"Point is that Mavis here is a hell of an actress. She can do this part better'n anyone here."

"Then she'll have to audition," said Esther.

"*She* din't." Marge threw a large thumb in Quill's direction.

"Yes, she did," said Esther. "I auditioned her. I'm the director, and I say who auditions and who doesn't."

"Quiet!" said Elmer. "Whyn't you tell us your experience, Ms. Collinwood. What exactly did you do at Doggone Good Dogs?"

John Raintree came into the room and settled unobtrusively in a chair. Doreen tiptoed in behind him. Quill drummed her fingers in irritation and wondered who else from the staff was coming to watch her debut as an actress.

"Best hot dogs in the South," said Mavis.

"Best in the whole damn country!" said Marge. "Good plain American food."

"I never knew you worked for somebody else before," said Betty Hall stiffly.

"Oh, yeah. Managed a whole chain of 'em down to Atlanta," said Marge. "Mavis was in the Mid-Atlantic region. She was Human Resources Coordinator and—"

"That's just fine, Marge," said Elmer Henry impatiently, "but we've got to get on with this rehearsal."

"Let me finish," said Marge, "*and* the best damn actress in the whole chain."

"Oh, I don't know about that," said Mavis modestly.

"Do they have actors in fast-food places?" asked Esther, in genuine bewilderment.

"Of course," said Marge scornfully. "We had an employee talent show every year and Mavis got the cash prize every time. Sang "The Doggone Good Dog" theme song. Go on, sing it for 'em, Mavis. She done a little dance, too," she said in a helpful aside.

"I don't have my costume or anything." Mavis sent a brilliant smile around the room.

Quill, acutely sympathetic to the agonies of performing in front of crowds, and still somewhat nettled over the "poisoned-guts" remark said, "Honestly, Marge. Let the poor woman sit down," surprising herself. If she kept this up, she could handle a dozen Mrs. Hallenbecks in a week.

"Go *on*, Mavis," said Marge.

"Well." Mavis cleared her throat and said confidently, "Now, y'all are going to have to do some *imagining*, and pretend I'm dressed as a hot dog." She winked at Dookie Shuttleworth, whose eyebrows rose in alarm. "The hot dog comes out in front of me, and out back—I'm in the middle of the bun." Then she sang, in a contralto:

> "You can slather me with mustard
> and a dilly pickle, too.
> Tickle me with onions,
> I'll be doggone good for you.
> I'm a plump and juicy red-hot
> In a toasted whole wheat bun.
> For less than two and fifty
> We can have a lot of fun."

She and Marge locked arms and swayed together in a lock-step.

> "Hot-Hot-Hot dog
> Doggone Doggone good.
> Bet you'd love our hot dogs
> Anyway you could."

Harvey Bozzel broke the silence. "Could use a *leetle* bit of editing, but it's good. Pretty good."

"Sing it again," said Gil Gilmeister huskily. "You looked great, Mavis. You, too, Marge."

Mavis tossed her head, and dimpled. Her dangling earrings clicked. She reminded Quill of someone: a chubby Vivien Leigh as Scarlett O'Hara. Quill cleared her throat and stood up. "This is a wonderful opportunity, don't you think? I mean, we practically have a professional right here. We'd be crazy not to take advantage of it. If you don't mind, Mavis, I think you'd make a wonderful Clarissa."

"We voted on Quill and we should stick with her," said Betty Hall. "Some newcomer just swanking on in here, even if she is a famous actress—I don't know how the town is going to feel about that."

"She's not a famous actress, Betty," Esther snapped. "She's a Human Resources Director."

"Whatever." Resentment was in every line of Betty's bowling jacket.

"Marge, you have the best judgment of anybody in the Chamber I know of," said Gil earnestly. "And I think this is a prime example of it."

"We gotta talk about that loan, Gil," said Marge jovially. "What d'ya think?"

"I move to have Mavis Collinwood take on the role of Clarissa in the History Days play," said Quill immediately. She ignored Myles's sardonic grin with the restrained dignity appropriate to an innkeeper rescued from public humiliation at the last minute.

"Second," said Gil.

Elmer called for a vote. Esther and Betty abstained, with what Quill identified as darkling glances, but the motion passed. Quill entertained a fleeting thought about the efficacy of Doreen's new commitment to prayer; she decided she was inclined to leniency in the matter of religious fervor. This was much more satisfactory than a tornado.

"I suppose we'll discover just how quick a study you are, Miss Collinwood?" Esther said stiffly. "Come, people, we're running behind schedule. Everybody at the pond in ten minutes."

Quill stopped John in the hall during the general exodus. "Do your plans include watching the rehearsal?"

He smiled faintly. "Not if you're a member of the audience rather than the cast."

"Thank you so much."

He glanced at her out of the corner of his eye. "Did you talk to the widows?"

"Yes."

"Is Myles going to continue with the background checks?"

"I'm not sure. John, Mrs. Hallenbeck's sitting by herself

by the fireplace." Quill looked back at the chattering crowd leaving the Inn. Mavis, expansive, was in the center. "I'll just speak to her."

She crossed the lobby and sat next to Mrs. Hallenbeck. "Did you get a chance to walk in the gardens today, Mrs. Hallenbeck?"

"Not yet. Mavis and I were going to go this afternoon, but she appears to be busy. Perhaps we'll go tomorrow." She folded her hands. "I'll wait until she is finished with her friends. The old are boring to you youngsters."

Quill was quiet a moment. It was pathetic, this small confession. "Would you like to walk down to the rehearsal with me? Only part of the cast will be in costume, but it might be kind of fun. I can't stay for the whole thing, but you're more than welcome to. There's always a crowd watching. Mostly townspeople."

"I'd like that very much."

It was one of those July afternoons that made Quill glad to be in Central New York in summer. The sky was a Breughel-blue, the sun a clear glancing light that made Quill's hands itch for her acrylics. As they came to the edge of the Falls Park and the small man-made pond that had been formed from the river water, Edward Lancashire picked his way over the grass to them.

"I'd call this a paintable day," he said by way of greeting.

"Do you paint, Sarah?" asked Mrs. Hallenbeck.

"I used to. Not much anymore."

"She was becoming quite well-known when she quit," said Lancashire. His dark eyes narrowed against the bright sun, he smiled down at Quill.

"A painter," said Mrs. Hallenbeck with satisfaction. "I knew you were quite out of the ordinary, my dear. I should like to see your work."

"My sister's work is more impressive," said Quill. "Are you finding the food to your liking, Mr. Lancashire?"

"Call me Edward. And the food's terrific."

"And what do you do?" asked Mrs. Hallenbeck.

"Oh. Reporting, mostly," he said vaguely. "What's going on down there?"

"This is the part of the play that's the witch test."

"The witch test?"

"Yes. When a person was accused of witchcraft, there was sort of a preliminary cut made of witches and non-witches. A real witch could swim. Innocent victims couldn't. So many American villages used the ducking stool as a test. The real witches swam to shore and were tried and convicted at a later trial."

"And the innocent victims?" asked Mrs. Hallenbeck.

"Drowned," said Quill.

"My goodness!" With a certain degree of ceremony, Mrs. Hallenbeck took a pair of glasses from her purse, fitted them on carefully, and peered at the makeshift stage by the ducking stool.

With the steadily increasing popularity of Hemlock History Week, the town had turned the area adjacent to the ducking pond into a twenty-acre municipal park some years before. An asphalt parking lot lay at the north edge, and half a dozen picnic tables surrounded the pavilion. The pavilion itself consisted of a large bandstand surrounded by enough wooden benches to seat two hundred spectators. The entire park fronted the Hemlock River; the Falls that formed such a unique backdrop to Meg and Quill's inn rushed gently into the river at the south of the park. The ducking pond was edged with concrete. A sluiceway was lowered to fill the pond in spring, and lifted to empty it in winter. A ten-foot fence of treated lumber stood at right angles to the pond's edge, where Harland Peterson parked his ancient John Deere farm tractor every year to power the ducking stool into the water. A chorus of cheers greeted him as the John Deere chugged into place behind the fence. He hopped out of the cab, waved his baseball hat to the crowd, and began hooking the ropes attached to the ducking stool to the metal arms on the front loader.

"That thing is old," Edward observed. "Fifty-six or fifty-seven at least."

"The Petersons are pretty thrifty," said Quill. She avoided Mrs. Hallenbeck's eye. Harland jumped back into the cab and raced the motor. Belching black smoke, the tractor jerked the front loader aloft. The ducking stool dangled freely in the breeze from the river.

"I thought a ducking stool was sort of a teeter-totter," said Edward. "The judge or whoever sat on one end, the accused witch on the other, and then the judge got up."

"Yes," said Quill.

"That's a lot simpler than using a tractor, isn't it?"

"Yes," said Quill.

"So why . . . ."

"Harland Peterson wanted to be part of the play. But he refused to dress up in a costume."

"And!"

"The Petersons have owned most of the town for generations. See that nice house there, over by the pavilion? Tom Peterson lives there. He's Harland's cousin. Harland donated the land for the park. And he owns a tractor."

"Ah." A look of ineffable pleasure crossed Edward's face. "I'm going to enjoy this."

Howie Murchison, Tom Peterson, and Elmer Henry ranged themselves in front of the stool. Esther dragged Mavis unceremoniously in front of them, shoved her head forward into a bowed and penitent attitude, then spoke earnestly to her. She stepped back, raised both arms, and dropped them.

"Take One!" she shouted.

"Are they filming this?" said Edward.

"Oh, no," said Quill cheerfully. "Esther sent away for a PBS videotape on directors' techniques. The Chamber argued for months about paying for it."

"Did they pay?" asked Edward, clearly fascinated.

"No. Marge said she'd tell Esther what to do for free."

"I ACCUSE!" roared Elmer Henry suddenly.

Mrs. Hallenbeck jumped.

"It's just the play," said Quill. "There's a whole bunch of 'accuses.' "

"I ACCUSE GOODY MARTIN OF THESE WILLFUL AND SATANIC ACTS!" Elmer hollered again. "THE DEATH OF MY GOOD MILCH COW! THE SICKENING AND DISEASE OF MY FLOCK OF HENS!"

"Crowd!" demanded Esther authoritatively. "The chorus, please!"

The crowd consisted of the eighteen Chamber members who didn't have major speaking parts. Quill noticed Keith Baumer had insinuated himself into the group.

Mumblings indicated the crowd was confused. Esther circulated briefly, issuing instructions, then stepped aside. "Take Two!"

"I ACCUSE!" roared Elmer, and recounted the death of several chickens, ducks, and sundry hogs.

"Crowd!" shouted Esther imperatively.

"Sink or swim! Sink or swim!" the crowd roared.

Mavis flung her hands over her head and fell to the ground with a thud. "As God is my witness! I'll never be hungry again!" Mavis shrieked dramatically.

Esther threw her script to the ground, hauled Mavis up by the collar of the print dress, and shook her finger in her face. "Take Three!" she said in loud disgust.

Elmer, Tom, and Howie declaimed in turn about the demise of their livestock. The crowd yelled "Sink or swim" until it was hoarse. With a defiant shake of her head at Esther, Mavis prostrated herself in front of her accusers and cried, "As God is my witness . . . I am innocent!"

"She got the line right this time," said Quill.

The "judge"—Gil in a black cloak, a tricorne hat, and a ruffled shirt—handed Mavis over for trial.

"Of course," Edward observed with a mischievous glance at Quill. "The French costumes. So much more attractive than those staid Pilgrims."

Screaming enthusiastically, Mavis was dragged to the ducking stool, roped in, and swung aloft. The front loader flipped forward, and Mavis slid into the pond. She emerged and swam to shore to loud applause.

"They go to the pavilion and have the trial next," said Quill.

"What happens there?" asked Edward.

"Well, she's tried. Convicted. There's this speech. Elmer comes out from behind the fence with a horse-drawn sledge and she's drawn off on it just long enough to substitute a dummy. The sledge comes back with a hooded dummy on it—they believed witches could hypnotize you to hell with their eyes. There's a procession to the foot of that statue of General Hemlock, and then a bunch of guys lower a barn door onto the dummy and the crowd piles stones on it."

"My goodness!" said Mrs. Hallenbeck. "The violence of these Pilgrims."

"Straight out of a Shirley Jackson story," muttered Edward.

Gil, his arm around a laughing Mavis, broke away from the crowd at the pond and headed toward them. Keith Baumer and Marge followed them like hopeful puppies.

"You're soaking wet, Mavis," said Mrs. Hallenbeck. "You should change."

"Don't worry your little ol' head about me," said Mavis with a broad smile. "So. What d'yall think?"

"You were marvelous," said Quill promptly. "It's going beautifully. If you don't mind, I'm going to take Mrs. Hallenbeck back to the Inn. I've got a lot of work backed up."

"Oh, we'll take care of Mrs. Hallenbeck," said Gil. He swept his tricorne off his head with a flourish. "Ma'am? Mavis has told me all about you. I'm eager to make your acquaintance. Mavis here suggested we take you down to the pavilion so you can watch the rest of the play. Then we're going along to Marge's diner for a bite of supper—Keith, Marge, Mavis, and me."

Mavis batted her eyelashes at Edward. "Why don't you come along, too?" She smoothed her print dress over her hips. "I am just dyin' to hear what you think of the rest of it. And Amelia? You're going to love Gil, here. I have to tell you he reminds me a lot of your late husband, good man that he was." She smiled even more broadly at Quill. "Now, what's that worried frown for? I've been taking care of this lady for a good many years now. She's in good hands, Miss Quilliam."

Quill, walking back to the Inn alone, had begun to doubt that very much.

"It's not that I have anything to go on other than this feeling, Myles," she said to him over a late dinner. "There's just something odd about Mavis."

"What, exactly?"

"The first day she was here, she was—I don't know. I thought. This poor woman is completely under Mrs. Hallenbeck's thumb. I even thought how awful her life must be, at this dreadful old woman's beck and call. But now . . ." She moved the salt and pepper shakers a little closer to the sugar bowl, then back again. The dining room was quiet. Most of the staff had gone home.

"Now, what?"

"Mrs. Hallenbeck isn't dreadful—just pathetic and lonely. And I don't think it's the Valium that's making Mavis so . . ."

"Slutty?" suggested Myles.

" . . . she's just *like* that!"

"Sheriff?" Davey Kiddermeister rapped at the dining room door and walked in. The youngest of the uniformed officers on Myles's force, his normally ruddy face was pale. "Sheriff? Gil Gilmeister's dead. They found him drowned over to the duck pond. Where the play was on this afternoon. He and Marge and a couple of guests from the Inn were at the Croh Bar. Guess they were getting into the booze pretty good."

"Dammit!" said Myles. He rose in a single powerful movement. "Quill. You *stay here*, understand me? I don't want you meddling."

Quill, a little numb with shock, followed them out the door.

CHAPTER 5

Davey raced ahead to set up the floodlights. Following Myles to the duck pond, Quill saw that the moon was a ghostly galleon riding the wine-dark sea. Bess, the landlord's daughter, she told herself in justification, would have been a lot better off if she'd *done* something rather than hanging out the Inn window fiddling with her hair.

"Myles."

Myles didn't bother to turn around, but threw over his shoulder, "Back to the Inn, Quill."

"T-lot t-lot to you, too," she muttered, jogging behind him. Then aloud, "If nothing else, I can see that the rescue team gets coffee."

The red lights of the ambulance spun wildly, bouncing off the cars and pickup trucks already jamming the small parking lot. Most of the onlookers were patrons-in-residence at the Croh Bar. Situated directly across from the Volunteer Firemens' garage, the bar acted as a kind of holding pen for rubberneckers.

There was a shout. The floodlights switched on. Quill stopped, dismayed. Gil's body lay face-down on the grass beside the pond, the ducking stool twisting slowly above him. Mavis and Marge, both soaking wet, huddled near the body. Keith Baumer was nowhere in sight. There was a short silence as Myles approached, then a babble of voices.

"Who pulled him out?" asked Myles.

Davey jerked his thumb at Marge.

"Andy Bishop here?" Myles crouched by the body.

"He's on his way, Sheriff," somebody called from the crowd.

Myles took a pen from his shirt pocket and pushed Gil's rucked-up shirt collar aside. Quill peered over his shoulder. There was a gash in the back of Gil's head. The water had washed it clean, and the purple lips gaped at Quill.

"Davey, I need a hand here." Myles grasped the body's shoulders, Davey the feet, and the two men turned Gil over.

Quill had never seen a drowning before; one look at the blue face, the foam at nostrils and mouth, and she turned quickly away. Myles cleared the area around the body with a few sharp words. Quill backed up, then walked around the fence that concealed Harland Peterson's John Deere tractor. It crouched like a metal Arnold Schwarzenegger, arms holding the front loader extending over the top of the fence. The front loader itself hung at a sharp angle, one end dangling free of the metal arm. Quill stood on tiptoe. The heavy shovel had worked loose. Partially dried blood glistened on the edge. Quill squinted at it in the glare of the floodlights. Blood, hair, and what may have been a bit of bone.

"Gotta close this off, Ms. Quill," said Davey.

"Where's the bolt?" asked Quill.

"Ma'am?"

"The bolt that held the front loader to the tractor arm."

Davey shrugged. "Into the river, maybe? It'd be swept away for sure. Sheriff wants to know if you could see to Mrs. Collinwood and Marge."

Marge and Mavis huddled under a blanket marked "Hemlock Falls Volunteer Ambulance." Quill sat down in the grass next to them and folded her arms around her knees. "You guys all right?" she asked. "Can I get you some hot coffee or anything?"

Marge snorted.

"What happened?"

Mavis began to cry. Marge herself was weeping silently, and impulsively, Quill put her arm around her.

"We were just practicin'," wailed Mavis, "for the play.

Just foolin' around. I swear I never dreamed this was gonna happen."

"And Gil sat in the ducking stool?"

Mavis gave a gigantic sniff. "He was saying my lines. Jus' jokin'. Hopped in the stool, and the next thing happened was that big ol' shovel came right down on his head. He fell into the pond and we went to drag him out, but we couldn't *find* him. Marge here kept going under water and pokin' around"— a convulsive shudder shook her—"and his *arm* or somethin' brushed my leg and I screamed."

"Was Keith Baumer with you?" asked Quill.

"*Him*," said Marge with contempt. "Took off like a scalded cat. I pulled Gil out, tried CPR. Didn't work. Mavis here called the ambulance from the pay phone."

A brand new white Corvette screamed into the parking lot and came to a screeching halt. The passenger door slammed, and a tall, skinny woman with bleached blond hair walked toward the body. Tom Peterson got out from the driver's side.

"Shit," said Marge. "Tom Peterson's brought ol' Nadine."

"Nadine is Gil's wife," said Quill in response to Mavis' bewilderment, "and Tom's her brother." *And Marge is Gil's girlfriend*, she said silently. "Maybe you two ought to come back to the Inn with me."

"Too late," said Marge practically. "Here she comes, and Tom with her."

Years of up-and-down dieting, combined with a permanent, free-floating discontent, had not been especially kind to Nadine Gilmeister's face. Quill noted with interest that her makeup was freshly applied, and her hair as elaborately styled as ever. It was after midnight, at a time when only innkeepers and late-night partiers were in street clothes, but Nadine had taken the time to put on a newly dry-cleaned jumpsuit. Although, Quill saw, at least she'd been upset enough to forget to remove the cleaner's tag from the collar.

Tom held Nadine's arm, greeted Quill with a nicely balanced degree of calm and concern, then said, "I was watching a videotape when I saw the ambulance light. I walked over here, and thought I'd better go get Nadine."

"Susan isn't home?" asked Quill.

"No. It's her bridge night. I think I can handle Nadine—but I may need to call on you, Quill."

"So this supposed rehearsal and business meeting was with you, Marge Schmidt," Nadine said.

"You know darn well it was, Nadine. We was both there when he called you."

"Both?"

Marge indicated the sodden Mavis. "Mavis. This is Gil's wife, Mavis."

Mavis, still crying, said, "The one runnin' the poor soul into debt?"

"How dare you!" shrieked Nadine. "And my poor Gil lying there dead as a doornail."

Tom looked nervously at Quill.

"A pretty well-insured doornail," said Marge. "Which is good for you, on account of he owes me a pile of money."

"Can you *believe* this woman?" Nadine addressed the stars. "I am standing right here and I cannot believe my ears. The man's not yet cold."

Marge glared up at her, then rose menacingly. "He'll never be as cold dead as you are living, Nadine Gilmeister." She took a deep breath.

Gil's relationship with Marge, as yet unacknowledged by either wife or girlfriend, appeared to be the next item on the agenda. Quill, sensing ill will, if not the potential for outright violence, stepped forward to take a hand.

"What is this dreadful noise!" demanded a familiar voice. "What has happened here? Mavis! Why in the world are you dressed in those wet clothes?" Mrs. Hallenbeck trotted out of the darkness, well-wrapped against the evening air in a plaid Pendleton bathrobe.

"What're you doin' here, Amelia?" asked Mavis sourly.

"If I may remind you, both our rooms overlook this view. The emergency vehicle lights wakened me. I knocked on your door. There was no answer. I deduced that you must be down here. What has happened?"

"Mrs. Hallenbeck." The authority in her own voice surprised Quill. She would have to practice more. "I want you and Mavis to come with me. Marge, I think you should check with the sheriff to see if you can go home now.

Nadine, I am so very sorry for your loss."

"Let's go, Nadine," said Tom. "You'll want to ride with . . . er . . . to the hospital."

Nadine glared at Marge. "The ambulance's waiting on me," she said. "I'll leave you to later, Marge Schmidt."

Marge took herself glumly off. Quill walked Mavis and Mrs. Hallenbeck back to the Inn.

Most of the Inn's guests had crowded into the lobby, and when Quill shepherded the widows in the front door, they volleyed questions. Meg, John, and Doreen were dressed, all three prepared to offer assistance. "But John said to stay here in case we had to evacuate or save the silver or something," said Meg. "What happened?"

Quill explained there'd been a drowning. The orthodontist's wife clutched her youngest offspring, an unprepossessing ten-year-old, and wanted to know if the Inn was all that safe for children. The orthodontist cleared his throat portentiously and said, as a medical man, he'd be glad to help if the accident had anything to do with teeth, gums specifically. Quill, engulfed in waves of tiredness from a second disturbed night's sleep, told everybody to please go to bed, and that breakfast in the morning would be on the house.

Keith Baumer, who'd apparently headed straight for the safety of the Inn's bar, volunteered to take the widows to their rooms. Edward Lancashire offered instead. Mavis, dimpling at them, said, "I swan!" with what she clearly thought was a delightful giggle. Mrs. Hallenbeck clutched Quill's arm and demanded that Quill see her to her room. "You must have some tea sent up, my dear, and we can have a nice, long talk."

"Quill's got an inn to run," said John. "I'll take you up, Mrs. Hallenbeck."

"Absolutely not!" said Mrs. Hallenbeck. "That is an intolerable suggestion! Quill, you will come up to my room at once."

"I'm sorry, Mrs. Hallenbeck," said Quill, "but I have my responsibilities here."

Keith Baumer, loud in confused explanations of why he had left the scene of the accident, escorted Mavis and Mrs. Hallenbeck upstairs.

Meg, after a close look at her sister's face, marched her into the kitchen and poured her a double brandy. John and Doreen trailed after them.

"What I don't understand is why the heck it took so long to pull Gil out of the pond," said Meg. "It's not that deep."

"Drink is the opiate of the masses," said Doreen, apropos of nothing.

"You're mixing up Marx with the Victorians," said Meg briskly. "And what do you mean, 'drink'? If this religious stuff you've come back from vacation with is teetotal, you can just forget it. Nobody wants you charging the bar and whacking the boozers with your mop."

"If Jesus turned water into wine for the Kennedys, then he blesses those that take a nip, on occasion," said Doreen loftily. She poured a hefty belt from the brandy bottle into a coffee cup. "What I meant is, those three was down to Croh's after eatin' at Marge's."

"*Real*-ly?" said Meg with interest. "Probably to help them forget what they'd had for dinner. But were they soused, you think?"

"I saw them," John volunteered. "I'd say half the town did. They were knocking them back."

"You were at Croh's?" said Meg. "Is that what you do on your nights off? I've never seen you take a drink here, John—not in all the months you've been here."

"Meg," warned Quill, "give it a rest."

"Eternal rest," mused Doreen, "rocked in the Everlasting arms."

"Poor Gil," said Meg. "Better everlasting arms than Nadine, though."

Quill choked on her brandy, and raised a hand in protest.

"So that shovel just whacked him on the back of the head and those two ladies were too smashed to pull him out of the water," Meg continued sunnily. "What a lousy accident."

"If it was an accident," said Quill. "And you didn't actually see it, Meg, so let's not joke about it, okay?"

"What do you mean, 'if it was an accident'?" said John.

"The bolt that attaches the payloader to the support was missing," said Quill. "Now, admittedly, that's an old tractor. A fifty-six or fifty-seven, somebody said. And the Petersons don't spend a lot on maintenance. But if it fell out, where was it? I investigated and I didn't find it."

"*You* investigated!" hooted Meg. "I should have sold all your Nancy Drews to Bernie Hofstedder in the sixth grade."

"Couldn't it have fallen into the river?" said John.

"It's not likely," said Quill crossly. "There's an enclosure there, remember? The bolt would have fallen inside the fence. I looked, and it wasn't there."

"It depends on *when* it came off," John persisted. "If it snapped under the tension of Gil's weight in the ducking stool, it could have flown quite a distance."

"Not that far," Quill said. "I looked at the one that was still in place on the other side of the tractor. That bolt has to weigh a pound at least. I just can't see something that heavy flying over the fence into the river."

"But who'd want to kill Gil Gilmeister?" said Meg. "I mean, other than the poor shmucks who bought cars from him. And how could anybody know that Gil and those two were going down to the duck pond for a drunken 'rehearsal'? More than that, how could this supposed murderer be sure that *Gil* was going to sit in the thing? The only person scheduled to use it was Mavis."

"The Devil's abroad tonight," said Doreen.

"Oh, it is not," said Meg. "Honestly, Doreen, just leave it to Myles. He'll do his usual bang-up investigation and clear it up in no time."

"Thorough, is he?" asked John.

"You haven't been with us long enough to see him in action," said Meg, "but he's just terrific. He was a senior-grade detective with the New York City police force before he moved here."

"He's too young to have retired," said John.

"He didn't retire, he quit," said Meg. "Just got fed to the back teeth. Said he was losing his sense of proportion. Thing is, he's got all kinds of great connections from his days on the force. What crime there is around here gets solved really fast."

"You didn't know about Myles, John?" asked Quill.

"Come to think of it, you two don't see much of each other," said Meg, "but you'll see him in action now. If Quill doesn't solve it first." She rolled her eyes at her sister.

John's face softened with what might have been a smile.

"I wish you luck, Quill. Here—" He dug his hand into his jeans pocket and dropped his Indian-head nickel into her palm. "Maybe this will help."

"From your grandfather, the Chief?" She wrapped her fingers around the coin. "Did you inherit any of his tracking skills? If we pooled our talents, we could solve this before Super Sheriff even files a report."

John was silent a moment. "I'll leave it to the experts. Good night, Quill, Meg." He touched Doreen briefly on the shoulder, an unusual gesture for him, and padded silently from the kitchen.

"Well, Hawkshaw, what now?" said Meg. "Shall we haul out the magnifying glass, the scene-of-the-crime kit, and the rubber hose?"

"The only thing I'm going to solve now is my fatigue. It's after one o'clock. I'm going to lock up and go to bed."

"I'll do it," said Doreen. "You look bushed. You too, Meg." She shook her head dourly, the omnipresent cigarette dripping ashes on Meg's wooden counter. "The Devil's presence is here tonight. Just like the Revrund Willy Max warned us in Boca Raton. I shall seek Satan out in the dark corners of this place."

"Be quiet about it," advised Meg, "or you'll wake up the guests."

"Maybe some of 'em should be woke up," said Doreen smacking her lips. "See the signs for their ownselves."

"The only sign I want to see is the face of my alarm clock at six A.M. tomorrow," said Meg.

Quill, agreeing, went upstairs to bed, and fell into an exhausted sleep. She was awakened by the shrilling of the house phone.

"Miss Quilliam? Sarah?"

Groggy with sleep, Quill blinked at the bedside clock. "It's eight o'clock!" she said into the phone. "Damn!" She shook the clock. The alarm, which had been set for six, burst into the morning silence like a chain saw. Quill smacked it against the night table and the ringing stopped.

"Miss Quilliam? It's me, Dina. You know, at the front desk. I'm sorry to get you up."

"It's way past time to get up," said Quill. Her thoughts soggy, she said belatedly, "Why are you whispering?"

"It's the guests."

"What?"

Dina raised her voice. There was a suspicion of a shriek in it. "The guests! They're milling around here like . . . like . . . hornets."

"They're angry? What hap—Never mind. I'll be right down."

She grabbed the first clothes at hand, a denim skirt and a navy blue T-shirt, hastily dressed, and headed for the lobby. The orthodontist, his wife, their little boy, Mavis Collinwood, and Keith Baumer were clotted in front of Dina. They did resemble hornets after prey. They broke into a buzzing whine of exclamations as Quill descended the staircase.

"Here she is!" Dina said. Relief washed over her like water over a thirsty prospector. "Miss Quilliam, there's this sort of problem . . ." She trailed off helplessly.

"Why don't you go into my office, Dina, and take care of the phones. Have you called John?"

"Yes, but he didn't answer."

"Call the kitchen and ask Meg to get someone to find him. Now—" She turned to the orthodontist, who seemed to have the lowest level of agitation. "How can I help you?"

"It's downright disgustin'!" interrupted Mavis Collinwood.

"Calm down, Mave," said Keith Baumer.

"Dr. Bolt, maybe you could explain?" said Quill.

"It's these messages. Little scraps of paper pushed under our doors." He held out a piece of paper. Printed in large block letters at the top of the page was: CALL 1–800–222—PRAY! Beneath it, Quill read aloud, "The Lord sees all evil! The Lord hears all evil! Thou shalt not steal!"

The orthodontist's ten-year-old son burst into noisy wails.

"Adrian," said his mother. She shook his shoulder imperatively. "Stop that!"

Dr. Bolt avoided Quill's questioning look. "We were due to check out this morning, as you know. We packed our suitcases and went down for an early breakfast. When we came back, the room had been cleaned, and we find this message." His chest swelled with indignation. "Now, look here, Miss Quilliam. I do not condone Adrian's appropriation of towels and ashtrays as souvenirs. My wife and I have already discussed this with him. On the other hand, I must register a serious complaint about your housekeeping staff going through my little boy's belongings."

"Oh, dear," said Quill.

"And on my bathroom mirror?" said Mavis indignantly. "I jus' stepped out this mornin' for a walk with Mr. Baumer, and when I came back . . . well, I don' want to even repeat what was written on my bathroom mirror. In soap!"

"It didn't say anything about Detroit did it?" said Quill.

"Don't you get smart with me, Miss High-and-Mighty," said Mavis. "I scrubbed that mirror clean. The ol' bat sees it, I'm out of a job."

"Where is Mrs. Hallenbeck?" asked Quill.

"Out for a walk," said Mavis sullenly. "Says she's been complimented frequently on her complexion and a walk helps. Lord!"

Quill apologized to the orthodontist, the orthodontist's wife, and gave a souvenir ashtray to the little boy, who stopped wailing and demanded a towel, too. She couldn't bring herself to apologize to Baumer. She took ten percent off the orthodontist's bill. She soothed Mavis, who flounced upstairs to see to Mrs. Hallenbeck, who may or may not have returned from her walk, and advised her to destroy any messages that may have been shoved under the old lady's door.

When the lobby was clear of guests, she took the master key, went up to Baumer's room and let herself in. A slip fluttered from beneath the door: AND HE CURSED THEM WITH MANY CURSES! THE PLAGUES OF EGYPT ARE UPON HIM! After a moment's thought, she checked the dresser drawers (clear of noxious items), the bathtub (ditto), and then stripped the bed. She removed two dead grasshoppers, a garden slug, and a lively cricket from between the sheets.

She marched to the kitchen. Meg was busy with a cheese soufflé, an apprentice holding a large whisk, and a copper bowl. Doreen, she said in response to her sister's evenly worded questions, had left for a Bible class or something. "No! The egg whites have to peak before you fold in the yolks or the damn thing'll be flatter than my chest!" She turned her attention to Quill, who had reiterated her desire to see Doreen. "Can't this wait?"

Quill began an explanation.

"Hand it over to John," Meg interrupted. "He's pretty good with her."

"Where is he?"

"I don't know!" said Meg. "Quill, will you get out of the kitchen? Whatever she did can wait until after the breakfast crowd leaves."

Quill sat in the dining room. She ate an omelette *aux fines herbes*, grapefruit broiled in brown sugar, and a scone. She drank two cups of coffee. She decided that she wouldn't string Doreen up by her thumbs. She even began to find the messages funny. The second cup of coffee convinced her that all Doreen needed was a new enthusiasm. Maybe she could suggest cross-stitch.

By nine, John still hadn't shown up, and she went to look for him. None of the staff had seen him. She knocked on the door of his rooms and received no answer. She went outside, thinking that perhaps he'd gone down to see Mike, the groundskeeper, but Mike was trimming the boxwood, and admitted he hadn't seen John at all that morning.

It was a glorious morning. The air was soft, the sun benign. The display of dahlias by the drive proved irresistible. Feeling a bit guilty, Quill took some secateurs from the gardening shed and spent a contented hour clipping dead heads, weeding, and aerating roots.

The mindless and beneficial calm that overtakes the dedicated gardener was interrupted by Dina. Quill sat back on her heels and smiled happily at her. "John show up?"

"No." Dina, who was affecting the seventies look this year, chewed at the ends of her long brown hair.

"Not more Old Testament doom, death, and disaster? Doreen isn't even here."

"No. Can you come to the office?"

Quill stored the secateurs, the trowel, and the gloves, and followed Dina back to the Inn.

"I heard about last night, and the night before that," she said, "and I thought, well, I'll just let her garden peacefully for a bit. But, Quill, this is a real mess. Maybe I should have come to get you before this."

"What's a real mess?"

"These cancellations!" The phone buzzed angrily. Dina

groaned. Puzzled, Quill picked up the phone and answered, "Hemlock Inn, may I help you?"

An outraged woman demanded the manager.

"I'm one of the partners in the Inn," said Quill. "Can I help you?"

Why, demanded the voice, had her tour group received a last-minute cancellation notice this morning? Did she, Quill, have any idea how disruptive this was? Did she, Quill, have any idea of the contortions required to find a last-minute booking elsewhere? As far as Golden Years Tours was concerned, the Hemlock Falls Inn was off their promotional literature. Forever. And everybody else in the tour business was going to hear about it. Immediately.

Quill hung up the phone.

"Another one?" said Dina. "That'll be the fourth."

"Have you seen John this morning?"

"Nope."

"Do you have the bookings ledger?"

"Couldn't find it. It's not behind the front desk, where I usually keep it, and it's not in the desk here. I *know* I had it this morning. It was on the counter, because all those people were checking out."

"There's a copy on disk in the computer," said Quill carefully. "Dina, I know you worked last night, but before you go, could you help me pull up the records on the PC and call everyone that's booked for this week? Just let them know that a . . . prank of some kind has been pulled. Tell them to disregard any phone calls they may have had. Tell them you're calling to confirm the reservations. If we split the list up, we can maybe salvage the week."

By noon, Quill thanked the exhausted Dina, sent her home, and totaled up the losses for the next business quarter. The caller had been busy; a dozen calls to the major revenue-producing tours had been made between eight-thirty and ten. The message in each case had been brief: the Inn was calling for John Raintree, to cancel confirmed reservations. Very sorry, but there's been a major problem. The Inn was closed. To those few customers who'd been loyal enough to inquire when the Inn would reopen, the message was curt: the Inn would not reopen.

CHAPTER 6

At first baffled, Quill searched the grounds, talked to the staff, and made phone calls to a few of John's accounting clients. By two o'clock, Quill's concern for John's whereabouts had escalated to irritation.

Quill went to the first-floor rooms John had occupied for the past year. She knocked, received no answer, then used her master key. She'd been in the rooms no more than two or three times, and each time wondered at the Spartan quality of John's personal life. Three suits hung in the closet; one winter, two summer. Two sports coats. A modest number of white shirts, a handful of ties, and other necessities barely filled the bureau drawer and the bathroom cabinet.

A photograph of a pretty Indian girl leaning on the hood of a car stood on the night stand; the print had faded a little. The car was a 1978 Olds Delta 88. John's diploma awarding him an MBA from the Rochester Institute of Technology was propped on the small desk. There were books on the shelf under the TV. *Aztec*, by Gary Jennings; *Beggars in Spain*, by Nancy Kress; dozens of science fiction and historical novels. There were perhaps half a dozen self-help books: all of them dealt with alcoholism.

Quill addressed the photograph. "I do not believe that this man did this," she said. "There is no way that I will ever believe John did this." The dark eyes stared back at her.

"We've got three questions to answer," Quill told her. "First one is, Where the hell is John? The second is, How did he get there? The third is, Who tried to pull the unfunniest joke in hotel history and blame it on him? Marge Schmidt? She wasn't even *near* the place this morning. Keith Baumer, playing tricks on his morning walk? Maybe Mavis—out of revenge for her fall from the balcony? When I get those answers, there won't be any more questions . . . just a major whack up the side of the head for whoever gets in my way."

Quill slammed outside to the gardens in a highly satisfying rage. She collared a clearly startled Mike the groundskeeper, who said No, he hadn't seen John; his car was gone, but he hadn't seen John leave. Balked, Quill went to find her sister.

"You're kidding!" said Meg. She was in the storeroom, stacking fresh vegetables in the wire bins. "Would you look at those Vidalias I got this morning? God, they're gorgeous! I'm putting French onion soup on the specials tonight."

"You can't, Meg," said Quill, momentarily distracted. "You use raw egg in the stock."

"So? Makes it richer. Did the Buffalo Gourmet Club cancel? That's an oxymoron if I've ever heard one. Remember last year when they had that food fight in the bar?"

"That was the Kiwanis from Schenectady. Are you listening to me?"

Meg breathed on a tomato, polished it with the bottom of her T-shirt, and set it on the shelf. "Yes, sweetie. I'm listening to you. John's gone. About thirty per cent of the business is gone because somebody pulled a jerky joke. But the bank hasn't called the mortgage or anything, has it? The business will come back. And we can get another hotel manager—the Cornell School's filled with wannabees. I mean, look at the luck I've had with the *sous* chefs from there."

"And salmonella hasn't poisoned anybody—yet."

Meg grinned and bit her lip. "Okay. I'll make onion soufflé. Or maybe just chop it up fresh with these beefsteak tomatoes. They're the most beautiful tomato in the world, these beefsteaks."

Quill sat on a hundred-pound sack of rice and put her chin in her hands. "So what do you think I should do?"

"What can you do? Myles is right, don't fuss so much, Quill. John will come back with a perfectly logical explanation, and if he doesn't—done's done."

"And those phone calls?"

"That foul Baumer is capable of anything, if you ask me. You turned down his gallant advances yesterday morning, didn't you? Well, in my vast experience of disappointed harassers, it'd be right up his mean, spiteful alley."

"You don't think it was Marge?"

"The bookings ledger was here this morning, and Marge wasn't. It would have taken her an hour to copy all those names and numbers. She wasn't here long enough last night to do it."

"And that missing bolt?"

"What possible connection could poor Gil's accident have with John running off on a toot, most likely, and a series of malicious phone calls?"

"I don't know," Quill said, "but by God, there is one."

Sitting at her desk, contemplating the display of Apricot Nectar roses outside her office window, Quill failed to find any connection at all.

She shuffled through her phone messages: nothing from Myles; one from Esther reading "The show must go on! Rehearsal at the Inn 4:00 P.M."; a few from tour directors wanting a chance to discuss the practical joke, which she set aside for Monday during business hours; and one scrawled on a piece of the wrapper for the paper towels the Inn bought in bulk: AND WORMS SHALL CRAWL THROUGH HER NOSE. "Doreen!" said Quill. "Dammit, *whose* nose?"

"Whose nose?" she repeated when she found the housekeeper scrubbing the toilets in 218. Doreen had listened stolidly to Quill's succinct summary of why she was *not* to impose her beliefs on the guests.

"That scarlet woman," said Doreen, "that whore of Babylon."

"I thought it was the whore of Detroit."

"Don't you laugh at me, missy. I need a little Bible study is all." She sat back on her heels and contemplated the gleaming porcelain with satisfaction. "I joined the Reverend

Shuttleworth's Bible classes this morning. Learn me a bit more."

"Let's get back to this wormy person," suggested Quill. "You haven't whacked the orthodontist's wife, have you?"

"They checked out. Nope. It's that Miss Prissy butter-wouldn't-melt-in-her mouth friend of the widow lady. Mrs. Hallenbeck's companion. A righteous woman, that Mrs. Hallenbeck, to my way of thinking. She shouldn't have to put up with a person bound for the Pit."

"You mean Mavis Collinwood? Where is she?"

"Bar. Acting no better than she should with that skirt-chasing salesman."

"Doreen, I've just finished telling you that the guests' behavior is no business of ours."

Doreen got up from the tile floor with a groan, and attacked the tub. "Will be if that poor Mrs. Hallenbeck has a heart attack from the sheer cussedness of that woman."

Quill, mindful of the alarming changes in Mavis' personality after her ingestion of Andy Bishop's Valium samples, went to the bar. The mystery of John's whereabouts would have to be put on hold. Besides, she could tackle Baumer about the phone calls. Meg was probably right.

Called The Tavern in their brochures, the bar was the most popular spot at the Inn, occupying an entire quarter of the first floor. The bar's floor and ceiling were of polished mahogany. Floor-to-ceiling windows took up the south and east walls. Quill had painted the north and west walls teal, and Meg had persuaded her to hang a half dozen of her larger acrylics on the jewel-toned walls.

When Quill left her career as an artist, she'd been heralded as the successor to Georgia O'Keeffe. "A small stride forward in the school of magic realism," wrote the critic in *Art Review*. The brilliance of the yellows, oranges, and scarlets of her Flower Series leaped out from the walls with exuberance.

Some weeks, when Quill longed for the rush of her old studio in Manhattan, she avoided The Tavern altogether; at other times, she sat in the bar and took a guilty pleasure in her work.

It was early for the bar trade, but the tourists had started arriving for History Days, and the room was full. At first, Quill didn't see Mavis and Baumer. When she did, she wondered how she could have missed them.

Mavis had bloomed like the last rose of summer. Gone were the prim collars, the below-the-knee print skirts, the spray-stiffened hair. Mavis' full bosom spilled out of a black T-shirt with an illuminated teddy bear on the front. Quill couldn't imagine where Mavis had tucked the batteries. The T-shirt was pulled over a pair of black stirrup pants. Mavis' high-heeled shoes were a screaming red suede with bows at the ankles.

"Coo-eee!" Mavis called, waving her hand at Quill. Nate, the bartender, gave Quill a wry grin and a shrug. Quill leaned over the marble bartop and whispered, "How long have they been here?"

"Through two Manhattans for the gentleman and two mint—"

"Don't say it!" groaned Quill.

"—juleps for the lady."

"Nobody drinks mint juleps, Nate. Not willingly, anyway."

"That's one dedicated Southerner, I guess."

"As far as I know, she's still taking that Valium Doc Bishop prescribed for her," said Quill. "Keep an eye on them, will you?"

"Hard not to," said Nate. "I can short the drinks, if you want."

"If you do, short the bar tab, too." Quill threaded her way through the tables and sat down next to Keith Baumer. "Did you and Mrs. Hallenbeck get a decent night's sleep, Mavis?"

"I did, I guess. I don't know about the old bat. She was up walking around awful early, I can tell you that."

"Best part of the day," said Baumer genially. "I'm up at six and out for a walk every morning. Get a head start on my work."

"Does your business include a lot of out-of-town phone calls?" Quill asked coolly.

Baumer showed his teeth in what might have been a grin. "Lots." He raised his hand and shouted, "Barkeep! Another round for us. And I'd like to buy you a drink, Ms. Quilliam. What's your poison?"

"Nate will bring me a cup of coffee. Mavis, about last night—"

"Wasn't it awful?" Mavis' eyes filled with ready tears. "That poor, poor man. I'd only met him that day. But he was such a friendly soul. So open, so candid in his needs. I declare, it was like seeing a dear friend pass."

Baumer gripped her knee with a proprietary air. "Comfort is what you need, Mave. And I've got just the ticket."

Mavis dimpled at him.

Nate set drinks and a plate of hors d'oeuvres on the table, a signal he had shorted the liquor in at least Mavis' mint julep. "Compliments of the house, Mr. Baumer."

"Hold it, hold it, my man. Let's see what we have here." Baumer poked disparagingly through the food. "Stuffed mushrooms, for God's sake. You'd think a place with this kind of reputation would be a little more creative, eh? And what the hell is this? Liverwurst?" He wiggled his eyebrows at Quill.

"Meg's Country Pâté," said Quill. "And that's pork rillette, and anchovy paste on sourdough."

Baumer stuffed a mushroom in his mouth, chewed, and grunted, "Not bad. I've had better. But not bad. Here, kiddo, sink your teeth into this." He offered Mavis a pork rillette.

Quill, contemplating Mavis, remembered that John had seen them at the Croh Bar. Was there any connection between John's disappearance and Gil's drowning last night? Her palms went cold. "I wasn't very clear on what did happen last night, Mavis. Was Mrs. Hallenbeck with you all evening?"

Mavis scowled. "Pretty near. We went down to Marge's for dinner. It *was* a business meeting, you know, whatever that Nadine-person thought. Gil wanted to talk with Amelia about investing in his business."

"She doesn't act like she has that kind of money."

"Who? Amelia?" Mavis snorted, leaving a significant portion of the pork rillette on her chin. "You've got to be kidding. She's loaded."

Quill, hoping for more information, raised a skeptical eyebrow.

"Well, she is. She held practically all of the stock in Doggone Good Dogs. Made out like a bandit when the company was sold."

"She did?" said Quill.

"Well, sure. Her husband must have left her a packet, although she sure acts like she's broke. Penny-pinching ol' thing." Mavis giggled uncertainly. Her eyes were glazed. Baumer solicitously helped her to the rest of her mint julep.

"So that's how you met her? You worked for her husband?"

"Who says so?" demanded Mavis suddenly. "Who says I worked for him? It's a damn lie!" She swayed a little in her chair, the teddy bear on her T-shirt blinking furiously.

Quill was going to have to sober her up before asking about John. And she sure didn't want to ask any more questions in front of the rude and inquisitive Baumer. "Are you sure you don't want to lie down, Mavis?" said Quill. "You know, Dr. Bishop thought you should take it easy for a few days."

Mavis got to her feet. She swayed a little, her face pale. "I declare, I do feel jus' a little bit woozy."

"Why don't you come and lie down in my room," said Baumer. "I can give you a back rub or something, help you sleep."

"I'll give her a hand, Mr. Baumer," said Quill coldly. "Come on, Mavis. Alley-oop."

"Alley-oop!"

Quill propelled Mavis firmly through the bar and up the short flight of stairs to two-sixteen. She knocked briefly on the door; when no answer came from Mrs. Hallenbeck, she used her master key and pulled Mavis inside. The rooms were dark, the drapes drawn.

"Who's there?" called a timid voice.

"It's me, Mrs. Hallenbeck. I've brought Mavis up for a nap." Quill eased Mavis, by now half-asleep, onto the bed. The connecting door opened, and Mrs. Hallenbeck peered fearfully into the room.

"She is not drunk again, is she?"

Quill pulled the bedspread over the blinking T-shirt. Mavis looked up blearily. "Amelia? I'm sorry, sugar. Guess I had a li'l too much to drink. We'll go for your walk in a bit. I jus' need a snooze." She closed her eyes, then popped them open again. "Amelia? You're not an ol' bat." She sighed, "I'm the ol' bat," and began to snore.

Even die-hard aging Southern belles look vulnerable in sleep.

Quill decided John couldn't possibly be involved with this woman, or what had happened last night. She knew, abruptly, that what she most wanted was the Inn back the way it was before Mavis' catastrophic transformation into Southern sex kitten of the year. And the key to that was Mrs. Hallenbeck.

"Mrs. Hallenbeck? Could I talk to you a minute?"

"Of course, dear. Please come in."

Quill followed her into 214, closing the door behind her. "Would you like me to open the drapes? It's a beautiful day outside." She pulled the drape cord, and sunshine flooded into the room.

Mrs. Hallenbeck was dressed for walking in a beige trouser suit. She sat down at the little tea table. Her face was stern. "So many terrible things have been happening, Sarah. I was just sitting here in the dark, thinking about them. What's going to happen next? That dreadful accident last night. That Gil person. And Mavis behaving so oddly." Her lips trembled. "Sometimes I think I want to go home. But then I think, what would I do without you, my dear, and your lovely paintings, and your wonderful care of me, and I know we're doing the right thing by staying here."

"As a practical matter, I'm afraid Mavis doesn't have much choice. She'll have to testify at the inquest. But right afterwards, you and Mavis can go on with your vacation."

"Oh, no," said Mrs. Hallenbeck firmly. "Mavis has behaved in a wholly unacceptable manner. I would like you to come with me, dear. That would be wonderful. We could have a very good time together."

"I have the Inn to run, and my sister to take care of," said Quill gently. "But surely you don't want to abandon Mavis after all you've been through together?"

"Mavis? I'm through with Mavis." Mrs. Hallenbeck shuddered. "Her friends make me suspicious. Sometimes I think she's going mad."

"Hardly that," said Quill. "But I do think she's not quite herself." Quill experienced a flash of doubt. What if Mavis *was* a con artist, out to bilk an old lady?

"Have you had these kinds of problems before in your travels? I mean, Mavis introducing you to"—Quill searched for the right, unalarming words—"potential investors?"

Mrs. Hallenbeck sent her a sudden, shrewd look. "You do not get to my age and stage, Sarah, by handing over large checks to boobs like that car salesman. That is not the problem, although Mavis would certainly like me to buy her friends for her. No. The problem is finding someone sympathetic to be with when you're old. Do you know . . ." Her lips worked, and the large blue eyes filled with tears. "I loathe it. How did I get to be eighty-three? Why, I look in the mirror, and I expect to see the girl I was at seventeen. Instead . . . this." She swept her hand in front of her face.

"You have a beautiful face," said Quill. "There is a great dignity in your age. We're all going to get there, Amelia. I just hope that when I do, I look like you."

Mrs. Hallenbeck looked at her. "Mavis used to say such things to me. When we agreed to be companions in our adventures, I thought that she cared for me. And now, everything has changed."

"She's been through quite a bit in the last few days. I think," said Quill carefully, "that she's one of those people who just reacts to the situation at hand. Do you know what I mean? Impulsive. That she'll be fine once the inquest is over and the two of you can leave. Things will be the same as they were before." The Cornell University evening course in Interactive Skills training had emphasized something called Identification as a "tool for change." Tools for change, Quill realized, were not tire irons, but nice, tactful lies that made people want to behave better. "Identification" was a lie that made people behave by telling them you did something you didn't, so they'd feel better about changing their ways.

Quill decided to try Identification. "You know, my sister Meg and I—we fight quite a bit. We say things we don't mean." Quill hesitated, searching for the most appropriate lie. "I'm the older sister. Sort of like you're the older sister to Mavis. And I know sometimes I get very bossy. You know, telling Meg what to wear, how to behave. I even yank on her salary once in a while, if she's not cooking exactly the things I think the guests want. But then I remember that Meg has her own needs and her own life, and that I have to let her be herself. And we get along just fine."

"You think I'm too hard on Mavis?"

Mrs. Hallenbeck, Quill realized, was very good at what the professor had called "cutting the crap." Quill patted her hand. "I should have known you'd be shrewd enough to handle poor Mavis. I should think," Quill said expansively, "that what Mavis is really looking for is guidance. She needs you, Mrs. Hallenbeck. One advantage of being your age is that you've had so much experience with people."

"Possibly you're right. I mean, about comparing this to you and your sister." She sat taller in her chair. "I shall take care of things. You know, Mavis and I have been together for many years. I shall reflect on ways and means."

Quill left Mrs. Hallenbeck and marched triumphantly to the kitchen. Meg was scowling hideously at the Specials blackboard, chalk smeared on her face.

"I am so good!" Quill said. She threw herself into the chair by the fireplace and rocked contentedly.

"What d'ya think goes best with the French onion soup?"

Quill stopped rocking. "Um. You mean the onion soup you weren't going to make because of the raw egg ban?"

"The soufflé's a bust. It's too humid for it. I know!" She scribbled furiously for a moment. "Potted rabbit."

"In this heat? Don't you think something lighter is better for July?"

"Lancashire's booked a party of two for dinner. And I've got fresh rabbit."

Quill rose majestically to her feet. Perhaps the improvised management tactics she'd presented to Mrs. Hallenbeck had been an inspiration; she'd never tried a firm hand with her sister before. "Meg, if you do not stop using raw egg in the food, I will dock your salary."

"You will, huh?" said Meg, unimpressed. Meg put the chalk down and looked consideringly at her sister. "I just might remind Doreen that you spend every Saturday night—*all night*—with a certain good-looking sheriff. She'll want to put worms up your nose, I expect."

"You wouldn't!"

"It'd be nothing less than my duty," said Meg with an air of conscious virtue. She gave her sister an affectionate grin. "So what are you good at? Not this detective stuff?"

Quill sighed. "No. Not this detective stuff."

"You agree that John's probably gone off on a toot? Poor guy, after being sober all these years, and what're you looking at me like that for? You think it's a secret? Everyone knows John goes to A.A. on Thursdays. You know that Gil's accident was just that. And you can bet that creep Baumer was *probably* the one who made those phone calls, out of sheer despair at your rejection of his uncouth advances."

"Ye-e-es," said Quill reluctantly.

"I thought you were going to make a courtesy call on Nadine Gilmeister," Meg said briskly. "One of us has to. And you're *very* good at that."

"I suppose you're right."

"So take a couple of brioches as a tribute to the funeral; get out of my kitchen and do it. Oh, Quill?"

Quill looked back.

"Stop by Tom Peterson's, will you? I stuck some of yesterday's delivery in your car. The meat's tainted."

"The meat?"

"Yes! The meat. It stinks. I can't serve it. Something must be wrong with those refrigeration units. Tell him I want fresh good stuff in the cooler *now*. Make him eat that stuff if he won't."

"Okay," said Quill meekly.

Gil's ostentatious white Colonial was in the town's only suburb, about four miles from the Inn. The street where the now-widowed Nadine lived was lined with cars, and Quill parked her battered Olds half a block away. Hemlock Falls citizens were conscientious about funerals and calling hours. Friends of the deceased rallied around the family, dropping by with a continuous stream of food.

The front door was partly open and she slipped in quietly. She set the brioches in the kitchen between a huge home-cooked ham from the Hogg's Heaven Farms, and a chocolate banana cream pie—Betty Hall's specialty dessert for Saturdays.

She was unsurprised to see Nadine dressed completely in black, something that was Not Done in Hemlock Falls, because it was considered a waste of hard-earned cash. ("So whattya gonna do with a black outfit anyways?" Marge Schmidt had been heard to opine. "Only place to wear it is up to Ms. Barf-your-guts-out-Quilliam's, and after a meal there, you don't have enough left to pay for the dress.")

Marge was, of course, conspicuously absent, but most of the Chamber was there, in force. Quill said hello to Mayor Henry, who nodded gravely, and waved at Howie Murchison, who was in close discussion with Andy Bishop.

A large poster featuring a close-up of Gil's grinning face usually stood by the showroom door at his dealership. Some thoughtful soul had brought it to the house, and it now stood in state by the fireplace, a black-ribboned wreath surmounting the legend "Drowned, But Not Forgotten."

"Not real creative," said Harvey Bozzel, a thick piece of brioche in one hand. "But God! What'd you expect on such short notice? And I've decided not to send a bill. Although the printer double charged for the overtime." Mementos of Gil lay scattered on a table underneath the poster. "Nice touch, don't you think?" said Harvey. "His wallet, his Chamber membership, stuff like that. I think Nadine's going to bury it with him. Except for the credit cards."

"Is all this from . . . ?"

"The body? Some of it," said Harvey. "Quill, now that we have a chance to talk, what about that ad campaign? I've come up with some really exciting ideas."

"Harvey, this just isn't the right time to discuss it."

"Monday, then? I could drop by around ten o'clock."

"Sure." said Quill.

"I'll bring some roughs for you. It's gonna be great."

"Excuse me," said Quill. She edged over to Esther West, who was standing by an impromptu bar set up on the credenza.

"So where do you think she got that?" said Esther bitterly, with a gesture toward the widow.

"The dress?" Quill peered at it. "Looks like DKNY."

"You'd think she'd have the manners to shop at home at a time like this," said Esther. "I have the nicest little black and white suit that's been in the window for ages that would have been perfect. Purchased in the hope of just such an occasion." Esther belted back a slug of what smelled like gin. "Now, where's she going to wear that thing after this funeral?"

Quill said she didn't know.

"Mayor asked me to write a short piece in Gil's memory," said Esther. "You know, after the opening ceremonies tomorrow." She adjusted her earring. It was mother-of-pearl, at least two inches wide. "Taste. That's what the mayor's after. I kind of like what Harvey wrote, you know? 'Drowned, but not forgotten.' But we can't just say that. I thought maybe something from *Hamlet* might go over well."

"*Hamlet*?" said Quill. "You mean *Hamlet*?"

"That play by William Shakespeare. There's a scene from it on my director's video. This Queen Gertrude is very upset over a drowning. She runs into the palace and has some very nice lines about a drowning. Very nice."

"The ones about Ophelia?" Howie Murchison, occupied with refilling his Scotch, winked at Quill. " 'Too much of water has thou, poor Ophelia; and therefore, I forbid my tears'?"

"You know that play, Howie? I think it's nice. And of course, that's what happened to Gil. Too much water. What do you think, Harvey?" Esther inquired of the ad man, who'd also come to the credenza for a refill.

"Well, Gil was bashed on the head first," said Harvey. "I don't know how creatively appropriate that drowning speech would be. I mean he *drowned*, yes. Too much water, yes. But he was hit on the head first."

"The rest of this play *Hamlet* seems to be people dead of sword wounds," said Esther critically, "and I don't suppose that would do."

"There's always 'Cudgel thy brains no more about it,' " offered Howie.

"Oh, no," said Quill involuntarily. She was afraid to look at Howie; she bit her lower lip so hard it hurt. "I'll just say something to Nadine. Excuse me again, Harvey."

A space around Nadine had cleared, and Quill went over to see her. "I'm awfully sorry, Nadine," she said soberly. "Is there anything I can do for you? Do you need someone to stay with you?"

"Thank you, no," she said. "I called Gil Junior, of course, and he's driving up from Alfred. He'll be here sometime this afternoon." The two women were silent for a moment. Abruptly, Nadine said, "He was a bad husband, Quill. He ran around on me, and never came home, and caroused too much, and I spent like a drunken sailor to spite him. And now everyone in the town thinks I'm awful. And I was, Quill, I was." Suddenly, she began to sob. The low murmuring in the room stopped. Quill put her arm around Nadine. Elmer Henry proffered a handkerchief. "I'll take her," said Betty Hall with rough kindness, and she led Nadine away.

Quill sighed, turned, and knocked over the table that held Gil's final effects. With an exclamation of chagrin, she bent to sort through the items that had fallen to the floor. Gil's wallet, still damp from the duck pond, had opened and its contents lay scattered. Quill picked up his driver's license (credit cards were conspicuously absent) and a few family pictures. She tucked several of Gil Junior back into the wallet, and flipped over a picture that had been folded in half. She smoothed it out.

A pretty Indian girl stared back at her. The girl in the picture on the night stand in John Raintree's room at the Inn.

CHAPTER 7

Quill smoothed the photograph flat. The girl was dressed in a pink waitress's uniform, leaning across a diner counter. She smiled into the camera, black hair long and shining, dark eyes bright. Was this a girl John had loved? What would a picture of John's girlfriend be doing at the scene of Gil's drowning? Quill took a deep breath. There had to be another explanation. John couldn't be involved with this. Could she have been a waitress at Marge Schmidt's diner? Could John or Gil have met her there? If that were true, this picture might belong to Marge, and not to Gil at all. No. Marge was Hemlock Falls' most notorious employer, running through waitresses and busboys with the speed of a rural Mario Andretti. And anyone who'd tuck her aged mother into a nursing home on Christmas Eve, as Marge had done, was not someone you could accuse of sentimentality. Marge wouldn't carry a keepsake of a favorite waitress. If she carried photographs at all, they'd be of cream pies she had known and loved.

Mavis and Keith Baumer were from out of town and had never met John before. Could the picture have belonged to either of them? Was there any connection between John and Mavis? What possible connection could John have with the companion to an elderly and wealthy widow?

That left Gil himself. Gil and John were business acquaintances, hardly friends. But John, a loner, had few friends.

Quill carried the photograph into the kitchen. Nadine stood at the sink, staring out the back window.

"Nadine, I just wanted to say goodbye. If there's anything at all that you need, please call me."

"Thanks for coming, Quill. I've been telling everyone I don't know when the funeral's going to be held. Myles said maybe a week or two."

"That long?"

"He wants to complete the investigation. There'll have to be an autopsy. Howie Murchison says that's standard in an accidental death. He won't be able to probate the will until the inquest is done, so I hope Myles is quick about it."

"Will you be . . . all right . . . until then?"

This was local code for money matters. Wealthy farmers were said to be doing "all right." Marge Schmidt was said to do "all right" out of the diner. Betty Hall, a junior partner, was held to be doing not so well.

"Things weren't going so well," Nadine said, confirming the commonly held belief that Gil's money troubles were real and not the grousing of a Hemlock businessman who felt it unlucky to look too successful. "Mark Jefferson at the bank said there's a couple of outstanding loans that have to be paid off, but Gil had a lot of life insurance. That's the one thing he kept up. Now Marge Schmidt"—spite made Nadine ugly—"had better have some damn good proof that Gil borrowed money from her. If she doesn't, she can whistle for it."

"Meg and I could probably find something to tide you over," said Quill.

"Thanks. But I can always call on Tom. He's been a good brother, by and large. Been supporting Gil for all these years."

Quill shifted uncomfortably. "By the way, Nadine, I found this dropped on the floor of the living room. Is it yours or Gil's?"

Nadine glanced at the photograph. Her expression froze. "My sister-in-law," she said shortly.

"Your sister-in-law?"

"John Raintree's sister, yes. She was married to my brother Jack. We don't talk about her or him, so just forget it, okay?"

"Sorry," said Quill. "I didn't know."

"You didn't?" Nadine lit a cigarette and slitted her eyes through the smoke. "John never told you?"

"No!"

"Then *I'm* not about to." Nadine crushed the cigarette into a used coffee filter in the sink.

Quill went back to the living room. She made idle conversation with the remaining townspeople, but the visitors were clearing out. She wondered if she'd ever know all the town's secrets, or if she'd always be treated like a flatland foreigner.

Quill looked at her watch. She needed to get back to the Inn and she still had Tom Peterson to tackle about the meat. Perhaps he might tell her about John's sister. She fingered the photograph. She should either leave the photograph here, or take it to Myles as evidence in the case. And if she did that, she'd have betrayed John, perhaps, to the inexorable machinery of the law. If she could just talk to John first, show him the picture.

Her bad angel, a handy scapegoat for childhood crimes and misdemeanors, and little-used until now, whispered, "Swipe it!" She did.

After a hurried exit from the Gilmeister living room, she drove to Peterson's Transport, wondering if the penalty for theft increased relative to the viability of the victim. "He's dead, *he* won't care," sounded like a practical, if graceless, defense. On the other hand, phrases like "impeding an official investigation" had an ominous ring to them. So did, "concealing the evidence in a crime."

I am hunted, beleaguered, and driven by time, Quill thought as she turned onto Route 96. It was four-thirty; she had to be back at the Inn before six for the Chamber dinner. Maybe she could just toss the spoiled meat in a convenient dumpster rather than talking face to face with Tom Peterson. But Meg would have a fit. Peterson would want to send the meat back to the supplier, who in turn would dispose of it, and process, thought Quill, will be process.

Petersons had owned much of Hemlock Falls at one time or another; as the family's fortunes declined, bits and pieces of their property had been sold off. Tom had leased the parcel on the corner of Route 96 and Falls River Road to Gil when they had gone into the car dealership together. The land abutted the warehouses and dispatch offices from which Tom ran his trucking business, a location convenient to Syracuse, Ithaca, and Rochester. Gil's hopes of a customer base far beyond Hemlock Falls had never materialized, but the dealership managed somehow from year to year. Quill wondered who, if anyone, would take it over now that Gil had passed on.

Quill pulled into the driveway to the dealership. The Buick flags were at half-mast, and a black-bordered sign had been posted on the glass doors: CLOSED OUT OF RESPECT FOR GIL, which Quill thought had a better ring to it than "Drowned, but not forgotten."

She drove the car around to the converted house trailer that served as a dispatch office for Peterson Transport. It was placed outside the chain-link fence that surrounded the warehouse. She parked the car, got out, took the smelly cardboard box from the trunk, and carried it to the trailer door. Freddie Allbright, whom Quill knew from his occasional appearances at Chamber meetings as a substitute for Gil and Tom, opened the door partway and greeted her with a laconic snap of his gum.

"Hi, Freddie. Is Tom in?"

Freddie jerked his head toward the inside of the trailer. "Mr. Peterson!" he shouted, not taking his eyes from Quill. "Compn'y."

"Quill." Tom rose from his desk and came forward to welcome her. "Come in. Sit down."

Quill sat down in one of the plastic chairs that served for office furniture and set the cardboard box on the floor next to it. The scent of raw meat filled the air. Freddie hulked in the doorway, snapping his gum.

Tom stared at him. "Freddie, I want you to go out and find that dog."

"Just dig hisself out again."

"Then find him and chain him up," said Tom deliberately. "He's the best security system we've got." Freddie slouched out of the trailer. Tom shook his head. "You never seem to have trouble keeping good help, Quill. Want to pass along your secret?" Since this didn't seem to be anything more than a rhetorical question, Quill didn't reply. Tom settled himself behind his desk and smiled. "What can I do for you?"

"Two things. One's kind of a pain in the neck, the other's more of a question."

"Bad news first," said Tom. "Then we can end on a positive note."

"This last shipment of beef was spoiled," Quill said apologetically. "I haven't brought the whole side, of course, just the fillets."

Tom blinked his pale eyes at her. "It's been awfully warm, Quill. Are you sure your cooler's working properly?"

"This was delivered yesterday," said Quill, "and your guys are great, Tom, they always bring it straight into the cooler. Meg takes the beef out to let it get to room temperature about three hours before the dinner crowd shows up. Anything that isn't used is disposed of that night. She said this stuff is tainted." Quill rummaged in the box and unwrapped a pair of fillets. "See the graininess at the edges?"

Tom raised his eyebrows and gave the beef a cursory glance.

"Meg and I both thought you might want to check the whole shipment."

Tom nodded. His hands fiddled impatiently with a piece of paper on his desk. Quill, exasperated at Tom's indifference, said tartly, "Can you give us credit for this, Tom? And we're going to need another delivery."

"I've got one coming in from the Chicago slaughterhouse in about twenty minutes. We'll have it up there within the hour."

"That'll be fine."

He smiled at her. "And the second request?"

"Oh." Quill, not entirely sure why she was uncomfortable, demurred a bit. "I just wanted to tell you how sorry I am that Gil's gone."

"Yes," Tom nodded. "Nice guy. Lousy business partner. That it?" He rose, clearly prepared to show her out. The piece of paper he'd been playing with fell to the floor. It was a matchbook. A full one. The cover was folded in threes.

Quill picked it up.

"Nervous habit," said Tom, "ever since I quit smoking."

"I'd like to have a pack with me. Just in case." Quill slipped the matchbook into her skirt pocket. "There *was* one thing I wanted to ask you, about your brother's wife?"

"Jack's wife?" Tom's eyes narrowed. With his thin lips and prominent nose, he looked more like a lizard than ever. "She's no longer with us, I'm afraid."

"They divorced?" said Quill sympathetically. "I'm sorry to hear that."

"Jack's dead," said Tom. "I don't know where that little bitch is, and I don't care."

Quill's face went hot with embarrassment. "I didn't mean to intrude," she said, "but . . ."

"None of your business, Quill. The past is past. Now, if you'll excuse me, I've got to check on Freddie. He's supposed to retrieve that damn German shepherd and plug the hole in the chain-link fence where it dug out. Has trouble remembering orders. I have to keep tabs on him every minute." Still talking easily, Tom had her out the door and in front of her car before she knew it. He opened the driver's door and waited for her to get in. "Any more trouble with the deliveries, you call me directly, Quill. See you tonight at the meeting."

Quill drove back to the Inn, the matchbook and the photograph safely in her purse. Something, she told herself darkly, was definitely afoot.

She parked in her usual spot by the back door to the kitchen, turned the ignition off, and thought through the events of the past few days. John, the ready recipient of all her confidences over the past year, her true partner in the sometimes harrowing responsibilities of innkeeping, had to be protected somehow. Quill knew there was an explanation of the picture, of Tom Peterson's matchbook, of Gil's death, if she could just buy a little time for John. She had to talk to him.

But first she had to find him.

The dashboard clock said six-seventeen. The Chamber was in the middle of a costume rehearsal, followed by dinner at six-thirty. She and Myles had a standing date Saturday nights—subject to various Tompkins County or Hemlock Inn emergencies—which started about ten. The rest of the evening left very little time to search John's room for further clues—such as, a nasty voice whispered in her head, the bolt from

Peterson's John Deere tractor. Quill bit her lip hard, and pushed the thought away.

She couldn't talk to Meg; the presence of *L'Aperitif*'s critic coinciding with a dining room oversold to History Days tourists would already have her bouncing off the walls. As it was, with John still missing and unable to serve as *sommelier*, Quill would have to scrape her off the ceiling.

Myles could help, of course—with an All Points Bulletin. But exposure to official questions raised by the presence of that photograph in the wallet of a drowning victim could only endanger John, at least until she knew the facts.

No, Myles was out of the question. Besides, she'd interfered with his investigations before. The wrath of Moses on discovering the defalcations of the Israelites was nothing to it. She would just have to handle this herself. There was one advantage to half of Hemlock Falls stuffing the Inn tonight— somebody must have seen John. If she kept her inquiries discreet, she might find him before anyone other than she and Meg knew he'd gone missing.

"Did John show up yet?" Meg thrust her head in the open car window. "Did he tell you where he'd been? Is he sober? Did you get the meat? And what the heck are you doing sitting in here doing absolutely nothing! Do you know what's *happening*?" Meg raked her hair forward in irritable bursts.

"What's happening?" asked Quill, calmly getting out of the car. "Are the *sous* chefs all here?"

"Yes!"

"And the wine and fruit deliveries okay?"

"Yes! Yes! Yes!"

"And the Inn's not on fire." Quill steered her sister back to the kitchen.

"No! Don't be such a smartass, Quill. We need John! Look!" Quill pushed the right half of the dining room door open and peered around it. Edward Lancashire, dressed in an elegant charcoal-gray suit, was talking to an equally elegant blonde by the windows overlooking the gorge. His wife, Quill bet. The dining room was filled with chattering tourists for the Early Bird specials. Quill squinted at a tuxedoed figure seating guests. Not John, but Peter Williams, the young graduate student who worked as headwaiter on weekends. Peter circled the room, quietly observant of the quality of service. Quill let out a small sigh of relief; Peter could pinch-hit as *sommelier* cum maître d'. All she had to do was distract Meg long enough to get her back to the kitchen. Once absorbed in her cooking, Meg would be oblivious to Armageddon and stop plaguing her with questions she couldn't answer.

"I've seen the woman with Edward somewhere before," Quill said mendaciously. "Is that one of the editors, do you think?"

"Oh, God," breathed Meg. "I'll bet it is! Where's *John*, dammit. They'll need an aperitif."

"I'll tell Peter to take care of them."

"Don't tell him they're from *L'Aperitif*. They're supposed to be incognito."

"And you go back into the kitchen."

"Right."

"And cook like hell."

"Right." Face as tense as any Assyrian coming down like a wolf on the oblivious Sennacharib, Meg flexed her hands and returned to the Aga.

Quill looked at her watch and dashed to her room to change. One of these days she'd get organized enough to leave time for a real bath, but two years at the Inn had honed her fast-shower technique. The desire for a leisurely soak fell prey to necessity more and more often.

Quill's rooms were simply decorated, designed as a refuge from the demands of her day. Natural muslin curtains hung at the windows. A cream damask-stripe chair and couch sat under the mullioned south window. A cherry desk and armoire stood in the corner. Beige Berber carpet covered the pine floor. The eggshell walls held two paintings, both by friends from New York, and a few pen-and-ink sketches she'd done as a student. Her easel stood in the southwest window, a half-finished study of roses and iris glowing in the subdued light. She spared the roses a perplexed frown, then showered quickly, subdued her curly red hair into a knot at the top of her head, and slipped into a teal silk dress with a handkerchief hem. The Saturday night before the start of History Days was traditionally fancy dress. The costume rehearsal was an excuse for the actors to parade their elaborate outfits for the admiration of the tourists and those citizens unlucky enough to be merely bystanders.

By the time Quill clattered down to the dress rehearsal, the Inn was filled with the low hum of guests.

Quill slipped into the conference room unnoticed. Two of the salespeople from Esther's store had spent the afternoon cataloging and tagging the costumes in the conference room and Quill walked into a room transformed. Portable clothes racks filled with gold silks, pink taffetas, green velvets, and enough ecru lace to choke the entire flock of Marvin Finstedder's goat farm lined the walls. All twenty-four cast members of *The Trial of Goody Martin* (eighteen whose participation was limited to the repetition of the phrase "Sink or swim!") squeezed together cheek by jowl. Esther laced Betty Hall into a fuschia chiffon townswoman's costume; Elmer Henry stood in front of a full-length mirror on wheels adjusting the gold lace on his cuffs; Howie Murchison paced gravely around the room, and flipped the lapel of his skirted coat forward to reveal a hand-lettered button that read "Colonial *I*ntelligence *A*gency" at anyone who'd stop long enough to read it.

"What do you think?" he asked Quill.

"It's just as nifty as the Empire costumes," she said diplomatically. The confusion would be an excellent cover for a few discreet questions concerning John's whereabouts. Howie was as good a person to start with as anyone else. "John had to run to Ithaca, and said he was going to drop off some stuff he picked up from the drugstore for me at your office, rather than take the time to come back here. Did he get there?"

"Haven't seen him all day," said Howie. "Sorry. Do you want me to call Anne and see if she can pick it up for you?"

"Oh no, Howie. Thanks. It'll keep until Monday."

All Quill learned in the next twenty minutes was that practically everybody in Hemlock Falls would be happy to send somebody else to the drugstore for her, which made Quill grateful for the neighborliness exhibited, but left her unenlightened as to John's whereabouts.

Nobody had seen him all day.

Quill surveyed the crowded room and wondered what to do next. Pointed questions of both Mavis and Marge concerning their activities last night would give her a better grip on what had happened. Had they seen John after they left the Croh Bar? Was he driving or walking? Was anyone with him?

Mavis, face pink with excitement—and, Quill hoped, nothing else—was being stuffed into her costume with the aid of a heavy-breathing Keith Baumer. Any interruption there would be fruitless. Marge was busy organizing the removal of the clothes racks to Esther's van outside with a verve to rival General Patton's drive to Berlin. Mrs. Hallenbeck stood proudly in the corner, dressed in the black cloak and broad-brimmed hat of A Member of the Crowd. "I have practiced 'Sink or swim,' " she said when Quill stopped to admire her costume. "Miss West seemed to feel that I would add verisimilitude to the mob scene. I shall shake my walking stick, like this."

"You were at dinner with Mavis and Marge last night, Mrs. Hallenbeck. What time did you come back to the Inn?"

"About nine-thirty. I retire every evening promptly at ten, and I insisted that they bring me back here well before that time."

"Everyone came with you?"

"Mavis had to go see Gil's partner, Tom Peterson. Keith Baumer, Marge, and Gil took me home. I left them at the lobby entrance. I believe Marge said something about going to a place called the Croh Bar afterwards."

"You didn't see my manager, John Raintree, with them at all?"

"The Indian? No. I did not. Do you think he could be involved with the accident last night?"

"No," said Quill firmly.

"Well, I'm sure you know best, my dear. You seem to have such an excellent head on your shoulders." She leaned forward and lowered her voice. "I am taking your advice. Regarding Mavis."

With the exit of the cast members in full costume to the dining room at six-thirty, Quill knew she should check the front desk, see to the wine cellar, and finally, beard the chaos in the kitchen. Instead, she went to John's room with the picture from Gil's wallet tucked in her pocket. She switched on the overhead light. The room was as she'd left it earlier in the day: silent, the clothes hanging neatly in the closet, the books and papers in the same places. The picture stood on the night stand where she had left it. Quill picked it up and turned it over. The cardboard backing was loose. She drew it carefully out of the frame. The picture from her pocket fitted the back. When she replaced the cardboard backing, it fit perfectly.

She held the frame in her hands, concentrating hard. It was all too obvious that both pictures had been kept here, in this frame. How had the one picture gotten from the frame to the duck pond, and from the duck pond to Gil's wallet? And why? Did John carry it with him, as a reminder of his sister? If he didn't, who took the picture from the frame? Had John or someone else dropped it at the duck pond while drawing the bolt to set a trap for . . . whom?

"Find anything interesting?"

The frame jumped in her hands. "Myles!"

He came into the room with that infuriatingly silent walk. "Let me see that."

"It's . . . just a photograph, Myles. Of John's sister."

"John's sister? I found this picture at the pond. Nadine said it was her sister-in-law. Gil was going to put it in the family album." He looked sharply at Quill. "It agitated her."

Quill bit her lip. Myles took both photographs and put them in his shirt pocket.

Myles set the frame back on the night stand. "I'd like to talk with him, Quill. Is he here?"

"How did you know I was here?"

He nodded at the uncurtained window. "I've been waiting for him."

"And you saw the light go on. Of all the sneaky—"

"This is serious business, Quill. We need to question him."

" 'We'? 'Question'? What the hell are you talking about?"

He looked at her silently for a long moment. "You'll know eventually, so you might as well know now. The computer's turned up a record on John."

"What kind of a record?"

"I don't want you involved in this, Quill."

"Well, I am involved, Myles. Not only is he the real manager of this Inn, but he's a friend. A good friend. And I think it stinks that there's some stupid accident in that damn duck pond with a bunch of drunks horsing around, and the first thing you think of is—Oh! 'Must be that Indian up to the Inn.' " Her mockery of local speech patterns nettled him, but she went recklessly on. "And *of course* you go to that blasted database and ask, not for Gil Gilmeister's jail record, or Marge Schmidt's or that fuzzy-headed Mavis', but John's."

"Tom Peterson saw him at the pond earlier that evening," Myles said levelly.

Quill was momentarily caught off stride. Then she said, "Of *course* he would. He probably did it! I was at Peterson's today. Look at this matchbook." She pulled it out of her skirt pocket and waved it at him.

Myles took it, his face grim.

"Tom Peterson was up in Mavis and Mrs. Hallenbeck's room," said Quill, recklessly. "*He's* the person you should be investigating. Not John. And everyone knows that Mavis was the one person who was supposed to sit in the ducking stool. You should be looking for Tom's motives!"

"Quill, I've told you before to stay out of this."

"But why pick on John?"

"He served eighteen months in Attica for manslaughter. He was released last year, just before he came to work for you."

She sat down on the bed. She knew her face was pale.

Myles sat down beside her and took her hand in his. "Is there anything else you want to tell me?"

She stood up to avoid the touch of his arm against hers; physical proximity to Myles always weakened her resolve. "Do you know the details?"

"Of John's case? No. I'm going to Ithaca to pull the files Monday. All I've got now is the computer record of the sentencing and time served."

"Will you tell me when you find out?"

"Will you tell me when John shows up?"

She glared at him, mouth a stubborn line.

Myles eased himself to his feet. "This could be a case of murder. Or it could simply be an accident. I don't have enough information. And without information, I won't know if it's murder or accident."

"What does your gut-feel tell you?"

"My gut-feel tells me I want to talk to everyone in the vicinity of the accident. And John was in the vicinity."

"That's not enough of a reason and you know it," Quill said.

"Quill!" Myles stopped, exasperated. "Listen to me. I'm going to tell you one more thing. And if I tell you, you've got to promise me that you'll let this alone. You agree?"

Quill put her hand behind her back and crossed her fingers. "Yes," she said.

"A couple of the boys down at the Croh Bar said John and Gil got into an argument about ten-fifteen."

"An argument? What kind of an argument? Over what?"

"It wasn't over what, it was a *who*." A reluctant grin crossed his face. "Mavis seems to be getting around quite a bit."

"John got into an argument with Gil over Mavis? I don't believe it." She hesitated. "Was he drinking?"

"Not according to the bartender."

Quill hadn't realized how tense she'd been until she relaxed. "I'll tell you what it was. I'll bet he saw how much Mavis was drinking on top of that Valium and tried to get her to go home."

"That sounds more like John," Myles admitted. "But no one seems to know what the argument was about."

"What does Mavis say?"

"That she doesn't want to talk without a lawyer."

"Can't you do something about that, Myles?" said Quill anxiously.

"Of course I can do something about that, if I can find a judge on a Saturday night in Tompkins County in the middle of July. Davey's gone to Ithaca to try and get the summons."

"Marge must have been a—what d'ya call it—a material witness. What does she say?"

"That she was in the ladies room, and missed the whole thing. Given the amount of beer they were drinking, it's not unreasonable. Now, I've told you more than I should. And you're going to butt out, right?"

"Mm," said Quill, nodding.

Myles narrowed his eyes at her. "I'll see you at ten unless Davey's back with that summons."

Quill gave him her most innocent smile.

Quill made John's rounds of the Inn before joining the Chamber members at dinner. The Inn's lares and penates, perhaps in sympathy with the stresses of the past forty-eight hours, were being merciful tonight—and, thought Quill, it was about bloody time. Everything was in order at the front desk. Guests who were booked to check in had checked in; those who were scheduled to leave had left, without noticeable depredations to the supply of ashtrays, towels, or shower curtains. All the staff that was supposed to had shown up on time, and the line waiting for tables was satisfyingly long but not intolerable; even the bar hummed with relaxed, not drunken, voices.

Nate poured her a half glass of Montrechat. Guiltily, she decided to hide out in her office and drink it slowly and alone.

A breeze blew in the open window, carrying the scent of lilies. She sorted through the events of the past two days. There were questions to be answered, all right. Mavis might refuse to talk to Myles without a lawyer, but she might talk to Quill, given the right investigative technique. She needed Mavis. And Myles. She finished the wine. She'd weasel information about John's prison time out of him, no matter what. Undeterred by the fact that she'd never once been able to get information out of Myles he didn't want to deliver, she went in search of Mavis Collinwood.

Saturday night at the Hemlock Inn dining room with an overflow crowd was a scene to bring joy to a banker's heart. As a rule, Quill didn't much care for bankers, whose affable smiles and neatly pressed suits hid hearts of steel when it came to matters of cash flow and lines of credit. Bankers were prone to the chilling repetition of the phrase "prompt repayment of the loan," just when it was most inconvenient to hear it. Bankers wanted to lend you money when you didn't need it, charged horrible interest rates when you did, and all too clearly preferred that two hundred meals with a profit margin of 75% be pumped out by a raft of *sous* chefs and dumped in front of gluttonous hordes instead of carefully chosen, beautifully cooked meals presented to a discriminating few.

To Quill, fully booked Saturday nights were an etching by Thomas Hobbes, a perception reinforced this evening because of the costumed Chamber members. But given the Rableiasian noise level and rate of consumption in the dining room, the First Hemlock Savings and Loan guys were undoubtedly pleased as Punch.

There was no accounting for taste.

A place had been set for her at the Chamber table and she sat down between Elmer Henry and Howie Murchison. Mavis was four chairs away. Keith Baumer had invited himself to the dinner and had squeezed himself next to her. His right hand was under the table, his left busy shoveling bites of Potatoes *Duchesse* into Mavis' open mouth. Mavis squealed at periodic intervals; Dookie Shuttleworth, eyes fixed on his plate, frowned disapprovingly on her opposite side. Directly across from Dookie, Marge and Betty slurped Zinfandel with abandon.

"Meg's surpassed herself with this lamb," said Howie to Quill, his tricorne tilted rakishly over one eye. "What's in it?"

Peter Williams set a plate of lamb in front of her. Quill unwrapped the tinfoil encasing the chops.

"It's coat dew agnes ox herbs!" said Keith Baumer loudly. Mavis and Marge shrieked with laughter. He waved the hand-written menu card at Quill and grinned sweatily. "Says so right here, Howie. But—oh!" He pulled a face of mock horror. "See Quill's face? Is it my French, Quill? Tell her how good my French is, Mavis."

"You *bad* boy!" Mavis shrieked, whacking him energetically with the menu.

Quill ate her lamb absent-mindedly, trying to figure out a way to get Mavis alone. An after-dinner brandy in the Lounge was clearly a bad idea—she was three sheets to the wind, if not four. Maybe Mrs. Hallenbeck could help. Quill glanced across the table. The widow was listening with glazed attention to Norm Pasquale, who was able, without any encouragement at all, to recite the entire high-school-band program-listings for the past twenty years. " . . . clarinets in 'Mellow Yellow' " Quill heard him say. He was up to 1976.

"Lemon?" said Howie in her ear.

"I'm sorry, what?"

"I said you don't want to eat your lemon, and you were about to." He took her fork, dumped the lemon slice on his plate, and placed the fork back in her hand.

"No. You're right, I don't. Howie, could you do something for me?"

He peered at her over his wire-rimmed glasses. "You *do* want that stuff from the drugstore. . . ."

"I want him"—she pointed to Baumer—"out of the way so I can talk to Mavis."

"I suppose I could take him into the Lounge for an after-dinner brandy."

"What a good idea," she said cordially. "It'll be on the house. As a matter of fact, why don't you give him several?"

Howie looked at Baumer doubtfully. "He's had quite a bit already."

"He's not going to drive anywhere, so I don't care if Nate has to carry him upstairs feet first. Drink," she said recklessly, "as much as you want, as long as you keep him occupied."

Quill stood up, tapped her water glass, and thanked the Chamber for its continued support of the Inn over the years. This was met with warm applause. She expressed her conviction that Sunday's presentation of *The Trial of Goody Martin* would be the best yet. This was met with enthusiastic shouts. She invited the members to have brandy and *crème caramel* on the house in the Lounge, which was met with more cheers, except for Marge, who rolled her eyes and yelled, "milk puddin'!" to no discernible purpose. Esther leaned across Elmer Henry and interpreted helpfully. "She wants to hold the meetings at the diner next year. She says these foreign puddings make Americans sick. She says . . ."

"Thanks, Esther. I get the picture."

In the general scraping of chairs, Quill edged around the table and grabbed Mavis by the arm. "I'm going to the ladies' room before I go to the Lounge. Want to come with me?"

"Why, sure, sugar."

Mavis moved like a rudderless boat, amiably correcting course as Quill guided her to the main-floor bathrooms. Inside, she peered blearily at herself in the mirror. "Shee-it. Would you look at this *hair*?" She patted the stiffly lacquered waves delicately. Quill, confronted with a real live opportunity for detection, wondered wildly where to start. What would Myles do? Ask to see some identification, probably, which was no help at all, since she doubted that much would be gained by asking to see Mavis' driver's license. Besides, she already knew Mavis.

Or did she?

"Mrs. Hallenbeck seems a little . . . difficult . . . at times. I really admire the way you handle her. Have you known her long?"

Mavis stretched her lower lip with her little finger and applied a layer of lipstick. "Long enough."

Well, that answer was loaded with information. Quill took a moment to regroup. "I was absolutely fascinated to learn that you and Marge are old friends," Quill tried again. "Have you visited her in Hemlock Falls before this trip?"

"That ol' girl don' like you too much," said Mavis. "Why you want to know that?"

"John Raintree mentioned that he'd seen you before . . . I *think*," Quill said hastily. "I may have misunderstood."

"That Indian fella? You know what we say down South?"

From the sly look in Mavis' eye, Quill didn't think she wanted to know what they said down South.

"Indians're worse liars than niggers."

Quill drew a deep breath. Doreen pushed the swinging door to the bathroom open, stuck her head in, and said brusquely, "You're needed, Miss Quill."

Mavis dropped her lipstick into her evening bag and closed it with a snap. "I better be gettin' back to that party." She grabbed Quill with a giggle. "Think I'm gonna get lucky tonight. That ol' boy Keith may be baldin' on top, but there's fire in that oven, or I'm Mary Poppins." Her grip tightened and her eyes narrowed. "So I'll be in the Lounge for a while, if you want to have a little more innocent girl talk." Her long fingernails dug painfully into Quill's wrist. "After that, I'll have a sign out—readin' 'Do Not Disturb.'" She released Quill's wrist. Bosom outthrust, she sailed out the door.

"Huh!" sniffed Doreen, skipping aside as the door swung closed. "That's one of them wimmen that needs her devils cast out for sure."

"What women?"

Doreen dug into her capacious apron pocket and thrust a fistful of pamphlets at Quill. THE LORD DESPISES THE SINNER WITH LUST IN HIS HEART! the first one thundered in scarlet ink. HE SHALL CAST OUT THE DEMON OF UNRIGHTEOUSNESS screamed the next. And third, YE SHALL EXERCISE THE DEVILS OF HOT DESIRE. The line art featured large men with beards shaking impressively large forefingers at big-breasted women. Lightning featured prominently in the background. "Oh, my," said Quill.

"We exercised a right number of devils at the meetings in Boca Raton," Doreen said in satisfaction. "Bit noisy, but those devils skedaddled out of the sinners like you wouldn't believe."

"It's *exorcise*, Doreen, not exercise."

"We got right sweaty doin' it," said Doreen indignantly. "I mean to show these to the Reverend Shuttleworth. He ain't got enough fizz in his preaching. I'll bet the Reverend would fill the pews right up if he had a bit of exercising in his sermons. Stop puttin' people to sleep. There's this 1-800 number he can call any time of the day or night to get the lowdown on this stuff." Quill opened her mouth to lodge a protest, and Doreen swerved into an abrupt change of topic. "You're wanted at the reception. What're you standing around here for?"

Quill gave up. "What's the problem?"

"Somebody's here to check in."

"I think we're full."

"Hey, do I run this joint or do you?"

A strong impression of smug hilarity hung around Doreen. Quill's misgivings strengthened to dismay when she arrived at the reception desk, Doreen at her heels. The woman who stood at the front desk was both sophisticated and annoyed, a combination that guaranteed trouble. Dressed in a short tight skirt, platform shoes, and a well-cut jacket, she had the smooth, expensive hair and skin that meant money with access to Manhattan.

"Are you the manager here?" she said crossly.

Quill cocked an eyebrow at Doreen; there'd been a lot of women like this at the gallery when she was painting, and if Doreen thought she'd see her boss discomposed, she had another think coming. "I'm Sarah Quilliam," she said, extending her hand. "And excuse me for saying so, but that's the most marvelous jacket I've ever seen. It simply *screams* Donna Karan. Not everyone can wear her as well as you do."

The fashion plate relaxed a little. "Darling, the cut hides the most awful flaws. She's easier than you think. Can you help me out here? I'm trying to check in, and this little person behind the desk keeps saying she has to ask the manager. Nobody seems to be able to find the manager, for God's sake."

Quill winked comfortably at the young Cornell student behind the counter. "He's on an errand for me," said Quill. "I'm the owner. What can I do for you? I'm afraid we're booked solid at the moment."

"But I've got a room."

Quill moved behind the front desk to check the bookings. The missing ledger had reappeared as mysteriously as it had gone. "And your name?"

"Celeste Baumer. Mrs. Keith Baumer."

If that was a snigger from Doreen, Quill thought furiously, she was going to do some "exercising" of her Inn's own devils: the housekeeping kind.

"She's got ID," said the Cornell student apologetically. "But I called Mr. Baumer's room, and he doesn't answer. Mr. Baumer's booked a single for the week, not a double, and John always told us to check with the customer when something like this happens."

"And he was right," said Quill. "Was your husband expecting you, Mrs. Baumer?"

"Oh, no." She exposed a bright row of teeth in what Quill took to be a smile. "I wanted it to be a surprise."

"Why don't you sit and have a glass of wine in the bar, Mrs. Baumer? On the house, of course. We'll see if we can find Mr. Baumer."

"Are you going up to his room?"

"Um," said Quill, "actually I think he's out on . . . on . . . a sales call or something."

"I've been on that damn train for hours. I want a bath and then I'll take you up on that free drink. But first I want to check in."

Maybe, Quill thought as she, Celeste Baumer, Doreen, and the Cornell student (who was carrying the suitcases) trooped up the stairs to the second floor, Keith Baumer left Mavis at the bar and was freshening up. Maybe he was making phone calls to his neglected customers. Maybe he'd fallen asleep dead-drunk. And alone.

Quill knocked on the door to 221.

"I don't think he's here," she said after a few moments.

"Open it up, darling," Celeste Baumer demanded. "You wouldn't believe how I have to pee."

Quill unlocked the door. Mrs. Baumer pushed past her and switched on the lights. Two twenty-one was decorated in Waverly chintz with scarlet poppies against a cream background.

The poppies on the tailored bedspread moved up and down with the briskness of waves on a breezy sea.

"Oops," said the Cornell student.

"Dang!" said Quill.

"You bastard!" shrieked Celeste Baumer with enormous satisfaction.

"Heh-heh-heh," chortled Doreen.

"God-*damn*!" shouted a nude and sweaty Keith Baumer.

Mavis screamed in a very ladylike way.

CHAPTER 8

July in Central New York is not the usual mating season for songbirds, but the repeated attacks of the cardinal flying into its own image on the sunrise side of Quill's bedroom window woke her at six. She squinted against the sunshine pouring in and addressed the bird. "That's not a hostile rival, that's you," she said.

Ta-Ching! The bird flattened its beak against its reflection, intent on assassination.

"Has the word gotten to the bird world, too? You think your sweetie's in here with some other guy?"

Ta-ching!

"You're related to Baumer, maybe, and have faith in the triumph of hope over experience."

Ta-CHANG! The bird, with one last mighty effort, hit the window and dropped out of sight. Quill got out of bed and peered out the window to the lawn. The cardinal lay on its back, feet up. It chirped, righted itself and flew at the window, beady eyes glittering.

Ta-ching!

Quill went back to bed and pulled her pillow over her head.

Myles, dressed in his grays, came out of the kitchenette carrying two cups of coffee. Quill groaned, sat up, and peered at him. "Are you going to let Mrs. Baumer out of the pokey?"

"Probably." He handed Quill a cup, then sat at the foot of the bed.

"You think it'll hit the papers?"

"Probably. The local's stringer's in town to cover the opening ceremonies of History Days."

"Oh, God."

"It'll blow over, honey." He rose, stretched, and drained his coffee. "Of course, you could always give up innkeeping as a profession and marry me."

"No, Myles."

"Or you could continue being an innkeeper and marry me."

"I tried marriage. It stinks. You didn't find marriage all that terrific, either."

"Youthful folly. On both our parts."

The cardinal hit the window again.

Quill got out of bed. Further sleep was impossible. "Would you like some breakfast? Meg's got an assistant in the kitchen that makes a mean Eggs Benedict."

"I'm going down to the jail to let Mrs. Baumer go. Unless you want to press charges for the damage to two twenty-one."

"I don't think so. I didn't like that lamp anyway, and I can fix the dent in the wall. Just a matter of replacing the sheetrock and repainting. I feel so sorry for her, Myles. I can't believe that jerk Baumer."

He kissed her, a process that always softened Quill's resolve to never marry again. "I don't know when I'll see you today, kiddo. Just relax and enjoy yourself."

"Easy for you to say—all you have to do is make sure that four thousand tourists in Dodge Caravans don't all crash into each other on Main Street."

"All you have to do is keep the doors barred against irate spouses, supervise the extra help, keep Doreen from rending Keith Baumer limb from limb in fine Old Testament outrage, hold your sister's hand if her soufflé flops, and generally wear yourself ragged."

"It's not that tough, Myles. Not when you've got good staff. And I've got good staff."

They both carefully avoided any mention of John Raintree. She closed the door after him and took a long leisurely shower, getting down to the dining room at seven o'clock. Meg was seated at their table for two by the kitchen door, and Quill went to join her. Meg had abandoned her leggings, ratty tennis shoes, and sweatbands for well-pressed jeans and a lacy top. She'd taken a curling iron to her dark hair, and wore a pair of gold hoop earrings.

"Well *you* look totally cool," said Quill.

Meg batted her eyelashes. "Guess who's going on a picnic with the best-looking gourmet critic in Hemlock Falls?"

"Really? Did you pack the basket?"

"Cold gravlax with my Scotch Bonnet salsa. Homemade flatbread, dilled potato salad. Nice chilly bottle of a sparkling Vouvray. Strawberries with that *crème brûlée* from last night. If we get a good seat for the opening ceremonies, I guarantee you that fourth star."

"Everything okay in the kitchen?"

"Frank's supervising. All we're going to get today is a zillion orders for roast beef sandwiches to go." She hesitated. "Any word from John?"

Quill shook her head.

"Jeez." Meg sighed. "Poor old you. At least you've got that creep Baumer out of your hair."

"Nope."

"Nope? Are you serious? After all that ranting and raving last night? I would have thought the son of a gun would be embarrassed to show his sniveling face in town."

"He's booked for the week. He's paid for the week. He'll stay for the week. That's what he said."

"In-credible."

"I assume it has to do with the sales convention at the Marriott." Quill sighed. "I can't think how that guy keeps a job."

"And the marvelous round-heeled Mavis?"

"Mrs. Hallenbeck said, 'booked for the week, paid for the week.' "

"They'll stay for the week?"

"Besides, I think both of them are looking forward to the play this afternoon. Ow!"

Meg kicked Quill's ankle as Keith Baumer, Mavis, and Mrs. Hallenbeck arrived simultaneously at the entrance to the dining room. Conversation in the dining room came to a halt. Mrs. Hallenbeck, Quill thought, was superb. She ignored Baumer with aplomb bordering on the magnificent. Mavis meekly trailing in her wake, she swept past Baumer—whose face was tinged a dusky pink—to their regular table. Head down, Baumer slunk to table eight.

"Oh. There's Edward," said Meg eagerly. Lancashire, in cotton Dockers, boat shoes, and a dark green denim shirt, walked in, and with a casual wave at Meg and Quill, began to come toward them. He stopped at the Hallenbeck table and spoke briefly to the widows. Mavis, in an off-the-shoulder tank top that showed more décolletage than her Empire-styled gown of the evening before, smiled invitingly up at him.

"Would you look at that!" hissed Meg. With a brief, apologetic glance at Meg, Edward pulled out a chair and sat next to Mavis. One of the Inn's impeccably trained waiters was instantly at his elbow with a cup and freshly brewed coffee. "How does she *do* it?" said Meg, awestruck.

Mavis flirted, giggled, and ignoring Mrs. Hallenbeck's imperious frown, beckoned to Baumer. Baumer shuffled over from his table and sat on Mavis' left. Sprightly conversation wafted through the air. Meg pulled at her lower lip. Quill looked at this familial symptom of deep thought in alarm. "Meg, I know that look. What are you going to do?"

"Me?" said Meg innocently. "Not a thing, sister dear, not a thing. Excuse me a moment." She sprang up and went into the kitchen. Quill swallowed her French toast, took a gulp of tea, and followed her hastily.

"A *lot* of tarragon, I think," Meg was saying to her *sous* chefs, "and what else? Ideas, guys, I need ideas."

"Baking soda instead of baking powder?" said the shorter one. His name was Frank Torrelli; his father ran a good restaurant in Toronto, and Frank was slated to take over the family kitchen when his apprenticeship with Meg was up. The taller one was a Swede from Finland, studying at the Cornell Hotel School on a green card. Bjorn's blond hair and blue eyes had the pale, icy look of plain water in a glass.

"Salt," said Bjorn. "A lot of it."

"Too obvious," said Meg. "I want subtle stuff. So he's not really sure what it is."

"I got it. I got it!" said Frank. He ran excitedly to the cupboard, pulled out a small bottle, and waved it in the air. "Eh? S'all right?"

"All right!" said Meg.

They burst into laughter.

"What's all this, then?" said Quill, feeling a little like a policeman in a medium-grade British mystery.

"Never you mind," said Meg. "Don't you have a lot of stuff to do today? Beat it."

"Peter's going to manage the front desk today. Doreen's taking care of the housekeeping staff. And I thought that Bjorn and Frank were in charge of the kitchen shifts." Quill folded her arms and leaned against the butcher's block. "One of the advantages of taking management courses at Cornell at nights is that you learn to empower your employees. So, I've got lots of time to spend with you guys, since you seem to be making all the decisions, anyway."

"Hey. Wouldn't your life be a lot easier if that miserable Mavis and sleazy Baumer beat feet?" demanded Meg.

"Well, yeah. Baumer at least." Frank had the mysterious bottle in his large hand and she couldn't see the label. Quill didn't know if she wanted to see the label. "But if Mavis doesn't stay the week, I have to play Clarissa. And you could rate my enthusiasm to be dunked and squashed right up there with getting nasty letters from the Board of Health. Not only that, but Mavis is going to be subpoenaed as a witness in Gil's drowning accident. So she can't leave."

"Just Baumer, then," said Meg. "We're just going to encourage Baumer to leave a leetle bit earlier than he had planned to. He's going to find the food not to his taste." Gales of giggles came from the *sous* chefs. Meg flung out both her hands at Quill's outraged expression. "Nothing illegal, immoral, or actionable. I swear."

"Please, Meg," said Quill. "Think of the bad publicity."

"From a guy whose wife shows up while he's in the sack with Mavis the Bimbo? From a guy whose wife whacks him up the side of the head with a lamp? He's lucky we don't turn him in to his company. *One* call to his boss at the Marriott, one call, that's all it'd take! He's lucky we don't sue him for damages. He's lucky he's alive!" Meg raked her hair back with both hands. Her cheeks were flushed. Her eyes glittered. Frank and Bjorn exchanged meaningful glances and melted into the background. "I will SHUT DOWN MY KITCHEN before I serve my good food to pigs like that!" Meg shouted. "I will THROW MY SPATULAS INTO THE FIRE!"

"Mornin'," said Doreen, stumping into the kitchen. She was wearing her best polyester pantsuit and a small straw hat. She put her hands on her hips and stared at Meg. "Well, missy. Looks like the Devil's got aholt of you."

Meg drummed her fingers on the countertop.

"You look nice, Doreen," Quill ventured into the charged silence.

"Been to see the Reverend," she said. "Givin' him tips on how to wake up the sinners. Gave him a couple of ideas for his sermon, he said." She went to the locker room to change into her work clothes. Her voice floated back to them. "Told him about last night. Said he'd never heard of such a scandalous thing." She reappeared, tying her capacious apron neatly around her waist. "Thinks that there Baumer's goin' straight to Hell. Along with Mavis. Called her a right fine name, too." She rummaged in her purse, withdrew a piece of paper, and squinted at it. "Wrote it down. Suckabus."

Meg started to laugh.

"Succubus," said Quill. "Oh, dear."

"Sounds nasty," said Doreen hopefully. "Innit? What is it, exactly?"

"Succubi are female demons," said Quill. "They visit afflicted men in the dead of night and . . . ah . . ."

"Sap their life force," said Meg with a wicked grin.

"You mean there's more than one?" said Doreen. "It's not just this Mavis Collinwood?"

"Quite a few in Times Square, when I visited," said Frank. He and Bjorn, noting the ebb of Meg's temper, had rejoined the women.

"They aren't real, Doreen," said Quill. "A succubus is a metaphor for the way the people of Old Testament times viewed a certain type of woman, and as far as I'm concerned, it's a bunch of male chauvinist hooey. I don't want any more discussion about sex vampires of Hemlock Falls, or for that matter, foul substances in Keith Baumer's food. I want everyone to go back to work."

"Yes, *ma'am*." Meg saluted. "Whatever you say, *ma'am!*"

Quill marched back to the dining room, ignoring the snickers from the kitchen with the dignity befitting a manager who had successfully quelled an employee revolt. A hoot of laughter with distinctly Swedish overtones modified her conclusion to a half-muttered, "Well, I told them, anyway."

She sat down at the table to finish her breakfast.

In a few minutes, Edward Lancashire joined her. "Ready for the big day?"

"It's not really a big day for me," Quill explained, "or Meg either. Everyone's checked in; the dining room, Lounge, and bar are all booked, and the staff knows what to do."

"It's the front-end preparation that's the toughest," said Edward.

"You'd know about that," Meg said cheerfully, as she rejoined her sister at the table. "You're not planning on dinner here tonight, are you, Edward?"

"No. I've booked a table at Reneès in Ithaca. Opening day of History Week is a little too raucous for me."

"You're going to the play this afternoon, though," said Meg. "We're having a picnic. Nobody should miss the play. And you shouldn't miss my gravlax. The Scotch Bonnet salsa is *fabulous*."

"Oh, I think everyone will be there," said Edward Lancashire. "Mrs. Collinwood. Mr. Baumer. The delightful Ms. Schmidt. I've eaten at her restaurant, by the way. It's quite good for American diner food. Perhaps even Mr. Raintree will join us? I haven't seen him around lately."

"He had some personal errands to run," said Quill hastily. "But I'm sure he'll be there, too. Nobody within fifty miles of Hemlock Falls misses *The Trial of Goody Martin*."

Seeing the crowds that afternoon, Quill revised her estimate upward; tour buses brought day trippers from Rochester, Buffalo, and Syracuse. Myles and his men cordoned off Main Street, and allowed cars to park on the shoulder of Route 96 outside the central business district.

The Kiwanis beer tent did a thriving business, the Lions hot dog stand ran out of buns at two o'clock, and the Fireman's

Auxiliary kiosk posted a triumphant SOLD OUT sign on the counter that had displayed wooden lawn ornaments of geese, pigs, cats, ducks, cows, and the rear ends of women in long print dresses. Gil's Buick dealership always took a booth for History Days. Quill, intent on finding out more from Tom Peterson about John and Gil, caught a glimpse of the awning over the late-model car that the dealership always planted in front of the booth. She wound her way through the tourists to it. Tom Peterson greeted her with a wave and a smile. Nadine sat under the awning, hands folded in her lap. Freddie, unexpectedly garrulous, was there, too.

"Missed you in church this morning," said Tom, who was a deacon at Dookie's church.

"John's out of town for a bit, and I got caught up," Quill apologized. "You know how it is in the summer. John's due back today, though. So I'll be sure to try next week."

"I wouldn't miss it, if I were you," said Freddie. "Something sure lit a fire under the Reverend this morning. Whooweee!"

Quill, intent on forming questions that would give her some clues as to Gil's relationship with the girl in John's picture, gave him an encouraging, if absent-minded, look.

"Hellfire and brimstone. Quite a little sermon." Freddie leaned forward and said in a low voice, "Just between you and me? Collections were up pretty near seventy-five per cent. The Reverend was as pleased as Punch, said the Lord was showing him the way to a resurgence of faith. And where there's a resurgence of faith, there's a resurgence of cash. Now, Miss Quill, wish we could come up with something for you that would give us a resurgence of cash. You think about tradin' in that old heap you've got for a good latemodel car?"

"You're taking over from Gil?"

Freddie shot an anxious look at his boss. "Just temporarily, like. Now, about that old heap . . ."

"Gil sold me that 'old heap' two years ago," said Quill indignantly. "It wasn't an 'old heap' then."

"Got to have the look of success in your business," said Freddie wisely. "Now, I could show you . . ."

Quill laid a hand on Freddie's arm and promised to look at

new cars. Then she walked up to Tom and said flatly, "Was Gil worried about the business?"

"Hell, we both were. I floated him a couple of private loans to tide him over first and second quarter. He expected business to pick up."

"Was that John's recommendation? The private loans?"

"John? He didn't have much to say about it."

"Does he audit all your books, Tom? You know, for the transport company and your private affairs?"

Tom's face closed up. "I don't know that that's really any business of yours, Quill. No offense."

Quill flushed. Great detectives of fiction were never accused of rudeness; she'd have to brush up on her technique. "I was just thinking of having John do my personal taxes, that's all. Wondered if you found him as good at that as he is at the commercial end."

Tom frowned. "Quill, you hired him. You know him better than I do."

"Just wanted your opinion," she murmured. She cleared her throat. "Will you have a new partner now? Did Gil leave key-man insurance, or do you get the whole dealership?"

"Quill, I don't know what game you're playing at. But you don't play it with me. I'm warning you." He held her eyes for a long minute. Quill gazed coolly back. He turned away from her. "Time for you to be going down to the Pavilion, isn't it? Wouldn't want to miss the play. Unless you'd rather continue to stick your oar into my personal business."

The sun was hot, but not hot enough to account for the heat in her face. Quill decided her chief irritation was with Myles, who had failed to clarify the embarrassing pitfalls awaiting inexperienced interrogators. She shoved the recollection of Myles's prohibitions against any kind of detecting firmly out of her mind, waved cheerfully at Nadine, who raised a hand listlessly back, and walked the two blocks to the Pavilion, absorbed in thought.

The open-air Pavilion was ideally situated for the presentation of *The Trial of Goody Martin*. Thirty wooden benches, seating three to four people each, formed a series of half-circles in front of a bandstand the size of a small theater stage. A forty-foot, three-sided shed had been built in back of the bandstand in 1943 to provide space for changing rooms, sets, small floats for parades, and band instruments. Between the shed and the municipal buildings that housed the town's snowplows, fire engines, and ambulances was an eight-foot-wide gravel path. The path debouched onto the macadam parkway that circled the entire acreage of the park. The action in *The Trial of Goody Martin* required that the audience sweep along with the actors and props in a path from the duck pond to the bandstand to the bronze statue of General Frederick C.C. Hemlock.

The statue of the man and his horse had been erected in 1868, two hundred years after the founding of the village. Something had gone awry in the casting process, and the General's face had a wrinkled brow and half-open mouth, leaving him with a permanently pained expression as he sat in the saddle. On occasion, roving bands of Cornell students on spring break heaped boxes of hemorrhoid remedies at the statue's base, which sent the mayor into fits. Most years the statue sat detritus-free, except for the six-foot heap of cobblestones piled at the foot and used to crush the witch each year.

The crowd was enormous, the benches jammed. Quill stood at the periphery and scanned the mass of people for Meg and Edward Lancashire.

Esther West jumped up on the lip of the bandstand, and shaded her eyes with her hands. She caught sight of Quill, pointed at her, and waved frantically.

Elmer Henry appeared out of the crush of people and grasped her arm. His face was grim. "You memorize that Clarissa part?"

Quill's heart sank. "Why?"

"That Mavis is drunker than a skunk. Esther don't want her to go on."

"Elmer . . . I . . ."

"You're the understudy, aren't you? You got to do this, Quill. For the town."

"Maybe we can do something," said Quill weakly. "A lot of black coffee?" The mayor looked doubtful. "Come on. She may not be drunk, Elmer; she may just have stage fright. I mean, look at all these people."

"That's what I'm looking at. All these people. We can't have the Chamber look like a durn fool in front of these folks. Do you know that some have come all the way from Buffalo?"

Quill plowed her way determinedly through the sightseers to the shed at the back of the bandstand, the mayor trailing behind. The shed was seething with a confused mass of costumed players and uniformed high-school band members. Harland Peterson's two huge draft horses, Betsy and Ross, stamped balefully in the corner. The sledge, the barn door, and the band instruments squeezed the space still further.

"Quill! Thank God! Do you see her, that *slut*?" Esther gestured frantically at Mavis, then clutched both Quill and a copy of the script in frantic hands. Sweat trickled down her neck. Mavis, blotto, swayed ominously in the arms of Keith Baumer. Her face was red, her smile beatific. Esther shrieked, "Can you believe it? Here's the script. You've got ten minutes until we're on."

Surrounded by Mrs. Hallenbeck, Betty Hall, Marge Schmidt, and Harvey Bozzel, Mavis caught sight of Quill and caroled, "Coo-ee!"

"Coo-ee to you, too," said Quill. "Esther, I can fix this. I need a bucket of ice, a couple of towels, and Meg and her picnic basket."

The ice arrived before Meg. Quill ruthlessly dropped it down Mavis' dress, front and back. Someone handed her a towel. She made an ice pack and held it to the back of the wriggling Mavis' neck.

Meg and Edward Lancashire joined them a few moments later. "Oh, God," said Meg. "Will you look at her?"

"You've got your picnic basket?" Quill asked through clenched teeth.

"Sure."

"You have those Scotch Bonnet peppers for that salsa?"

A huge grin spread over Meg's face. "Yep."

"You have your special killer-coffee?"

"Uh-huh."

"Then let's get to work."

The Scotch Bonnet had the most dramatic effect. Mavis gulped the coffee, squealed girlishly at the reapplied ice pack, but howled like a banshee after Meg slipped a pepper slice into her mouth.

"Language, language," said Meg primly.

The two sisters stepped back and surveyed their handiwork. Mavis glared at them, eyes glittering dangerously.

"And Myles claims you can't sober up a drunk," said Quill.

"Actually, he's right," said Edward Lancashire. "All black coffee does is give you a wide-awake drunk. I don't know that Scotch Bonnet has ever been used as a remedy for drunks before. I'd say what you've got there is a wide-awake, very annoyed drunk."

"You can write about it in your column," Meg said pertly.

"Well, Esther? What d'ya think?"

"I think we've got ourselves a Clarissa," said Esther grimly. "Just in case, Quill, I want you to study that script. She'll make the ducking stool, but I don't know about the trial. C'mon, you."

In subsequent years, Chamber meetings would be dominated periodically by attempts to resurrect *The Trial of Goody Martin*, and it was Esther West, newly converted to feminism, who firmly refused to countenance it. "Anti-woman from the beginning," she'd say. "It was a dumb idea in the first place, and a terrible period in American history, and we never should have celebrated it the way we did. Now, *Hamlet*—that play by William Shakespeare? I've always wanted a hand in that."

Mavis handled the ducking stool and the swim with a subdued hostility that augured well for the artistic quality of her impassioned speech at the trial to come. Marge Schmidt, Betty Hall, Nadine Gilmeister, Mrs. Hallenbeck, and others in The Crowd, may have yelled "Sink or swim" with undue emphasis on the "sink" part, but the audience failed to notice a diminution in the thrust of the whole performance, and joined in with a will.

Elmer Henry, Tom Peterson, and Howie Murchison dragged Mavis the forty feet from the pond to the bandstand, and the trial itself began. Dookie Shuttleworth, surprisingly awe-inspiring in judge's robe and wig, pronounced the age-old sentence:

"Thou shall not suffer a witch to live."

Mavis soggily surveyed the audience, smoothed her dripping gown over her hips, and addressed the judges. "My lords of the Court, I stand before you, accused of the crime of witchcraft . . ."

So far so good, thought Quill, perched on a bench in the front row. The *s*'s are mushy, but what the heck. Half the crowd's mushy from the heat and the beer.

"A crime of which I'm innoshent!" She burped, swayed, and said mildly, "I'm not a crimin'l. Jush tryin' to get along. Good ol' Southern girl in the midst of all of you"—She paused and searched for the proper phrase. "Big swinging dicks?" she hazarded.

"She's off script!" screamed Esther.

Apparently finding the response from the audience satisfactory, Mavis raised her middle finger, wagged it at a blond family of three in the front row, and took a triumphant bow.

Quill pinched her knee hard, a defense against giggling she hadn't needed since high school.

Dookie thundered his scripted response, "Scarlet whore of the infernal city! Thou shalt die!" then called for the sledge. Harland Peterson drove Betsy and Ross to the side of the stage, the straw-filled sledge dragging behind them.

Mavis spread her arms wide, in her second departure from the script, and leaped into Harland's arms. He staggered, cussed, and dropped her into the straw. Responding to a harmless crack of his whip, Betsy and Ross phlegmatically drew the sledge down the path behind the shed.

As the business of trading Mavis for the hooded dummy went on in the back, Howie, substituting for Gil, read the grisly details of the sentence aloud, straight from the pages of the sentencing at Salem three hundred years before. " . . . planks of sufficient weight and height to be placed upon the body of the witch . . ."

Harland Peterson appeared at the edge of the stage, scowling hideously. He waved at Howie, who ignored him.

" . . . and the good citizens of this town to carry out the justice of the Almighty . . ."

Harland gestured again, furiously.

" . . . and the law of the Lord is as stones, and as mighty as stones . . . *What*, Harland?"

"Barfed on my boots! I ain't drivin' that sledge! You git

somebody else to drive that sledge." He stomped off. Howie looked around helplessly. The crowd sniggered.

Harvey Bozzel, teeth displayed in a wide shiny grin, jumped off the stage and reappeared some minutes later on the front seat of the sledge, reins in hand. There was a scattering of applause. "Gee!" he hollered firmly. Betsy and Ross turned obediently to the right. Meeting the wall of the municipal building, they stopped in their tracks.

Ripples of laughter washed through the audience. Quill stole a look at Elmer and Esther out of the corner of her eye and pinched her knee. She was going to have an almighty bruise.

"Haw! you durned fool. Tell 'em to haw!" Harland yelled.

"Haw!" said Harvey, in a more subdued manner.

Betsy, or perhaps it was Ross—Quill couldn't tell for certain—flicked an ear, gazed inquiringly at her partner in harness, then pulled to the left. This brought the forward edge of the sledge frame into view. Failing further direction, Betsy and Ross continued to pull left, and the sledge frame hit the shed side with a thud.

"Giddyap!" roared Harland at his horses. "Ignore the durn fool up there."

Ross, or perhaps it was Betsy, snorted, shook his head in genuine disgust, and pulled straight in response to the man who fed him oats twice a day—not to mention the occasional sugar cube. The sledge with the dummy finally emerged intact from behind the shed.

"You got that, Harvey, you idjit?" Harland shouted as he spelled out the commands to make them clear. "H-A-W means *left*. G-E-E-U-P means *right*. 'Giddyap' means *straight*."

Betsy and Ross broke into a rumbling jog. "Giddyap" was something they understood. The dummy bounced on the sledge, black hood flapping in the breeze.

" 'Giddyap' twice means faster," Harland said in a normal tone of voice. "Never knew you was such a durn fool, Harvey."

The band broke into the strains of Gounod's Funeral March and the procession moved down the path to General Hemlock without further incident.

Quill wondered if she should check on Mavis. If she'd gotten sick to her stomach, she was going to feel a lot better, and she might want to see the conclusion of the play. On the other hand, Mavis sober was probably meaner than Mavis drunk, and she had taken grave exception to the dose of fiery pepper. Quill decided guiltily to spare herself the experience.

She strolled on down to the statue, behind the crowd.

Howie demanded the laying on of the barn door, while Dookie and Elmer beat a slow and solemn rhythm on a large drum. The dummy, indefinably lifelike, sprawled in the straw. The sacklike hood had been drawn tightly around the high neck of the dress.

She heard the thunk of stone on wood, and the final prayers of the "judges" condemning the witch's soul to hell.

The crowd usually entered into the spirit of the thing, and so it was with no surprise that Quill saw Keith Baumer heave a stone weighing a good hundred pounds onto the stones already piled high, to shouts of Go!Go!Go! from the crowd.

She saw the stage blood seeping from under the wooden planks.

It was the smell that alerted Quill: the coppery, unmistakable scent of blood—mixed with worse odors. The crowd quieted, then stirred uneasily, like water snakes in a still pond.

The dummy's hand stiffened, convulsed. The nails turned blue.

For a few terrible moments, Quill saw nothing else at all.

CHAPTER 9

"Squashed flatter than a bug on a windshield," said Marge, awed.

Myles had taken immediate control, separating those townspeople and Inn guests nearest the stage from the audience at large and sending them to the Village Library. Davey Kiddermeister escorted them to the ground floor, then set up a methodical interview system. One by one, each of the group was called and disappeared into the librarian's office behind the checkout desk.

Pale and sweaty, Keith Baumer paced to the front window and looked out at the Pavilion, where Myles was getting names and addresses from the out-of-towners. "Are we gonna put up with this? Who does that damn fool think he is?" He borrowed a cigarette from Harland Peterson and lit it with shaking hands. "He's going to hear from me on this one. I know people."

Mrs. Hallenbeck coughed and waved her hand elaborately in front of her face.

"You can't smoke in here," Esther West said.

Baumer stubbed out the cigarette with an angry glare. "Murchison, you know about these things. What are our rights here?"

"I practice family law, Baumer," said Howie dryly. "Probate, real estate. I'm not much on problems like these."

"It wasn't anybody's fault."

"That rock you heisted onto the shed door was a hundred pounds if it was twenty," said Harland Peterson brutally. "I'd say it was your fault."

"But you have to have knowledge beforehand," said Baumer. "I had no idea she was there. You people all piled the rocks along with me. If there's criminal negligence here, we're all in it together. I'd like to retain you as counsel, Murchison, until my own lawyer gets here from New York."

"'Fraid I can't help you," said Howie.

Quill wondered at the sudden drop in Baumer's buffoonish façade; he was pretty quick to stand on his rights. Had he been in trouble before?

Tom Peterson came out from the librarian's office. "He wants to see you next, Quill." He looked at the assembly. "Don't worry everybody, Deputy Davey's keeping it short."

Elmer stopped Quill as she headed to the office. "Emergency meeting at the Lounge tonight, Quill? Chamber's got to discuss this."

Quill nodded her agreement and went into the librarian's office.

Davey sat at Miriam Doncaster's desk, his black notebook an incongruous official object among the china ducks, geese, and dogs that the librarian collected. "Will you sit down, please, Ms. Quilliam?"

Quill sat in the straight chair in front of the desk and folded her hands in her lap.

"Your name and home address, please, and don't tell me I already know it like Tom Peterson just did, because I have to go through this exactly the same way with everybody, or Myles'll have my head on a platter, like that poor fella that messed with the stripper."

Quill took a moment to sort this out. Davey was a faithful member of Dookie's church. He must mean John the Baptist.

"Sarah Quilliam, the Hemlock Falls Inn, Four Hemlock Road, Hemlock Falls," she said. "My zip code . . ."

"Don't need no zip code." Breathing through his mouth, Davey peered at the notebook. "May I see your driver's license, please?" Quill fished in her purse and handed it over. Davey made a check mark in his notebook without looking at it, and handed it back. "Did you know the name of the deceased?" he read aloud.

"Mavis Collinwood."

"Do you remember what she was wearing when she left the stage on the sledge? Before Harland pulled her around to the back?"

"A long, black cotton gown. A white ruff around her neck. A black cloth cap tied with strings under her chin."

"Anything else?"

"Well—" Quill blinked at him. "Shoes . . . stockings . . . and, um, underwear?"

"Thank you. Please leave the library without speaking to anyone out there. Except to tell your sister that she's next."

"That's all?" Quill rose to her feet.

"Yes, ma'am."

"Do you think you could interview Mrs. Hallenbeck next, Davey? It's been a long day for her, and she's had quite a shock."

Davey's eyebrows drew together; an obdurate state official following an inflexible routine. "Myles told me to do these interviews of the people who actually knew Ms. Collinwood in this exact order. Mrs. Hallenbeck's at the bottom, right before the people who were next to the stage."

"Why isn't he interviewing the people who piled rocks on the barn door?" asked Quill, exasperated.

"I don't know, ma'am. Just doing my job."

"You'll be doing your job a lot better if you let me get that little old lady back up to the Inn so she can recover from the shock," said Quill with asperity. "I'm sure Myles would want you to see to the needs of the elderly."

"He did tell me to make sure she was comfortable. I got her a glass of water. And a cookie." Davey slowly erased a line from the bottom half of his notebook and laboriously wrote at the top. "I'll see her right after your sister and Mr. Lancashire."

"Would you tell Meg and Mrs. Hallenbeck that I'll wait for them outside?"

"Yes, ma'am. And you're not supposed—"

"To tell anyone you belted me with a rubber hose to extract important information."

Quill walked outside and sat on the steps of the library. Across the green lawn of the park four lines of tourists stood restlessly in the July heat. Myles had assigned uniformed officers to take the names and addresses of members of the audience. Others patrolled the lines, seeing that the elderly had a place to sit in the shade, and taking little kids to the Porta-Johns. Quill figured the interview took about three minutes, minus the demands she'd made of Davey, and did some calculations on her fingers. At eighty people an hour, it'd be several hours before she could ask Myles what the heck was going on.

Meg bounced out the library door. "Edward will be out in a minute," she said. "I told him we'd wait for him. What do you suppose that clothes stuff was all about?" she continued, coming down the steps to sit at Quill's side. "I mean, who cares what she was wearing? Does Myles ask people in a car crash if the driver was wearing designer jeans, or what?"

Quill, who had been wondering the same thing herself, let out a gasp.

"Well?" Meg demanded.

"The hood."

"The hood?"

"The hood. Meg, *somebody put the hood on Mavis*. She was never supposed to wear the hood. She was supposed to ride on the sledge to the back of the stage, jump off, put the dummy in her place, and stroll on out to watch the rest of the fun and games. But Harland came stomping out complaining that she'd thrown up all over his shoes, and then Harvey said he'd drive the sledge. Mavis could have passed out on the sledge, which would account for the fact that she was there instead of the dummy, but she had no reason to put on the hood."

"Wow," said Meg. "Oh, wow. Murder. Oh, my God. Who did it?"

"How should I know?" demanded Quill. She watched the sheriff's patrol across the green. "All kinds of people had motives to murder Mavis."

"Who?"

"Who? I'll tell you who." Quill, upset, couldn't think of anyone but John and Tom Peterson. But they had wanted Gil dead, hadn't they? Or had they? "Celeste Baumer for one."

"I thought she went back to Manhattan after Myles let her out of jail."

"Maybe she didn't. Maybe she stayed here, lurking until an opportunity presented itself."

"Dressed like she was, she'd stick out a mile. Who else?" Meg's eyebrows shot up. "I know! Mrs. Hallenbeck!"

"Why? She's out a companion, and I really doubt she'd find it easy to get another one. She's terrified of being alone. Not to mention the fact," Quill added sarcastically, "that she's eighty-three years old and more than likely a grandmother six times over."

"The Grandmother Murders," said Meg. "I like it."

"Now Keith Baumer—*there's* a murderer for you."

"Too obvious," said Meg. "I mean, he was the one who lifted the heavy stone onto her."

"Not if he wanted to divert suspicion from himself." Quill locked her hands around her knees. She could see Myles's broad shoulders in the distance. "Maybe Mavis was pressuring him to marry her, or something."

"I wish John would get back," said Meg, who obviously wanted to avoid a serious discussion as Quill did. "This is a mess. Do you suppose they'll cancel the rest of History Days?"

"I don't know." Quill rubbed her hands over her face. "Maybe I'm crazy. Maybe it *was* an accident. Mavis was so drunk, she could have put the hood on as a joke or something, and then passed out on the sledge."

"Myles will take care of it." Meg sat up and brushed the seat of her jeans briskly. "Let's walk over and ask him what's going on."

"He'll just tell us to butt out, Meg. He always does." Quill was seized with a desire to get back to the Inn, and jumped to her feet. "Where's Edward? He's been in there quite a while. Did he go in right after you?"

"Yep. I'll go check."

"Meg, we're not supposed to go in there. Davey said . . ."

"Bosh!" Meg jumped up, disappeared into the building, then reappeared a few moments later with Edward Lancashire.

"Mrs. Hallenbeck just went in to see Officer Kiddermeister," he said in response to Quill's inquiry.

"You were in there a long time," said Meg. "Did he ask you the same questions he asked us?"

"I'm sure he did," Edward said easily.

The door to the library swung open, and Mrs. Hallenbeck felt her way carefully down the steps. Quill went up and took her arm. "Are you feeling all right? This must have been such a shock!"

"This has been quite an experience," the old lady said. "Most interesting. I warned her that liquor would be the death of her someday—that, and those pills." She gazed around with satisfaction. "It's a lovely day."

"Did Mavis drink much, Mrs. Hallenbeck?" Edward asked.

"A cocktail every evening, without fail. I myself neither smoke nor drink, nor put any drugs in my body," she said firmly. "I am often complimented on my youthful appearance. It is the result of taking care of myself. Shall we walk to the Inn? I could use a cup of tea."

"Would you like me to call the van from the Inn, Mrs. Hallenbeck? It's all uphill." Quill was worried about her in the heat.

"What a thoughtful child you are, Sarah. You take such good care of me. No. I shall walk. I walk four or five miles a day most of the time. I am frequently complimented on my stamina."

The four of them set off at a rapid pace, Mrs. Hallenbeck leading the way.

"Had you known Mavis long?" asked Edward of her.

"Oh, yes. She worked for my late husband, you know. Had a title—Human Resources Director or somesuch. Quite a stupid woman, really, when you think about it."

"Such a terrible way to die," murmured Quill, half to herself.

"Perhaps the sheriff will find some evidence on the barn door," suggested Edward.

"I did not so much as pick up a stone, so I clearly am not responsible," said Mrs. Hallenbeck with immense satisfaction. "But that terrible Baumer person. Someone should put people like that in jail. Imagine being responsible for an accident like that."

They reached the bottom of the incline to the Inn. Mrs. Hallenbeck looked girlishly up at Edward. "I believe I'll take this handsome young man's arm up these little stairs."

Edward presented his arm with a gallant gesture, and the two sisters fell behind. The words "frequently complimented" floated back to them more than once, and Meg muttered crossly, "I don't think that woman's elevator goes all the way to the top, Quill."

"Meg, she's eighty-three years old. We can't imagine what that's like. All the people that she grew up with, her husband, her friends, are either gone or going. The line between life and death must seem very thin to her, each day more of a struggle to stay on this side and not slip to the next."

Meg started to hum the portentous strains of "Pomp and Circumstance," and Quill told her to shut up. "That doesn't make you think of fat guys with double chins making speeches full of hot air?" said Meg innocently. "It does me."

"I'd rather think about what to serve the Chamber tonight."

"Something comforting, but not depressing," said Meg. "Pasta in sauce ought to set Marge right up. As long as I don't have to make it, smell it, or eat it. Frank'll make it."

"Pasta in sauce," said Marge with satisfaction some three hours later. "Finally something I rekonize."

"Very diplomatic," said Howie dryly. "Traditional village fare for weddings, anniversaries, and funerals." He rolled a forkful around in his mouth. "Do I detect fresh basil? The last of the Vidalias?"

"Do I detect bullshit?" asked Marge, raising her eyes to the ceiling. "Or is it Heinz spaghetti sauce, like any sensible person uses."

"We need to get to the purpose of this meeting," said Elmer Henry. He rapped the gavel and stood up. Seventeen faces stared back at him. "This emergency meeting of the Hemlock Falls Chamber of Commerce is now in session. Will you lead us in a prayer, Reverend?"

"He's not here," said Betty Hall. "He called his own emergency session of the deacons at his church. Said he'll be right along as soon as it's over."

"So Tom Peterson isn't here either," said Elmer. "And

Myles is off on his investigation. We have enough to vote, Quill?"

"You need a certain portion of the membership," said Quill hesitantly. "I'm not sure just how many."

"Two-thirds," said Howie impatiently. "There's twenty-four active members."

There was a pause while everyone figured this out.

"We're two short," said Esther, which, unknown to Quill, helped enlighten Mark Anthony Jefferson, the vice-president of the Hemlock Falls Savings and Loan, as to Esther's cash-flow troubles.

"No, we're one over," said Marge promptly, which would have surprised Mark Anthony not at all. "So, do we cancel the rest of the History Days or what?"

"If I might say something," said Harvey Bozzel. He stood up, tucked his hands boyishly in the back pocket of his cotton Dockers, and composed his features into a grave, but not solemn, expression. "We've experienced a terrible tragedy here. Just terrible. And we sincerely mourn the passing of this celebrity in our town."

"Celebrity?" said Betty Hall. "She was a paid companion to that old lady. What's with the celebrity stuff?"

"She was a professional actress," Harvey said gently.

"She was a dancing hot dog!" said Betty. "I don't call that being a celebrity."

"A story . . . now, Ralph, you can help me on this . . . that will probably be picked up by the national media."

"A TV station was here," admitted Ralph Lorenzo, editor and publisher of the *Hemlock Daily News*. "But it was just the affiliate from Syracuse."

"With the proper handling," said Harvey, "this can be a story of national scope." He ran one hand through his styled blond hair and asked rhetorically, " 'Does an ancient curse haunt the peaceful village of Hemlock Falls? Story tonight at eleven.' With absolutely no disrespect to the dead, think of the publicity." He lowered his voice and looked at them earnestly. "Think of the good it can do the businesses of Hemlock Falls. Quill, has anyone decided to shorten their stay with you because of this?"

"I thought it might," said Quill, "but no. Everyone seems

to be ghoulishly interested in what's happened."

"No, no, no, no, no. Not ghoulish, Quill. It's the universal need to validate your own existence. In the midst of death, there is life. This is a well-known phenomenon in advertising."

"It is, huh?" Harland Peterson banged his fist on the table. "If you're talking about keeping this play going all week, I say it ain't right and it ain't fit, and I'm going to vote against it."

"I have to agree with Harland," said Quill. "This is capitalizing on—"

"On an accident that could have happened to any one of us," said Harvey. "Quill, if you had decided to go on, it could have been you! Don't you see? You get on the expressway after a tractor-trailer hits a bus—you drive more carefully. These occurrences, terrible as they are for the victims, can help prevent such things from happening again. Now, if the town were to approve a small advertising budget, I'd be happy to handle the necessary press releases, to interface with the media, perhaps conduct tours of the fatal spot."

The members responded with vehemence. Marge offered the practical opinion that it'd be good for the diner business, and probably the Croh Bar, too. Howie Murchison drew an analogy between Harvey's proposal and the behavior of ghouls; Miriam Doncaster offered a precise definition of ghoul and agreed with Howie. Freddie Bellini, the mortician, said death was a decent business and he wasn't going to sit still for nasty shots from lawyers and librarians. Quill abandoned any pretense at taking notes and wondered if John Raintree had been in a car wreck, and maybe that was why he'd gone missing.

Myles walked into the room and the squabble stopped abruptly. He was still in uniform. The lines around his gray eyes had deepened a little, and his mouth was grim. Quill thought he looked terrific, like Clint Eastwood riding into town to deal out frontier justice to the mob. He pulled a chair up to the table and sat down.

"We were just discussing the rest of History Days," said Elmer. "Talking about whether or not to continue with the play. What do you think?"

Myles shrugged. "We've found all we're going to find at the site. Go ahead."

Quill would have preferred a response more in the heroic mode. A man who looked like Myles should wither the Harvey Bozzels of this world with a phrase or two of devastating pith. A direct blaze of contempt from his steely eyes would do it, too.

"I'm hungry," said Myles. "Any more of the pasta around?"

Quill handed him her plate. "Take mine."

"So we have the sheriff's support," said Harvey. "I can work up a fee schedule for you right now, and then we can take a quick vote."

Myles wiped his mouth with Quill's napkin. "You don't have my support. I said the site's not off limits."

"What's your opinion, then?" asked Esther. "Harvey said you don't close the expressway after a car accident, so why should we lose the business from History Days?"

"I don't have an official opinion. My personal opinion is that we've had two deaths in the past forty-eight hours and that's no cause for celebrations of any kind."

"We can always tell when it's not an election year, Sheriff," said Harvey nastily. "These two accidents could have happened anywhere, at any time. . . ."

"They weren't accidents," said Myles. "Gil Gilmeister and Mavis Collinwood were murdered." Myles swallowed the last of the pasta and stood up. The silence was profound. "Quill, you're to notify me if any of the guests here at the Inn check out. Any of you here have planned to take any time away from the Falls, let Davey know first." He stopped at the door, and looked directly at Quill. "I'm going to need to talk to John Raintree. There's an APB out on him. Any of you see him, call me."

"Murdered!" said Miriam Doncaster.

"Bullshit," said Marge. She wiped her forehead with her napkin.

"S'cuse me," said Ralph Lorenzo, "seems to be a story here." He jumped up and ran after Myles, almost colliding with Dookie Shuttleworth and Tom Peterson as they came into the conference room.

"Forgive us for being late," said the Reverend Shuttleworth.

"We had a most important meeting at the church."

"Sheriff says Gil was murdered, Tom," said Howie Murchison.

"Gil?" Tom stood uncertainly for a moment. The Reverend Shuttleworth took his arm and put him into a chair.

"Murder," said Harvey Bozzel. "Can't see that anybody would want to murder Gil, and if they did, whacking him over the head with that front loader was a piss-poor way to do it."

"That Mavis Collinwood, too," said Elmer. "Marge, you were there at the duck pond. What the hell happened?"

"You know what happened," said Marge sourly. "Sheriff's full of baloney. Coulda been me, coulda been Mavis sat in that ducking stool. You have some gripe with Gil, Harland? You set that tractor up somehow?"

"That tractor's been used for thirty years, and it's got another thirty in it. Ain't nothin' wrong with that tractor!" Harland roared.

"We must not assign blame," said Dookie Shuttleworth. "This is just further evidence that there is some devilish device at work here in town. Quill, the deacons and I have decided to hold a prayer breakfast. This distressing news makes it all the more urgent that we do so. Would the dining room at the Inn be available to us tomorrow morning? For perhaps forty people?"

"Of course, Mr. Shuttleworth," Quill said. "I'll speak with the kitchen about the menu."

"The church is not exactly in funds at the moment," he said apologetically. "Perhaps we could work something out?"

The wail of a siren jerked Quill upright.

"That's the ambulance!" said the mayor. "What the heck? What's happening to the town now?"

Quill ran into the hall and out to the front lobby. Two paramedics burst in through the door. The woman, a substantially sized brunette Quill had seen in town before, said, "Room two twenty-one, miss?"

"This way," said Quill. They followed her up the short flight of stairs. Two twenty-one was Baumer's room. Quill, her heart pounding, rapped on the door as she opened it with her master key. "Mr. Baumer!" she called. "It's Sarah Quilliam. Are you all right?"

"In here!" Baumer's voice was whispery, faint. Quill froze with anxiety bordering on outright fear. Some lunatic must be abroad in Hemlock Falls. Maybe Harvey Bozzel was right. The paramedics shoved her unceremoniously out of the way and charged into the bathroom.

Quill sat down on the bed and took several deep breaths.

"Was that the ambulance?" Meg stood at the open door. She snapped her fingers nervously, a habit which had irritated Quill since their childhood. "Is Baumer okay?"

"Yes, to the ambulance, and I don't know about Baumer," said Quill. "The paramedics are in there with him." Thumps and mumblings from the bathroom indicated the presence of too many people in too small a space. "Have you seen him tonight?"

"Umyah."

"What do you mean, 'umyah'? Was he at dinner?"

The brunette opened the bathroom door. Her partner, a thickset guy with a mustache, supported Keith Baumer. Baumer's face was furious. And green. Quill couldn't decide which condition was uppermost.

"This," Baumer rasped, "is the hotel from Hell." The male paramedic dumped him unceremoniously on the bed. Baumer groaned theatrically and closed his eyes.

Quill, who had a growing, uneasy suspicion about the cause of Baumer's illness, asked the medics what happened.

"He has food poisoning," said the brunette. "We got a sample." She held up a clear tube. Quill averted her eyes from the loathsome contents. "I just think he ate sumthin' that didn't agree with him."

"He have anything with raw egg in it?" asked the male medic. The tag on his white coat read O. DOYLE. "This could be salmonella."

"Salmonella," agreed his partner. "Deadly stuff. Ought to take him to the hospital." She nodded her head in gloomy relish. "Might not last the night otherwise."

"There is no salmonella in my kitchen," snapped Meg. "And if he's sick, it's because he grossed out on my food. Pork roast, potatoes *duchesse*, asparagus with hollandaise—and the eggs were cooked, thank you. He started the meal with sausage-stuffed mushrooms, and ended it with a chocolate *bombe*, and nobody's gut can take all that, even a cow, which has four stomachs instead of that guy's one."

"He looks a little better, Mr. O'Doyle," said Quill, eyeing Baumer with hope.

"It's Doyle, ma'am. Oliver Doyle. And I think he does, don't you, Maureen?"

"I'll take his temperature." She opened a black bag, took out a thermometer, and rolled up her sleeves. "CAN YOU HEAR ME, MR. BAUMER!"

"I can hear you fine," he snapped. "It's my stomach, not my ears."

"CAN YOU ROLL OVER ON YOUR STOMACH FOR ME? WE'RE GOING TO TAKE YOUR TEMPERATURE." Maureen advanced on him, the thermometer held aloft.

"We'll wait in the hall," said Quill. She shoved Meg out of 221, across the hall, and flat against the opposite wall. "What the hell have you been up to, Meg!"

"Nothing," said Meg, meekly.

Quill knew her sister's literal mind. "Then what have Frank and Bjorn been up to?"

"A little creative cooking, that's all," said Meg. "Nothing remotely harmful."

Quill stood back and glared at her, hands on her hips. "That little bottle. What's in it?"

Meg opened her mouth, closed it. "Ipecac," she said. "A very weak solution."

Maureen and Oliver came out of 221, closing the door behind them. "Temperature's normal," said Maureen regretfully. "Pulse is normal. And he only threw up five or six times and he's not gonna heave again, he says. Told him to stay in bed for a few days, eat boiled eggs and tea, maybe a little toast."

"Aw, Maureen, the guy's going to be fine," said Doyle, "just ate something that didn't agree with him. I seen guys a lot sicker come out of the Croh Bar and work the late shift at the paint factory, no problem."

"Still got to report it to the Board of Health," said Maureen. She waved the test tube. "Send this in for samples." She brightened. "Might be salmonella. Just a teensy little bit."

"Nah." Doyle shook Quill's hand. "He heaves again, give Doc Bishop a call. You won't need us. Bit of a waste of time, this. Took me away from a great video and the girlfriend."

"You must let the Inn make a contribution to the ambulance fund," said Quill hastily. "I mean, on top of the one we give every year." Quill drew them to the stairs. "And we'll take good care of Mr. Baumer. We'll see that he stays in bed a couple of days. Meg will see to the menu herself."

"Told him you prob'bly wouldn't charge him," Maureen tossed over her shoulder as they carried their equipment out, "on account of you wouldn't want a lawsuit or nothing." She waved the test tube aloft in farewell.

"Thank you," Quill said to the closed door, "very, very much." She turned to her sister. "What were you thinking of?"

"That we'd get rid of him!" said Meg with spirit. "Have him move to the Marriott or something. Let them put up with him."

"Good plan," Quill said cordially. "Excellent plan. I like a plan that means we're going to have to wait on him hand and foot for the next three days. *For free!*"

"Tell you what," said Meg with a charitable air. "Since you're so upset about this, let me take care of it. You don't have to worry about a thing."

"That's big of you."

"It's the least I can do."

A shout came from behind the closed door of 221. Quill smiled sweetly. "That call's for you."

The Chamber members were eating lemon tarts when Quill returned to the Lounge. She sat down, looked at the yellow custard filling, and pushed it away.

"Everything all right?" asked Howie after a moment. "Elmer wanted to come stampeding to the rescue, but I convinced him that another eighteen bodies stuffed into your front lobby would only confuse matters."

"Seventeen," said Marge. "I hollered at Ollie Doyle out the window. Said your sister finally poisoned somebody."

"Don't be absurd, Marge," said Esther. "What we have to worry about is whether a murderer's running around loose in Hemlock Falls. He might be staying right here at the Inn!"

"The only person who'd want to murder Keith Baumer is his wife," said Quill. "And she went back to Manhattan this morning after Myles let her out of jail." Well aware of the town's propensity for gossip, she came to a decision. She ground her teeth, looked Marge in the eye, and said, "You were right. My sister thought Keith Baumer was the ultimate pest. So she put ipecac in his food." She shut her eyes, waiting for the barrage of indignation sure to follow.

"Really?" said Betty Hall with interest. "Marge tried that once with this smartass yuppie from New Jersey that kept sending his food back. Worked a treat. Never saw him again."

"Made him pay the bill, too," said Marge with satisfaction. "Tell Meg baking soda in the scrambled eggs works just as good. And there's no mess to clean up."

"Well, we all hope that Meg's efforts are rewarded," said the Reverend Shuttleworth. "There are certain signs about the man that are very disturbing, very disturbing. There is strong evidence that he was an instrument in the downfall of that poor creature who went to her reward this afternoon. And I have your Doreen Muxworthy to thank for first bringing them to my attention."

"The staff at the Inn aims to please," said Quill. "Mayor, if the meeting is going to go on much longer, I'll need to leave you to your coffee. I've got to see to some things."

"Yes. With John being accused of these murders, you will have many extra duties," said the Reverend Shuttleworth. "The members were telling me about this APR."

"APB," said Quill, "and John has *not* been accused of these murders, Mr. Shuttleworth. And I'd appreciate it *very* much if you all understand that. Myles just wants to talk to him. That's all. He has . . . evidence germane to these incidents."

Nobody would meet Quill's eye. She wondered just exactly what had been discussed while she was occupied with Baumer. "You've known him for years," she said. "He grew up in this town. He does the books for half the businesses in town. You've trusted him in the past. Has he ever betrayed that trust?"

Mark Anthony Jefferson cleared his throat. "Well, that's just it, Quill. We've been talking the matter over and—" Quill drew breath to protest, and Jefferson held his hand up.

"Please. He knew, for example, quite a bit more about Gil's car business than Tom here—his own partner—did. I'm going to go over the books tomorrow with Tom, at the bank, to see if there may have been any irregularities that Gil could have discovered."

"You have no basis for that belief," said Quill hotly. "None!"

"It's wise to take precautions," said Mark Anthony. "As for Ms. Collinwood . . ."

"He'd never even met Mavis Collinwood before she came here!" said Quill. "This is all—There's a word for it. Howie?"

"Supposition?" said the lawyer.

"No!" Quill knew her face was red with anger. "Slander!"

Howie looked at Marge and raised his eyebrows.

"I'll tell her," said Marge gruffly. She rocked back in her chair. "Mavis told me something about John that you have to know, Quill. I'm sorry to be the one to do it, too, because although I ain't sure about this fancy schmancy kwee-zeen you all serve, you've been a good enough friend and neighbor over the years. And you know I'm mostly joking when I give you a little bit of hassle over stuff. The way I figure, we've got a friendly rivalry, that right, Howie?"

"You ought to get to the point, Marge," said Howie.

"John was the head of the accounting department for Dog-gone Good Dogs some years back. After my time. Mavis figured he was the one who embezzled near three hundred thousand dollars from their company. Then he disappeared and nobody saw hide nor hair of him for a couple of years. Mavis was that shocked when she met him here at your Inn." Marge looked around the table. "So what we figure is, John had himself a real good motive to get rid of both of them, Mavis and Gil."

Quill left them sitting there without a word.

CHAPTER 10

Quill wanted a place with no phones, no people, and no problems. When being nibbled to death by ducks, she thought, the best thing to do is leave the pond. Meg was the sort of person who'd mince the ducks into pâté, and not for the first time, Quill envied her sister's direct, assertive approach. For Meg, all odds were surmountable.

Even murder.

She left the Inn and walked to the gazebo in the perennial garden. Evening was coming on like high tide on a still night, the purple-blue darkness flowing over the Falls' ridge to touch the crescent moon. The dark hid the colors of the roses, but their scent recalled their names, and their names their sturdy beauty—Maidens' Blush at its peak; the damasks Celsiana and La Ville de Bruxelles in full bloom; the hybrid teas Tiffany and Crimson Glory a constant undernote, as they had been all summer. Quill's hand flexed as though it held a paint brush. She sat in the gazebo and let pictures of new paintings drift through her mind's eye. The heart of a Chrysler Imperial rose would make a wonderful painting—a man-made rose with a man-made shape at odds with the essential nature of flowers. It would give the painting an energetic irony. And the color—an aggressive, insulting, dangerous red.

Like blood seeping from under a barn door.

"Ugh!" said Quill into the dark. She asked herself the logical question: Who wanted Mavis dead? She shut her eyes and thought about the scene of the crime as a painting. The bandstand with the three witnesses—Howie, Elmer, and Tom Peterson; Dookie, in the judge's seat, the crowd immediately in front of the bandstand.

Who in this picture had the opportunity to kill?

Baumer had been standing extreme stage left. If he'd looked over his right shoulder, he would have seen the sledge stop and Harland dismount. He could have waited until Harland stomped around stage right to accost Howie and tell him he wasn't going to drive anymore.

Did Baumer take the chance to pull the hood over Mavis' slack mouth and dulled eyes?

Tom Peterson had been standing at Baumer's elbow after he moved off-stage. The two men hadn't known each other, and hadn't spoken together, at least not in the replay Quill saw before her. Tom, too, could have ducked around the stage and gone into the semidarkness of the shed. Except that Quill could find no link between Tom and Mavis. And Mavis had been the target of the murderer, who had succeeded the second time, after failing the first.

Harvey Bozzel had jumped from the stage to the rescue like some half-baked Dudley Do-Right. The crowd had surged forward when Harvey made his dramatic gesture, and Baumer and Tom Peterson had disappeared in the melee.

Quill concentrated hard: Mrs. Hallenbeck, Nadine Gilmeister, Marge Schmidt, Meg, and Edward Lancashire had all been shoved back as the crowd moved forward.

There was herself, of course, sitting on a bench with two teenaged girls who'd been restless during the trial scene, and able, in the confusion, to walk away unnoticed. "And I sure as heck didn't do it," said Quill aloud.

So all of them had been close enough to slip around the bandstand and assist Mavis Collinwood down the gravel path to death at the foot of General Hemlock.

Who had been at the scene of *both* crimes? Tom Peterson, Nadine, Mrs. Hallenbeck, and Edward Lancashire had all been in the vicinity, but Marge and Baumer were the only two who'd been there at the time of both killings. Unless one of the others had *returned* to the scene.

Mrs. Hallenbeck certainly wanted Mavis alive; "Old age is lonely," she'd said. "You have no idea how lonely. And Mavis is a warm body in the house. She's nowhere to go, but to me. Do you know how hard it is to find a healthy, reasonably responsible person to take care of me?"

It was conceivable that Mrs. Hallenbeck had accomplished the murder, but there was no motive. Quite the reverse.

Did Tom Peterson want Mavis and Gil dead? Had he tried three times to kill her? She knew the car business was in trouble. Had Mavis and Marge offered to buy Tom out, using Mrs. Hallenbeck's money? Was there a reason that Tom couldn't/wouldn't sell? He said he'd been home watching a videotape the night Gil died, and his wife was gone for the evening. His house was the only residence even close to the park; he could have watched the three of them mooching around in the park; he could have slipped out, loosened the bolt, watched Gil's death, and taken the bolt with him. He'd have been back home in less than ten minutes.

What was the motive? Tom would have wanted Mavis alive, and able to buy Gil out.

What about Nadine? Quill thought long and seriously about Nadine. It didn't fit. In almost any other marriage, jealousy would have been a dandy motive. But it would have been Marge, not Mavis, who Nadine would have wanted out of the way. Besides, Nadine had been shopping in Syracuse with her sister the night of the ducking-stool incident. Her parking validation from the Mall had the time on it; she couldn't have physically been there in time to do the first murder.

And finally, Edward Lancashire. Quill could see no reason why the food critic for *L'Aperitif* would want to kill Mavis Collinwood. But he had the opportunity. And he'd been asking a lot of questions.

Marge was a most attractive candidate for both murders. Quill scrupulously cleared her mind of prejudice. You didn't pursue a potential murderer because the potential murderer called your sister Megia Borgia, and threatened you and yours with polyester-suited employees from the Board of Health. You investigated reasons why persons of such lousy taste would hate the victim.

"One," said Quill to the Sutter's Gold rosebush at her elbow. "Marge and Mavis worked together at Doggone Good Dogs. Marge claims Mavis told her three hundred thousand dollars was missing. And that John took it. What if Marge had taken it? And what if Mavis found out?" Everyone in town wondered why Marge did so well out of that little diner. She'd lent money to Gil more than once. Even Esther West had once confided to Quill that in times when the banks clamped down on lending, Marge was a good, if usuriously inclined, source of cash. Marge's behavior was definitely suspicious. She loved Gil—or did she? Gil owed her money. Her activities and motives *both* would have to investigated. Maybe Marge had been after Mavis all along. Gil could have hopped on that ducking stool *before* Marge could stop him. Quill shuddered at the thought of Marge screaming No! as Gil went drunkenly to his death.

Quill began to feel better. She was getting that I'm-really-good-at-managing-people feeling so often rebutted by the skepticism of her nearest and dearest. She jumped up and moved briskly along the gravel path, hands clasped behind her in the best Sherlock Holmes tradition.

Baumer. Another prime candidate. Quill pulled at her lower lip. She'd read with great interest various books on the personalities of murderers. Motive was frequently rooted in the character of the killers; given a variety of motives in a given number of people, only one would kill. Just considering his character, Baumer fit better than anybody. At least, he'd been positioned right; of all the members of the audience at the *Trial,* he was in the best position to pop backstage and hood the bird, so to speak. And he'd been with Mavis, Marge, and Gil the night of the duck pond killing. But why? No reason to kill Gil, but, like Marge, perhaps Mavis had been his target. Would he kill to keep his marriage together? Was he afraid that word of his shenanigans would get back to his boss?

"Probably not," said Quill, this time to the concrete fish pond by the French lavender. "But it wouldn't hurt to explore possibilities." She could start tomorrow, ask some tactful, discreet questions of Baumer's employers at the sales conference at the Marriott; go to the diner and confront Marge; investigate Peterson.

Quill heard the sounds of people leaving the Inn. Car doors slammed in the distance. Voices shouted goodbye. Motors revved, taillights blinked red; the Chamber members had gone home.

Feeling it was safe to go back in the water, Quill went to the kitchen and laid her conclusions out for Meg.

Meg sipped coffee—she was immune to the effects of caffeine, and had been known to drink her special blend to put herself to sleep—and drew circles on the pastry marble with her forefinger as Quill narrowed the number of suspects to two.

"So I'm going to go to the Marriott tomorrow and start with some questions about Baumer's past. The other thing I can do is have Doreen search his room for that bolt. And I thought I'd drop by the diner. If Marge is lying about John's connection to Mavis and Doggone Good Dogs, she did it under the guise of presenting an olive branch. I'll just walk into the diner for lunch, waving my own olive branch, and asking innocent questions."

"Have you talked this over with Myles?"

"Of course I haven't talked it over with Myles. You know that Myles is practically prehistoric in his attitude towards women's ability to do certain things."

"I haven't noticed that at all," said Meg. "He's got two patrolwomen in the Sheriff's Department, he voted for our woman senator in the last campaign, and he does his own housework. Doreen's after him all the time to hire her cousin Shirlee to clean for him. He cooks for you all the time, and I remember distinctly, Quill, that he took his two little nieces to Disney World all by himself last year. Myles isn't a male chauvinist. He doesn't want you messing in his police work, because you're an emotional, biased *person*. His bias is *not* gender-specific."

"I am *not* an emotional, biased person!"

"Yes, you are, Quill! You're a crusader. You've always been a crusader. Remember the protest?"

"Meg, don't bring up the protest."

"I remember the protest . . ."

"Meg, you always bring up the protest. That was thirty years ago, for Pete's sake, and you bring it up when the least little thing happens."

" . . . I was four years old. *Four years old*! You had me protesting the Vietnam war in front of my *kindergarten*. Here I was, this totally innocent little kid whose big sister had this sign STOP THE WAR with the *R* backwards, and we made the six o'clock news. Mom was so embarrassed she didn't go out of the house for weeks afterward. The neighbors thought she put us up to it."

"Dad thought it was great," said Quill stiffly. "He sneaked me a Mars bar when he came to get us at the police station."

"You never told me that," said Meg. "I never got any of it, either." She regarded her sister with exasperation. "Your analysis of the situation is clean, cool, and precise."

"Thank you," said Quill.

"It's also bogus. You're ignoring one screamingly obvious set of facts which bring the whole house of cards to the floor, Hawkshaw."

"And what's that?"

"John," said Meg. "John appears to have the best motive of all. What about that picture!"

"Why should the fact that Nadine and Tom's sister-in-law was John's sister have anything to do with anything?" said Quill crossly.

"Because you were the one that 'deduced' the picture really belonged to John, and Gil had it! Honestly, Quill. It makes perfect sense to me that if Gil saw it lying on the ground, he'd pick it up and put it away so he could return it to John later. It also makes perfect sense that the Gilmeisters knew about John's prison sentence and never told anybody. You know what Hemlock Falls is like. Nadine would be embarrassed to the tops of her ears to have everyone know they'd had an ex-con in the family. I love you, Quill, but there's caramel where your brains should be. You're letting your friendship with John get in the way of the facts." She shook her head. "I'm beat. I'm going to bed. I'll see you in the morning."

There was a mass of telephone messages under her door. Quill flipped on the overhead lights and sank into the Eames chair in front of the fireplace and riffled through them. The insurance adjuster would be by in the morning to examine the balcony. She could hand off the task of showing him around to Peter Williams. Myles had called; he was in Ithaca until Tuesday. The forensic lab tests on Saturday had been positive for sulfuric acid, which meant, thought Quill, that it was highly possible there'd been a first attempt on Mavis' life. She paperclipped that message to the three from Mrs. Hallenbeck, inviting her to dinner, to a cup of late-night tea, and then to breakfast tomorrow morning. "We must talk," each message read.

"That we must," Quill said to herself. "About our bill, about Mavis. About what you discussed at dinner with Mavis, Marge, and Gil."

She scrawled a short list. "Things To Do—Monday: Hal; Pet; Mar; Baum," and muttering the names HalPetMarBaum like a charm against disaster, fell into a deep, dreamless sleep.

The phone rang. Quill jerked awake. The digital clock radio blinked two-thirty. Quill regarded it with baleful eyes and picked the phone up. "This is Quill."

"Is Myles with you?"

"John!"

"He's not there?"

"No. He's in Ithaca and won't be back until Tuesday. John, I've been so worried about you. Where are you?"

The line went dead. Quill jiggled the cutoff button. Two quiet taps sounded at the door. Quill jumped up and flung it open. John stood there, white shirt rumpled, tieless, his sports coat filthy. The gray shadows under his eyes made his cheeks gaunt and his expression haunted.

"Come in and sit down," said Quill. She ushered him into the room and shut the door. John slumped on the couch and rubbed his hands over his face.

"You look exhausted, John. Have you had anything to eat?"

"A Big Mac, this afternoon."

"Meg will have a fit."

He chuckled. "Actually, it tasted pretty good. Sometimes you just get a craving for junk food, you know?"

Quill paced restlessly around the room.

John watched her for a moment, forearms on his knees. "I want to tell you about my prison sentence."

Quill sat in the Eames chair, relieved.

"I went to my rooms first, before I came to see you. I wanted to show you a picture I have there, but the police . . ."

"Yes, I know."

"Then you know about my sister?"

"I didn't know who she was, John, until I showed it to Nadine. Myles found the one of her in the waitress uniform at the scene of . . . where Gil drowned."

"By the pond?"

"Yes. I matched it with the one you had in your room."

"Gil was going to put it in the family album. He never had much sense. So, that explains the APB. Myles thought it connected me to the scene of the crime."

"Yes, John. Where have you been all this time?"

"I made some—acquaintances in prison. There's a network, if you know who to talk to, where to look. That's one of the things I did while I was gone. I spent a lot of time trying to find out why Mavis came here, what she was after, what she'd been doing since I saw her last at the company."

"So you did work together, then?"

"For about six years. It was just after I got my MBA from RIT." He shook his head. "I really thought I was going places, then." His face shuttered closed. Quill waited patiently.

"We were a close family, growing up," he said. "My dad worked the high steel and was gone a lot. My mom stayed home. My sister Elaina was quiet, shy, never dated much in high school." John stopped, sighed, then went on. "I was a rowdy kid in high school, ran around with a bunch of guys who got into stupid small-time things. Lifting cigarettes from drugstores, joy-riding in other people's cars. I straightened up my senior year, and left all of it behind me when I got the scholarship. All but friends, one in particular, who married my sister. Tom Peterson's brother, Jack." He looked at Quill, the skin drawn tight over his cheekbones.

"My dad died in a fall from a high beam. My mom passed on soon after that. Cancer. Elaina had no one but me. And Jackie, of course. Jackie who got into the booze every Saturday night, then every Friday and Saturday night, then every day of the week and came home from the bars and beat her.

"She never said a word. Not for all the time I was in school, not for the years I started working my way up to D.G.D.'s headquarters. I'd drive in from headquarters in Syracuse. We'd get together now and then, and I noticed things, as you will, in passing. A black eye. A fractured elbow. A cracked rib. Falls, she said, or clumsiness. Any one of the million transparent excuses you hear from battered women."

John stared at his clasped hands. "I was into the booze pretty good myself. Earning good money. On my way up. Ignoring all the signs that told me I was in trouble, refused to believe I was another alcoholic Indian. I'd beat the stereotype, right?

"I dropped by Elaina's one Saturday afternoon. Hadn't seen her for a couple of months. I'd been to a sports bar with some of the guys from the company and we'd gotten into the Scotch. Somebody had called me at the bar. Said there was trouble. I knocked on the front door and waited. Nobody answered for a long, long time. I went around to the back. I looked in the kitchen window. The place was a mess; pots and pans all over the floor. There was a huge smear of chili on the ceiling, from where a pot'd been thrown off the stove, I guess.

"Elaina lay face down in the middle of the kitchen floor. I kicked in the lock. Went to her. Called her name. I turned her over." A shiver went through him. It didn't reach his face. Quill swallowed, and dug her nails into her hands.

"Tomatoes get hot. He'd thrown the chili into her face, after hitting her with the pot, I guess. She was burned, from her temple, here"—he touched his own—"to her chin. Later, we found out that she'd lost the sight of one eye. That pretty face. Gone.

"I shouted. I shouted again. I could hear the TV yowling from the living room. I ran in. Jackie was passed out on the couch. His mouth was open. He was snoring. There was tomato sauce down his shirt, on his hands. I beat him to death. And they sent me to prison."

Quill was cold. She couldn't speak. "Why don't I make you something to eat?" She went to her small kitchenette and busied herself. When she returned, she brought a small bowl of soup.

John sipped it, then said, "It didn't make a big splash in the papers. But everyone in the company knew, of course.

And that included Mavis. "Mavis had a nice little sideline going."

"She was Human Resources Director, wasn't she?" Quill's voice was rusty. She cleared her throat.

"The employees had a joke. That she directed the resources into her own pocket. Nobody knew how much money she made, but she was in a position to find out things. And she did. Have a little problem with your former employer? Mavis would approve your hiring on the condition that ten per cent of your pay check be turned over to her, every Friday. Swipe a few cartons of frozen meat from the storeroom? Same deal. You couldn't turn her in without turning yourself in. And nobody complained, of course. Nobody in management knew, or at least I like to think they didn't. *I* sure didn't find out until I came to work here. She tracked me down and gave me a call."

"She was blackmailing you?"

"Mavis was blackmailing everybody. By that time, she'd weaseled herself into the old lady's back pocket, and when the old man was alive, you couldn't touch her. Mavis had something on the guy who took over the accounting after I left—I don't know what it was, but it gave her access to the books. And she cooked them. Three hundred thousand dollars were missing soon after I went to jail. After I got out, she called me, and sent me documents that "proved" I'd been systematically bleeding the company during my time as head of accounting. A small monthly stipend, she said, would keep this news from my current employer."

"I wouldn't have believed it for a second," said Quill indignantly.

"No? How well do you know me? I've been here less than a year, Quill. And if you'd been approached by a woman with proof of my prison trial, my alcoholism, and 'proof' I'd diverted three hundred thousand dollars for my private use, what would you have done? What would anybody have done? I would have stopped you from hiring someone like that myself."

"I would have asked where the three hundred thousand went," said Quill. "The way you live it's obvious you haven't got it."

"Mavis had that covered, too. Elaina is . . . not right. She's been in a hospital down in Westchester for a long time. The state pays a part of it, but it's not enough." He reddened. "Gil and Marge and most of my clients pay me in cash. My income from my business is unrecorded, and I pay it directly to the institution. It'd be a bit of a job to prove where that money came from—and get a lot of other people into tax trouble."

"So between Mavis and your sister, it must be quite a stretch to make enough money to live."

"I live pretty well, Quill. Except for the lack of junk food. I think we should try to convince Meg to add potato skins to the appetizer menu."

"The kind loaded with Baco-s," said Quill. "No problem."

"You want to tell her, or shall I?"

"Flip you for it."

The lighthearted game wasn't working. Quill set her coffee cup on the end table. "So you must have been pretty upset when she showed up here."

"Quite a motive for murder," John agreed. "Quill, on my sister's life, I didn't kill Mavis. And I didn't kill Gil."

"Then we'll have to figure out who did."

"The woman of action," mused John. "I haven't seen you like this before, Quill."

"Well, there aren't that many crimes to solve in Hemlock Falls."

"Just put one in front of you, and you drop your normally diffident manner and charge?" John asked. "I mean, I *have* heard the story about the kindergartener's protest march, but I thought it was apocryphal, at least until now."

"Hah," said Quill. "Let me bring you up to date."

She summarized the discovery of the photograph among Gil's effects, the conversations with Tom, Nadine, and Myles, and Marge's disclosure at the Chamber meeting. Her review of the deadly conclusion to *The Trial of Goody Martin* was succinct but accurate.

"So you believe that Baumer and Marge are the likeliest suspects, with Tom Peterson running a poor third just because he had the opportunity."

"Don't you? I mean, that matchbook's pretty significant."

"There's an old saying in the audit business, Quill: 'Follow the money.' When I left here Friday, I was in a panic." He smiled slightly. "Not usual for me, I know. But I thought if I could find out what happened to that three hundred thousand three years ago, I might be able to discover who was being squeezed by Mavis badly enough to kill her."

"It did occur to you, didn't it, that Mavis took it herself?"

He hesitated. "It's possible. But I don't think so. I have a friend who's pretty good on the computer. We got into Mavis' financial records this morning. If she did have it, she doesn't have it now. Mavis is just about broke. She needed that job with Mrs. Hallenbeck."

"But what about the money you sent her?"

He shrugged. "A couple of hundred dollars a month. I found that, all right, along with a few other contributors to Mavis' nest egg, who are more than likely in the same position I am myself. She appeared to be taking in about eight hundred a month. That's enough to keep her in red lipstick and mid-range designer clothes, but that's it."

Quill hesitated to ask the next question. Somehow, theorizing in the perennial garden was a lot different than a cold discussion of facts with your accountant. "What about Marge? Was she being blackmailed, too?"

"I don't know. I was reviewing records of deposits, Quill, and they don't list the origin of the money in any bank I ever heard of. If I have a little more time, I can take a look around Marge's accounts." He shook his head. "I have a hard time believing it, though. Two hundred a month is a pretty slim motive for murder. Then there's the fact that I *like* Marge. I've known likable murderers in the joint, but I can't believe she'd have to resort to killing Mavis to get rid of her."

Quill explained her theories. John, unlike certain sheriffs she could name, listened with interest.

"Baumer's a possibility. The guy dresses like he's on the edge. Tom Peterson? I don't know. The partnership . . ." He stopped.

Quill waited. "What? What about the partnership, John? Don't stop now. We may solve this, just sitting here!"

"You mustn't repeat any of this, Quill. When people hire me to handle their books, they trust me with a fundamental part of themselves."

"You're worried about my finding out about Gil Gilmeister's financial affairs, when you're being hunted for murder?" Quill said. "Oh, for goodness sakes, John. That's absurd."

"Not to me."

Quill bit back her laughter, figured she never in this world would figure out why men behaved the way they did, and promised never to reveal to anyone the state of Gil Gilmeister's general ledger. "Plus," she said dramatically, "I hereby absolve you of the least little suspicion that You Did It. No one with that kind of honor system could possibly have swiped that bolt. And since you weren't even here when Mavis was . . . you know . . . you're totally in the clear."

John looked at her gravely for a moment. "Let's get back to the partnership. Gil and Tom have a fifty-fifty partnership in the business, not ideal for a number of reasons, because they had to agree jointly on every decision they made, and sometimes the interest of one partner conflicts dramatically with the needs of another. This was very true in Gil's case. Nadine was quite a consumer, and Gil's drinking problem didn't help matters either. Towards the end, Gil was drawing heavily against the equity in his part of the business; and business isn't all that good to begin with."

"The cash loans came from Marge?"

"Yes. And I'll say this for her, Marge Schmidt is a hell of a good businesswoman. She didn't let her affection for Gil stand in the way of liens against the units."

"You mean Gil borrowed money from Marge against the cars he hadn't sold?"

"Against the cars he sold. You know most of the profit from that business comes from the car loans."

It seemed to Quill that John's admiration of Marge's business acumen was misplaced, and that the nature of business itself was perverse. Marge's stranglehold on Gil's business was a *good* thing? She forebore comment and said, "But none of this has to do with Tom Peterson's half."

"No. Although Tom was getting fed up, and looking actively for a new partner. Funny thing was, he wasn't helping Gil get the loan he needed from the bank. They require an audit, and Tom kept ducking me, putting me off. Gil knew this. Gil also knew that Tom could force Marge to call those loans in by threatening to take his profitable side of the business elsewhere. He was even talking about setting up in competition with Gil. Marge had lent Gil a lot of money, and it'd be a case of her business or his. As I said, Marge is good. She wouldn't let her and Betty's ship go down to save Gil."

"So my theory about Marge and Mavis bringing Mrs. Hallenbeck's millions into Gil's business wasn't all that farfetched."

"No. Although from the little I knew of Mrs. Hallenbeck when I worked for the company, she'd be a hard sell. She was a tough cookie right from the start. Nobody was real surprised when old man Hallenbeck locked himself into the garage and turned the car motor on."

"Oh," said Quill softly. "How terrible!"

"Yes. She's got the life, though, doesn't she? Or she did. Doggone Good Dogs was sold to Armour's. She retired with a tidy sum, to say the least. And she had Mavis to run her errands for her."

"Not anymore," said Quill.

"Will she find someone else?"

"I don't know—it's very difficult. There's very little help for the elderly these days—unless they're willing to accept a nursing home, and I can't see Mrs. Hallenbeck doing that."

"It'd be a heck of a *nice* nursing home, with her money."

"But none of that explains why Tom Peterson would have a motive to kill Mavis."

"There's something funny going on." John's habitual self-containment kept him on the couch; any other man would have been pacing the room. He allowed himself a slight frown. "I knew Mavis was coming. She called from the gas station in Covert to tell me that we had to discuss what she called a 'rearrangement' of the payments."

"You paid her once a month?"

"Yes. To a post office box in Atlanta. The envelope was addressed to Scarlett O'Hara."

"Good grief," said Quill. "It figures."

"She was . . ."—John hesitated, searching for the right word—"ebullient. Chattering." He moved his thumb and forefinger together rapidly to indicate mindless babble. "Said the money was rolling in from every side."

"She's got the wrong heroine in Scarlett O'Hara," said Quill. "Behaving much more like the rapacious Evita, don't you think?"

John dismissed this excursion into light-mindedness with a tolerant twitch of his mouth. "I guess. The point is, Quill, she chose Hemlock Falls for a purpose. Not just because I was here. I got the impression that she'd come to some crossroads."

What, thought Quill, would be considered a career milestone for a professional blackmailer? "She must have come across something that would really feather her nest. Big money," she said aloud. "More than you could afford. And since she obviously came to Hemlock Falls for a reason, it must have to do with people she knows here. Something that Marge is involved with?" Quill guessed. "Something Tom Peterson is involved with?" She jumped to her feet. "*John!* The matchbook! The memo from the D.O.H.!"

"The mysterious folded-into-threes matchbook?"

Quill waved her arms excitedly. "You said that Tom was ducking an audit. That you couldn't get his personal finance statement out of him. That Gil was getting desperate, because without it the bank wouldn't give him a loan. That's fact one."

John nodded. Quill began to pace around the room. "Fact two is that the matchbook showed up on the balcony. He must have been there. He must have tried to push her over the edge."

"Wouldn't Mrs. Hallenbeck have seen him?"

"She said she was in the bathroom. He's been in our back room any number of times, delivering meat; he'd seen the drum of sulfuric acid. If Mavis called him, like she called you, he'd have a lot of time to set it up. The register's out all the time at the desk; he could have found out what room they were staying in, no problem. And he was here in the Inn while Mrs. Hallenbeck and Mavis were at dinner. And he lives right across from the pond. He said himself he was home alone. And of course, he was right there at the play."

"But what's his motive? And how would he know Mavis before she came to the Falls?"

"Did his brother work for the company?"

"For a while. He was a salesman. Most kids from Hemlock Falls end up either at the paint factory, or working for Doggone Good Dogs."

"And Mavis knew all the dirty secrets." Quill stood still, closed her eyes, and concentrated hard. "Meat . . ." she said slowly. "Tainted meat. That D.O.H. memo Marge was waving at me said something about tainted meat. E. coli bacteria. I went to Tom's to check on the shipment of beef that Meg said was spoiled. Tom got very weird about it. Doggone Good Dogs is a large customer for meat shipments. Help me out here, John."

Quill opened her eyes and discovered that Indians could turn pale.

"Jesus Christ," said John. "That's it. The beef is delivered directly to the franchise from the slaughterhouse. The franchise is the point of inspection. We had a real run on rejections from the restaurants just before I . . ." His lips thinned. "I was just about to take our inspector out to an Ohio supplier when . . ."

"Elaina happened."

"Yes."

"But what would Tom Peterson want with tainted meat?"

"Resale," John said. "Selling meat to third-world countries would give you the biggest money. Reselling to small restaurants and diners wouldn't be worth it. But if you shipped the containers offshore . . . I don't know, Quill, this is all guesswork."

"We'd need proof," said Quill. "What if we checked out Peterson's warehouse?"

"There'd be no need for him to have the trucks move through here."

"Somehow we got some of it," said Quill. "Isn't there some indication where the stuff came from? If we could find the truck that had the stuff we got, wouldn't there be some bill of lading, or whatever, that would tell its point of origin?"

"The carcasses are tagged," John said. "But there's all kinds of ways to fake the documentation. Except for the tattoos."

"The tattoos?"

"On the carcasses. They're stamped by the USDA. If they've been rejected, there's a code for that. It's inked onto the carcass. Of course, it can be cut off, but if we could find a whole carcass we'd have proof."

"I'm going over there," said Quill. "Right now. Coming with me?"

John grinned. "Sure. What the hell?"

"What the hell," Quill agreed. "Just give me a few seconds to change into my burglar outfit."

"We'll need a rope, a camera, and a flashlight."

Quill pointed to the credenza. "Camera and flashlight in there. Rope's in the car trunk."

Quill re-emerged from her bedroom minutes later dressed in a black turtleneck, jeans, and running shoes. "Do you think I should black my face?"

"No. But it's a good thing you're not blond."

The July air was soft and still. John and Quill crept to her car. After a fierce whispered discussion about who should drive, Quill started the motor, and kept the lights off until they reached the end of the drive and turned on to Route 96. Quill's heart was beating faster than usual. Her palms were damp. Her sense of time was warped; the ride to the Peterson warehouse seemed endless, but when she pulled into the gravel road to the buildings, it seemed as though no time had passed at all.

"Park behind that shed," said John in a low voice. "We'll walk up on the grass. It'll be quieter."

In the open air, Quill felt exposed, sure that a floodlight would go on and a siren sound any minute. "Over the top, Ma," she hissed at John's back. She bit her lip to keep the nervous giggles down.

"Only you," John whispered, "would do Jimmy Cagney imitations at a time like this."

The chain-link fence loomed up at them. John put both hands in the wire and leaped lightly upward. The wire *chinged* in the darkness. John clung for a moment, then moved rapidly toward the top, his feet finding purchase where Quill could see none at all. She grabbed the fence, and the wire bit into her palms. John dropped lightly to the other side. Quill pressed her face close to his. "I don't think I can climb this," she mouthed. "There's a dug-out spot a little farther down. I'm going to go under."

She followed the line of the fence to the hole where the German shepherd had made his escape, and wriggled under. Her long hair caught in the torn wires at the bottom, and she bit her lip to keep from yelling. She rolled free and got to her feet. John was already at the warehouse door.

"Can you pick the lock?" she said into his ear.

He shook his head. "It's bolted from the inside." He pointed up, then motioned her to wait. He unwound the rope at his waist and made a quick lasso, spun it rapidly a few times, and tossed it into the air. It caught on the roof joist. He pulled the rope taut, then rappelled quickly up the side of the building. The thud of his tennis shoes on the metal wall sounded like thunder. He disappeared through a ventilation duct. Quill pressed herself against the building and quivered. The moments before John opened the door seemed endless. She let out her breath, only half-aware that she'd been holding it, when she heard the quiet click of the bar being drawn from the inside door.

Moonlight leaked through the open ventilation shafts in the roof, picking out the cab of a semi truck and four Thermo King refrigeration units. John took her hand, and they made their way carefully across the floor.

"If anyone comes in," John said very quietly, "roll under the cab and stay there."

Quill nodded. "These things are locked, aren't they? How are you going to get in?"

"There's a maintenance door under the roof. Give me a leg up."

Quill crouched down and cupped her hands together. John put his hands on her shoulders, stepped into her cupped hands, and sprang up. Quill staggered back; he was unexpectedly heavy.

She waited, searching the darkness. It was quiet. Too quiet. Quill bit back hysterical giggles. Time stretched on. Suddenly, a dark shape appeared at the back of the unit. Adrenalin surged through Quill like a lightning strike.

"Safety door," said John. "You can open the units from the inside once you get in."

"God!" said Quill, "did you find anything?"

A low growl cut the air. Quill's breath stopped. John grabbed her hand. The growl rose, fell, and turned into a snarl.

"The dog's back," said Quill. "Oh hell!"

John thrust her behind him. Quill could smell the rank, matted odor of an animal neglected. The snarl spun on, a sinister, mesmerizing purl of sound. John flattened himself against the metal unit and pulled her carefully with him. The snarl died. Quill could hear the dog panting. It wriggled out of the dark, ears pinned against its head, lips pulled back, eyes slits of red in the moonlight. The dog sprang. John hurled himself in front of her. Quill, her lip bloody from the effort not to scream, swung the flashlight hard and connected with the dog's thick furry skull. The animal shrieked and dropped back. The door to the unit was slightly ajar. Quill swung it open, scrabbling frantically in the frigid air. She pulled a box from the unit. It fell to the ground. Packages of hot dogs spilled into the dirt. The dog shook its head and got to its feet.

"Good doggie," said Quill, "nice boy." Moving carefully, eyes on the dog, she bent and picked up the frozen hot dogs, rolling them to the dog like bowling balls. The dog sprang on the meat, both paws protectively over the package. It glared at them. The growl heightened to a snarl, the snarl to a bark which split the air like a hammer.

"Okay," gasped John. "It's not going to charge if it's barking. Back off, slowly. Don't run until we get outside."

He forced Quill behind him. She held on to his arm; he grunted in pain, and she let him go. Her palms were wet and she smelled blood. The dog's barking grew intermittent, interspersed with snarling gulps of the frozen meat.

They reached the warehouse door. Backed out slowly. Quill slammed it shut. Lights in the trailer snapped on.

They ran. John forced Quill under the fence and followed her. Freddie Allbright shouted into the dark. Quill fumbled for the keys to the car, threw herself into the driver's seat, and was out on Route 96 before John had the passenger door closed.

"Good Lord," said Quill, when they were back in her room. She peeled John's shirt back from his forearm. "He got one good chomp in, didn't he?"

"It was worth it," said John. "There's a carcass there with the reject stamp." He waved the camera. "And I got the pictures. Now, Quill, I have a favor to ask. I'll need until Tuesday at least to go through Tom's financial records. Myles is gone until then, right?"

"Yes."

"I'm going to turn myself in. But not for another forty-eight hours. I'd appreciate it if you gave me some time."

"Gave you some time? You mean, you think I'd turn you in? John, how could you?"

"How could you not?" he said wryly. "You can't harbor a fugitive. I wouldn't let you, anyway."

"Just tell me where you're going to be, so I can report on my progress to you. I'm going down to the Marriott tomorrow, and I'm going to pump Mrs. Hallenbeck for everything that she knew about Mavis' affairs. Peterson's got to be connected with her somehow. And . . . now, this is the worst sacrifice of all, John." She paused impressively. "I'm going to eat lunch at the Hemlock Hometown Diner—Fine Food and Fast. Are you grateful, or what?"

For the first time that evening, a real smile crossed John's face. "Pretty noble, boss."

" 'Pretty noble'? I'd say that's incredibly noble."

There was a hard, imperative knock at the door.

"I didn't lock it," Quill hissed, then loudly, "Just a moment, please."

The door swung open and Mrs. Hallenbeck walked into the room. "So!" she said. "You finally caught him!"

CHAPTER 11

Mrs. Hallenbeck marched into Quill's quarters frail, rude and triumphant. Quill, astonished, looked at her watch: six-thirty in the morning.

"You didn't answer my phone messages," said Mrs. Hallenbeck. "I thought perhaps you didn't get them. I woke up and Mavis wasn't there to get my coffee. I always have just one cup, cut with hot water before I take my walk. Would you get it for me, please?" She sat down in the straight-back chair near the easel, and frowned at John. "What are you doing in Sarah's room? Have you spent the night here?" She lifted her chin. "If you have, I shall think twice about offering Sarah the opportunity to be in my employ." She smoothed her linen trousers with a precise hand. "Now. Tell me why I shouldn't call the police immediately. Everyone has been looking for this man."

Quill, unable to think of an adequate response, heated a cup of weak coffee in the microwave and handed it to Mrs. Hallenbeck. She sipped it and gave it back to Quill with a demand for more hot water. "You are extremely dirty," she said to John. "I suppose you have been hiding out."

"Do you remember me, Mrs. Hallenbeck? I thought you might have when you checked in three days ago, but you didn't say anything. Did Mavis tell you about me?"

"I thought I'd seen you before. I mentioned it to Mavis. She said I was mistaken. I am rarely mistaken."

"I worked for your husband a long time ago, in the accounting department."

"My husband?" Mrs. Hallenbeck didn't seem to hear John. She mumbled slightly. Her eyes clouded. She held her coffee cup out to Quill with a wordless demand that it be taken away. Quill put it in the small sink in her kitchen, and wondered what to do. Finally Mrs. Hallenbeck said in a querulous voice, quite unlike her usual crisp tones, "You remember my dear Leslie? Of course, he would have been Mr. Hallenbeck to you. Well, I don't recall you specifically. There were so many employees. They all simply adored Leslie. As I did."

Quill and John exchanged a cautious look.

"I only met Mr. Hallenbeck once a year, at the company Christmas party," John said. "I saw you there too, of course, but we never spoke before you came here."

"I should have remembered you if I had. I am frequently complimented on the accuracy of my memory."

The spell, or whatever it was, seemed to have passed. Quill wondered at the harshness of memory; a husband's suicide would be an intolerable burden to bear, the guilt horrific. Had John's quiet reference to her dead husband touched off memories too painful to bear?

The morning sun poked an exploratory finger through the southeast window. Its light made Quill aware of just how old eighty-three was. Blood, muscle, and bone all shrink, she thought, as though a tide has ebbed. Does the spirit shrink, too, and the healthy young become the senile old? Or does it wear away, as the physical does, to leave bedrock character behind? She thought of her own mother, and her mother's loving, changeless heart trapped in a body diminished, but not conquered, by age. She couldn't begin to make sense of it, and wouldn't bother.

"You have not yet given me a reason as to why the police haven't been called. What are you going to do about him?" Mrs. Hallenbeck jerked her chin at John. Her eyes were suddenly clear and shrewd. "He's wanted for murder, I understand."

"It's a mistake," said Quill. "And John's going to clear that up. He'll be back managing the Inn again. In the meantime I'd appreciate it if you wouldn't say anything about seeing him here. We're keeping it a bit quiet until John gets a chance to talk to the sheriff himself."

"So you're going to solve the murders. Huh! It's obvious to me that he did it. Killed that Mr. Gilmeister and Mavis, too." Her eyes widened in alarm. "You're not going to kill me, are you?"

"But he didn't, Mrs. Hallenbeck. He's innocent. And why in the world would anyone want to kill you?" The doubt was back; perhaps she was senile.

"I know things, of course. I know all about Mavis, and what she was like." Her hands shook. Her lips tightened in disgust. "Dreadful girl. I should have fired her years ago. I am far too tender-hearted. It's very easy to take advantage of me." She looked at Quill out of the corner of her eye. "As an example, I believe it was Mavis who staged that little— ah—incident with the balcony for the insurance money. I'm afraid she's done it before. If that is so, I have a great deal to make up for. You will, of course, present the bill for repairs to me. Sometimes I believe that all the trouble that has come since then is a result of Mavis' foolishness. If I had kept better control of her, if I had refused to allow her to go out with those appalling people, the rest of this would never have happened." She pursed her lips, and said anxiously, "You don't think people will blame me, do you? I confess to feeling a small portion of responsibility for what happened to her, and to Mr. Gilmeister. I believe the trap on the ducking stool was set for her. I should have managed her better. But I've never had a head for people like Leslie had."

Quill, reeling from the news that Mavis had made a career of conning hotels, couldn't respond for a moment.

"I don't think that's true, Mrs. Hallenbeck," said John. "I didn't know you well, and you know what employee gossip is like, but everyone agreed that you were probably better at managing the business than your husband. And successful business is all about how well you manage people. Mr. Hallenbeck always used to say that at the Christmas parties. My boss, Carl Atkinson? You may remember him. He had the greatest respect for your abilities. Someone with your kind of intelligence doesn't suddenly lose it. You can't blame yourself for Mavis' behavior."

Mrs. Hallenbeck smiled primly.

Moving quietly, as though not to startle a small animal, John got up from the couch. "Can I get you another cup of coffee?"

"Just a little, perhaps. Quite weak. I am very sensitive to caffeine."

Quill heard John making a fresh pot. She waited. She wasn't entirely sure what he was up to, with these flagrant compliments, but at least Mrs. Hallenbeck hadn't reached for the phone to call the cops yet.

"I think," said John, coming back into the room, "that Mrs. Hallenbeck could be very helpful in the investigation to clear my name."

"Oh," said Quill, enlightened. "Yes. Absolutely."

"I?" said Mrs. Hallenbeck with a gratified inflection.

"The reasons for Mavis' murder must rest in her past. I left the company a long while ago, Mrs. Hallenbeck, and I have very little idea of what went on in the past five years or so. You were there. You knew Mavis. You've even had her living with you for . . . how long?"

"Just a year. My son insisted that I have a companion to live with me."

"So, you know her better than any of us. Now, Quill and I have a suspicion that Mavis was a blackmailer."

"Wouldn't surprise me in the least," said Mrs. Hallenbeck. "I had a suspicion of that right along."

"You did?" said Quill, fascinated. "And you didn't get rid of her, or anything?"

"Well, she wasn't blackmailing me. And Mavis could be a great deal of fun, you know. Huh. Blackmail. *Who*, do you suppose?"

"That's what we were hoping you could tell us," said Quill. "Had you heard her mention Marge before, for example? In any way that would lead you to believe that she had something on her?"

"Marge Schmidt? No. I mean, of course, they worked together way back when. Margie was good, I'll give her that. Never had a proper respect for me or for Mr. Hallenbeck, but then, with that background, what can you expect? Blue-collar all the way, high-school education, no proper home life at all. But she was quite efficient at running the East Coast operations. I told Mr. Hallenbeck he should offer Marge more money when she quit. The profit margin in that was never the same after she left. I would guess," said Mrs. Hallenbeck with a twinkle, "that Mavis met her match in Marge Schmidt."

"You must have a good reason to suspect Mavis of blackmail," said John. "Think back. Any phone conversations, or letters, or people she mentioned? Especially if you've seen them here."

"Gil Gilmeister never worked for Doggone Good Dogs, for example?" said Quill. "Or Tom Peterson?"

"Oh, no. The first time Mavis met Tom was at the play rehearsal when Marge introduced him to both of us."

"And then you went to dinner with Gil at the diner."

"Yes. Marge had a loan outstanding against Mr. Gilmeister's half of the auto business. She suggested that I buy him out. Mavis knew that my investments hadn't been doing too well lately. The market these past few years has been simply appalling. I used to get quite a decent return on my portfolio, and it's been halved. *Halved.* I'm seriously considering suing my broker."

"How did you leave it with Gil?" asked John.

"I wasn't averse to a good return. I told Mavis to speak to his partner, Tom Peterson, to get an idea of what the business could do under decent management."

"Did she speak to him?"

"Yes. She was never one to let grass grow under her feet, I'll tell you that. Mr. Gilmeister, Marge, and Mr. Baumer brought me back to the Inn, while Mavis went across the green—to whatever it is that you call it. . . ."

"The Pavilion," supplied Quill.

"Yes, where the—incident occurred—to speak to Tom. Gil was most anxious for a quick decision. He didn't seem a bad sort, apart from his drinking problem. Whereas Keith . . . Tcha! A dreadful employee and a dreadful man."

"Keith," said Quill stupidly. "You mean Keith Baumer?"

"Yes, do you know him? Of course, he's staying here, isn't he? He was there when Mavis . . ." She shuddered. "I know there is a great deal of violence in the world today. I know at my age I should be more immune to it. But I cannot get the incident out of my mind. I dreamed about it, last night."

"Mrs. Hallenbeck!" Quill uncurled her clenched fists and forced herself to speak in a normal tone of voice. "Did you know Keith Baumer before you met him here at the Inn?"

"Of course. He was Meat Manager for the Central portion of the United States."

"For Doggone Good Dogs?"

"Yes." Mrs. Hallenbeck's tone was impatient. "As I was saying, I wonder if I should see that nice Dr. Bishop about my disrupted sleep. I've never needed much sleep, even as a young woman, but—"

"Mrs. Hallenbeck," said John. "You may have solved the case!"

"I?" A look of utter confusion crossed her face. "What do you mean? What did I say?"

"When did Keith Baumer work at Doggone Good Dogs?" John was marvelous, thought Quill, quiet, unexcited, yet properly deferential.

"Is it important?" said Mrs. Hallenbeck, her cheeks flushed. "You mean he and Mavis may have known each other before? That they had arranged to meet here? Of course! *Mavis* suggested we come to this place. There could be some reason for him to . . . to have made the accident happen? Well!" She was obviously pleased with herself. "I have an excellent memory. Let me think a moment. He was Meat Manager for about four years, approximately ten years ago, before your time, Mr. Raintree."

"And Mavis was Director of Human Resources at that time?"

"Not then. She was part of the department. She moved on to become Mr. Hallenbeck's assistant. Human Resources was headed at that time by a fiery young woman, most impractical. A Democrat, I believe. At any rate, Keith was fired under a cloud, as they say."

"Not embezzlement?" said John.

"No. Something to do with the way things are run nowadays. Stupid laws, when it's usually all the woman's fault. The way these young girls dress!"

"Sexual harassment," said Quill, "it figures."

"That was it. How clever of you, Sarah."

"How clever of *you*!" Impulsively, Quill walked over and gave her a hug. "This could be it, John!" She sank to her knees beside Mrs. Hallenbeck's chair. "Listen. We're going to need some time to track down Baumer's movements. My guess is that we can discover enough evidence to put him for a long, long time."

"You mean you think he killed Mavis?" She looked old and bewildered. Her lips moved soundlessly for a moment and then she looked at John. "I thought *he* killed Mavis!"

"No, Mrs. Hallenbeck, that's one of the things you are going to help us to accomplish. Remember? We're all working together to clear John's name."

"We're investigating," said Mrs. Hallenbeck with satisfaction. "You and I."

"And John. It's almost seven-thirty now, Mrs. Hallenbeck. Why don't you go down to the dining room? Meg and I usually eat about now, and you can join us. Just ask Peter to seat you at our table. Tell him I told you to sit there. I'm going to bathe and change, and then I'll join you." She helped the old woman out of her chair and escorted her to the door. "Remember. John isn't going to go to the police until the sheriff gets back. We have twenty-four hours to solve these murders. So part of your job as a member of the investigation team is not to let anyone know that John's come back."

Mrs. Hallenbeck nodded wisely. "I'll be downstairs, waiting for you, and"—she leaned forward and whispered in Quill's ear—"I shall be on the alert for clues."

Giddy from both lack of sleep and relief, Quill collapsed on her sofa with a sigh when the door closed on Amelia Hallenbeck.

John, more reserved, said, "It's not over yet. I'm going to spend the rest of the day with my hacker friend. I'll pull Baumer's address from the register and see what we can find in his financial records. But, I don't know, Quill. This all seems pretty tenuous."

"I'll talk to Marge, Tom Peterson, and Baumer himself, after I get back from the Marriott," said Quill confidently. "John, we'll solve this by the time Myles gets back. Let me know where I can call you. Is your friend in Ithaca or something?"

"No. Here in town. I'll give you the phone number." He wrote it down and handed it to her.

"You mean all this time you've been in Hemlock Falls?"

"Yes. And yes, Quill, I was within a block of the Pavilion when someone pulled that hood over Mavis' head. To someone like Myles, I'm still the ideal suspect. I had means, motive, and opportunity, for both murders."

He left as quietly as he had come. The coffee John made was untouched. She gulped two quick cups. Then she stripped out of her robe and nightgown and gritting her teeth, took a shower as cold as she could stand it. She dressed and went downstairs to breakfast. Meg would be fascinated with recent developments.

Meg, smoking one of her infrequent cigarettes, was propped back in her chair at their table, staring at the wall over Mrs. Hallenbeck's head. Mrs. Hallenbeck herself was tucking into a soufflé. Quill dropped into the chair next to her; she noticed through her haze of fatigue that Meg's hair was flat.

"Morning, Meg."

Her sister's gaze dropped from the wall to Quill's face with the suddenness of a bird after a worm. "Have you entirely lost your mind?" Meg demanded.

Quill put down her orange juice. Mrs. Hallenbeck couldn't have told Meg about John already. "I don't think so. Why?"

"Why? WHY?! We've got *forty people* showing up for breakfast in twenty-two minutes. Expecting food, I'll bet. Does anyone need to tell the chef about forty people arriving for brunch on a Monday when we average twenty servings in the dining room total, if we're lucky? Well!?"

"Forty?" said Quill bewildered.

"If that sanctimonious prat Tom Peterson hadn't called to confirm he had reservations, they would have all shown up to eat what? What, Quill?! Do I send out to the Burger King down the road for what they laughingly refer to as breakfast croissants?"

"Dookie's prayer meeting! Meg, I'm so sorry, it completely went out of my . . . ."

"Do you know what I've got in stock? Do you? Doughnuts! Four dozen Little Debbie doughnuts that the bread guy left here by mistake. Those doughnuts are so filled with artificial crap that people's arteries seize up just looking at them!"

"Meg, I'm *really* sorry. Honestly, there's been so much going on, it just . . ."

"Fell out of what passes for your mind." Meg stubbed out her cigarette, raked her hair back with both hands, and shoved herself away from the table. "This is just *it* for my reputation. Just *it*. You want me, I'll be in the storeroom. Hanging from the rafters."

The swinging door to the kitchen banged shut. Silence descended on the dining room.

"That is a very rude young woman," said Mrs. Hallenbeck.

"It's just Meg," said Quill. "You watch. She's probably whipped up a bunch of omelettes, or quiche, or Eggs à la Reine, and the deacons will think they've died and gone to heaven."

"You don't seem perturbed by the temper tantrum."

"Meg's cooking is her life. She takes it seriously. It's part of what makes her great. Running this kitchen is the best thing that ever happened to her."

"She should be married," said Mrs. Hallenbeck. "It would settle her down. You wouldn't have to spend so much time taking her abuse."

"She was married. To the sweetest man I've ever met. He was a stockbroker, and I swear, when he died I thought Meg was going to die. But we invested in the Inn together, and you wouldn't believe the change in her. It took a year or more for Meg to get over his death. The cooking was what did it."

"How did the young man die?"

"Automobile accident. He was thirty."

"She should manage on her own," said Mrs. Hallenbeck. "If you'll pardon an old woman's interference, my dear, she needs to lead her own life. You've cocooned her here."

"Do you think so?" Quill's eyelids drooped and she jerked herself awake. "Sorry, I used to be able to stay up all night in college. I seem to have lost the knack."

Mrs. Hallenbeck patted her hand. "Why don't you go up and take a nap? I will sit here and be alert for any unusual circumstances. I have a notepad, right here"—she tapped her black purse—"and I will write down anything untoward."

"You know, I think I will. I'm sorry we missed our breakfast"—Quill yawned—"but you're right. I'm not going to be much good at investigation if I'm falling asleep on my feet. I'll just check and make sure that everything's set up in the Banquet Room for the prayer meeting, and then take maybe an hour's nap."

"I will meet you for tea," said Mrs. Hallenbeck, "at five o'clock." Quill got up, and she added, "You know, my dear, you might think seriously about retiring from the Inn. It's a great responsibility, far too much to carry alone. Perhaps we could talk, at teatime, about other things you could do. Painting for instance. When do you ever have time to paint?"

"Not much recently, that's true. But I love the life, Mrs. Hallenbeck. It has a lot of rewards that might not be obvious to the outside eye. The Inn is a very peaceful place, you know. The past few days are definitely an exception. Our guests are almost always nice, like you, and come here to relax. Like this prayer meeting this morning," said Quill earnestly, aware somewhere in her sleep-deprived brain that she was rattling on, "—nice people, church people, peacefully praying in the Banquet . . ."

"Ah, Quill?" Peter Williams tugged at her elbow. Quill blinked at him. "We've got major trouble with the prayer meeting."

CHAPTER 12

"They came in a van about half an hour ago," said Peter as they walked through the lobby to the Banquet Room.

"They?" said Quill. The coffee she'd drunk to stay awake must have been decaf; either she was asleep on her feet or Peter didn't make sense. "They who?"

"Right out there." He pointed to the front door.

Quill opened the door and went outside. A white Chevy Lumina van was parked on the drive. The side panels were lettered in a screaming orange. "We Save Sinners!" Quill read aloud. "Call 1-800-222-PRAY!" She walked slowly around the van. "THE ROLLING MOSES—The Rev. William Maximilian" was printed on the hood in black Gothic letters intertwined with lightning strikes. Quill shut her eyes and opened them again. The design was still there. And the phone number. They were both very familiar.

Those pamphlets Doreen was carrying around in her apron pocket.

The license plates on the van read "Florida, the Sunshine State." The inspection sticker was a year out of date.

"Quill?" Peter called to her from the lobby. He sounded worried. "They're starting the prayer breakfast now."

Quill drifted slowly back in. "I don't think I want to know what's going on," she said dreamily. "I'm on overload. As a matter of fact, I'm going upstairs to take a quick nap."

She thought of her nice comfortable queen-sized bed with the muslin comforter and the cool white sheets.

Peter hesitated. "I'm the last one to judge by appearances . . ."

"Yes," said Quill.

"But these guys showed up at the prayer meeting this morning. They look pretty . . . unsavory, I guess you'd say. They said Doreen had called that 1-800 number and they were here to . . . to . . ."

"To what?"

"Perform an exorcism," said Peter.

"A *what*?"

"To rid the Inn of succubi and other stuff. I thought we'd better sit in."

Quill walked the short length of the hall to the Banquet Room. Most of the deacons were already there; Quill saw Harland Peterson, Elmer Henry, and Tom Peterson and smiled "Hello."

Dookie Shuttleworth stood by the open door, looking confused. He started forward when he saw Quill, took her hand, and patted it warmly. "We haven't seen you in quite a while, Quill. Please come in and join us." He drew her into the Banquet Room.

Despite the short notice, Meg and the kitchen crew had done themselves proud. The staff had set up a long buffet table; Kathleen Kiddermeister was making crêpes to order at one end. Chafing dishes filled with The Sausage, bacon, caramelized apple, puffed potatoes, and a large Heavenly Hoggs Ham were displayed along the rest of the table length. Bowls of fresh strawberries and blueberries sat in the center of round cloth-covered dining tables set with Spode china. The room was filled with most of the regulars of the Hemlock Falls Word Of God Reform Church—and a few who weren't. Doreen sat at a table with Esther West. The ubiquitous Keith Baumer had apparently invited himself and was swallowing food at an enormous rate. Quill decided testily to put the cost for Baumer's breakfast on his bill instead of the one that went to the church.

She paused to reconsider. She wouldn't throw Baumer out. She'd perform a charitable act. Let Baumer horn in if he wanted to. She was becoming more and more convinced that he was the best suspect of all. She was not averse to supporting the admonition to let the condemned eat a hearty meal; the food in prison would be a punishment all the greater in contrast.

The happy, contented buzz of satisfied breakfast-eaters bathed Quill in a warm glow. "Isn't Meg terrific?" she said aloud.

"She is wonderful!" said Dookie. "After this delicious breakfast, Quill—such a generous contribution to the church, my dear—I had no idea when I mentioned our money troubles that you would give us so much!"

Quill had forgotten her promise to fund the breakfast. She waved away the uneasy feeling that she'd been giving away a lot of free food since John had been gone. "Reverend Shuttleworth, there's a van outside . . ." Quill stopped, not sure how to continue.

"Yes. The Rolling Moses." The confused expression returned to Dookie's face and seemed to settle there. "They said Doreen Muxworthy called them early yesterday to tell them a succubus was inhabiting the Inn and their help was needed to get rid of it."

"Doreen?" said Quill, keeping her voice low with an effort.

Dookie brightened. "The Reverend William Maximilian said these—er—performances have a very positive effect on the urge of the congregation to donate to worthy causes. We agreed to split the collection plate today—and since we're in desperate need of funds, Quill, I thought perhaps . . . Ah! Here is the Reverend Mr. Maximilian now. Mr. Maximilian, I would like to introduce Miss Sarah Quilliam, who has so generously donated today's breakfast."

"Good eats. God bless you, sister."

The Reverend Mr. Maximilian breathed heavily through his open mouth. He was fat, hairy, and his five o'clock shadow rivaled the late Richard Nixon's. Quill hadn't seen sideburns like that since Elvis Presley gave his farewell performance.

The Reverend Mr. Maximilian engulfed her hand with his own sweaty palm and held on to it. "Rev'rund Shuttleworth is mighty lucky in his flock, little lady. Red hair like that means a passionate nature. A passionate nature. I hope you are going to join us for the service?"

Quill's response was a noncommittal "Um."

"And these are my helpers in the Lord. Byron? Joe-Frank? This little lady owns the Inn."

Guys a lot like Byron and Joe-Frank parked their Harley Davidsons outside the Croh Bar on Saturday nights. Joe-Frank had tattoos on his heavily muscled upper arms that said PRAISE GOD on the left and PUNISH SINNERS on the right. Byron's black leather jacket covered any tattoos he may have had, and just barely concealed a blackjack on his hip. His lack of visible skin ornamentation was made up for by the ring in his nose.

Quill nodded politely. She sat down next to Mark Anthony Jefferson, prey to misgivings.

"Fellows in Christ!" Dookie tapped a water glass with a spoon for attention. "We are privileged to bring a unique guest to our meeting today. I would like to introduce to you my brother in Christ, the Right Reverend Mr. William Maximilian. Willy Max has come to us all the way from Newark, New Jersey, where he was administering to another church such as ours—a church in trouble."

Dookie's eyes brightened as he warmed to his favorite topic. "Declining attendance, scanty donations, all these things are troubling the church here at Hemlock Falls, my friends. We have brought Reverend Mr. Willy Max here to support our spiritual renewal—to help us cast out the demons of avarice and miserliness, and invite in the angels of charity and openhandedness."

Elmer Henry cleared his throat in a marked manner. Dookie concluded rapidly, "Ladies and gentlemen, Willy Max and the Church of Rolling Moses!" Dookie led the applause and sat down.

Willy Max rose to his feet, tucked his thumbs into the substantial flesh hanging over his cowboy belt, and surveyed the room in silence. His brow beetled. His lower lip thrust out. He scanned the crowd, one by one, until the silence was utter. Absolute. The Banquet Room became as silent as a Carmelite nunnery at lunch. "I don't know about angels of charity," he said slowly, "I know about scarlet wimmin, and the Devil who sends them to torment our poor male flesh. Brothers and sisters," intoned the minister, "let us bow our heads and pray."

Obediently, the congregation bowed its head as one.

"Lord? It's me here, Willy Max. Your servant. Once again, Lord, I offer praises for the light of knowledge and redemption. Like Paul on the road to Damascus, Lord, I was struck down in stone by a vision of Hell. ('Cept it was in that CPR class in Sarasota, Lord, and not on a road a'tall.) Lord, we are poor cree-turs and wicked. We have fallen into temptation and into snares. . . ."

"Snares . . ." said Byron and Joe-Frank together.

"The snares of lust." His voice rose, beefy hands clasped. "The traps of temptation, the *pits* of *promiscuity*!" he thundered. "There are those among us who have been plagued by visions of the Scarlet Woman of Babylon at night . . . is it not so, brothers and sisters?!"

"Amen," said a few of Dookie's flock tentatively.

"There are those among us who have been *inflamed* by the thought of wimmin. Scarlet-lipped, rouged and scented wimmin."

"Amen." The chorus was swelled by several more parishioners as the plates were cleared.

Willy Max raised his hands to the ceiling. His voice slid upward like the tenor sax at the start of *Rhapsody in Blue*. "YOU HAVE BEEN DRAWN TO SALACIOUS AND HURTFUL LUSTS!"

"LUSTS!" shouted those citizens of Hemlock Falls who had finished their breakfast.

"WHO AMONG YOU IS DRAWN TO DAMNATION?"

A surprising number of voices said they were.

"ARE WE NOT ALL SINNERS IN THE EYES OF THE LORD?"

General agreement was expressed by the majority.

Willy Max began to move about the room, face red, arms waving. "BRING ME A SINNER, LORD, THAT I MAY SHAKE THE DEMONS FROM HIS SOUL! GUIDE ME, LORD! SHOW ME THE BLACK-HEARTED BUCKET OF SLIME."

"Right here!" said Doreen, pointing at Keith Baumer.

Baumer put his fork down, gazed around with a bemused expression, and said feebly, "Look here . . ."

Max raised his eyes beseechingly to the ceiling. "Who, Lord, who?"

"*Him, Lord, him!*" Doreen screamed.

"Uh, just a minute here," said Baumer. "I'm an agnostic."

"THIS IS THE ONE, REVRUND. THIS-HERE'S THE SINNER." Doreen grabbed Baumer by the tie. His eyes bulged. Doreen pulled. Baumer rose from his seat. Some hours afterward, opinion was divided as to whether this was strictly voluntary, since strangulation wasn't held to offer a genuine alternative to repentance.

"Have you lusted in your heart?" Willy Max demanded.

"Urgh," said Baumer.

"HAVE YOU LUSTED IN YOUR LOINS!" then, in an aside to Doreen, "Leave him go, sister."

Doreen released Baumer's tie. Byron and Joe-Frank grasped him by both arms, perhaps in a humanitarian attempt to prevent him from falling.

"Fall to your knees and PRAY!" hollered Willy Max. Byron and Joe-Frank assisted Baumer to his knees with good-humored alacrity.

"ooOOOOHHHLORD!" Willy Max shouted. "Shake these dee-mons from his breast!"

Joe-Frank tapped Baumer's knees with the blackjack. Baumer fell flat, face-up.

"GET THEE BEHIND ME, SATAN!" Willy Max implored the ceiling tiles. "BOYS! PUSH THE DEVIL OUT!"

Byron held Baumer's head. Joe-Frank thumped Baumer's chest and stomach with both fists, an ecclesiastical tribute, perhaps, to the CPR class where Willy Max had first received divine inspiration.

"Help-me, help-me, help-me," Baumer wheezed, in time with the thumps.

Tom Peterson scowled. Mayor Henry jiggled one large knee up and down. Harland Peterson's lower lip stuck out like a granite ledge. Dookie Shuttleworth's expression was an interesting mixture of agony and apprehension.

"Shake the demons outa him!" yelled Byron.

"Yay, bo!" Joe-Frank responded enthusiastically.

"Mr. Maximilian?" Dookie Shuttleworth got to his feet. "Mr. Maximilian!"

The bikers stopped pummeling Keith Baumer. Willy Max gazed benignly at Dookie. "Yes, Revrund?"

"The ah—devils—seem to have flown. I think perhaps if you could sit down . . ."

"There's a whole lot more shakin' to go on," said Willie Max sternly. "And a lotta prayers to holler."

Dookie picked his way apologetically to the front of the room. He gave Keith Baumer a hand and drew him up, then patted him on the shoulder. "Sit down, son."

Baumer sat down, mouth moving soundlessly.

"And you, Mr. Maximilian, we'd like to thank you for your support, but I think . . ."

"Hell!" Baumer gasped, to mildly disapproving looks from his near neighbors.

" . . . it's time for you and your followers to go now."

Quill held her breath. There was a moment's tense silence. Elmer Henry, Harland Peterson, and Davey joined Dookie, shoulder to shoulder. Byron and Joe-Frank cracked their knuckles ominously. Harland Peterson reached out one large hand and removed the blackjack from Byron's grasp like a mother taking a bottle from a beloved baby.

Quill wondered if she ought to pull the fire alarm.

"Thank you, brothers and sisters," said William Maximilian finally. "We'll leave you now, to continue on our mission. Revrund Shuttleworth, with your permission, sir, we'll pass the plate before we go."

"I think not," said Dookie sternly.

There was a murmur from the assembly. Quill was impressed. She had never seen Dookie so decisive.

"You're all crazy," said Baumer, who had recovered his breath. Then, perhaps unjust in this sweeping oversimplification, "You're a bunch of fuckin' maniacs!" He stood up, swaying a little, and marched to the door; he turned and glared at William Maximilian. "You'll be hearing from my lawyers, you son of a bitch."

Quill stepped aside to let him pass. One eye rolled wildly at her. He shook his head, as if to get rid of flies. He wobbled down the hall, headed straight, Quill surmised, for the checkout desk and the Marriott on Route 15.

"Brothers and sisters," said William Maximilian, "we'll bid you all farewell."

Quill followed them down the hall, through the lobby, and

out the front door. Joe-Frank, Byron, and Willy Max got into Rolling Moses. Joe-Frank turned on the ignition and gunned the motor. Rolling Moses took off like a cat with a stomped-on tail. She turned to Peter Williams, who had accompanied her, propelled, had she known it, more by concern for the look in her eye than a desire to make sure of Rolling Moses' departure.

"Bring me," she said, "Doreen."

"Yes, ma'am."

Quill took a few deep breaths. "And Peter? Mr. Baumer will undoubtedly be checking out. Will you make sure you know where he's headed? He's a material witness to the murder at the Pavilion, and Myles will want to know where he is."

"Yes, ma'am."

Quill went to her office and sat down behind her desk. Doreen tapped at the door, was given leave to enter, and came in.

"Now, I know what you're thinkin'," said Doreen engagingly.

"You can't possibly know what I'm thinking," said Quill coldly. "What I'm thinking is illegal in this state."

"First of all, the Reverend din't have those two with him in Boca Raton," said Doreen, "Honest. He had two helpers from the Sunset Trailer Park. Nice ladies." She paused reflectively. "Not as good at thumping as that there Joe-Frank." She heaved a deep sigh. "*Second* off, *I* din't call them."

"If you didn't, who did?" said Quill evenly.

"I dunno."

There was a short silence.

"So, am I fired?"

Quill remained expressionless.

"If I ain't fired, you gonna fine me?"

Quill picked up the stapler and depressed the arm. Three staples littered her desktop before it jammed. She set it back into place.

"You want me to think twice about this here Rolling Moses religion," guessed Doreen.

"I don't want you to think twice. I want you to forget it. I want it totally, absolutely, entirely erased from your memory. I want no more harassing of the guests. No more Bible verses in soap on bathroom mirrors. No more bugs in the beds. I don't give a damn about the seven plagues of Egypt. This is Hemlock Falls, and there are no grasshoppers, no locusts, no SLUGS allowed. Got that?"

"Got that," said Doreen. "I was kinda going off this, anyways. Thinking maybe of taking up Amway."

"Why do you have to take up *anything*!" shouted Quill. "Especially now, when I need you and Meg to be relatively sane and even-tempered."

"Somethin' happen?" said Doreen alertly.

"Yes." Quill took several deliberate breaths. She knew Doreen to be absolutely trustworthy in every area but her brief and violent enthusiasms. Well—pretty trustworthy. On the other hand, she didn't have a lot of choice. Someone had to search for clues, and she didn't have the time. "John's back."

"Ayuh," said Doreen.

"I haven't had a chance to tell Meg. But Mrs. Hallenbeck knows."

"That one!"

"It was an accident." Quill briefly recapped her conversation with John, leaving out the personal details, but including the sudden invasion of Mrs. Hallenbeck's and her intention to investigate.

"Sheriff is after 'em," said Doreen. "We don't have much time for this here investigating."

"No, that's one of the reasons why I was furious about the evangelist. All those management courses I take, Doreen, I'm supposed to put you on probation for stuff like this. And here I am trusting you with something that's vitally important. It's John's life we're talking about here. I mean, they don't execute people anymore in this state—but another prison sentence? We have to do something."

"Even if he *had* killed that Mavis . . ." Doreen began darkly.

"Well, he didn't," said Quill, "and what we have to do is look for that bolt. The one from Harland Peterson's tractor. There's no way it could have fallen into the river, Doreen—and I know Myles and his men didn't pick it up at the scene. So the killer's got it. Motives for Baumer are piling up. I want you to pay particular attention to his room when you look."

"You got it. I'll search the whole dang Inn."

"If you find it, be sure not to pick it up with your bare hands," warned Quill. "There may be fingerprints. Use your work gloves and put it into a Baggie or something. And, Doreen?"

"Yes'm."

"There's really no need to mention this to the sheriff, or Deputy Davey, or any of the patrol guys."

"You don't want them to find out? I thought we were helpin' them."

"Well, we *are*; it's just that some people might think it was interfering with an official investigation or something." Aware that her management training courses were stern in the admonition to at all times maintain an executive demeanor and that she was, perhaps, being a bit tentative where direct and aggressive behaviors were what led to Maintaining Control of Employees, Quill folded her hands on her desk and said briskly, "Then you'll report back to me the instant you discover something *essential*. It isn't worth it to waste time coming to me with *nonessential* information, like Keith Baumer's swiped towels, or something. Come to me when you discover facts that will help us get this investigation over."

"Like the instant I do?" asked Doreen, her eyes on the window behind Quill's desk.

Quill, nettled by the inattention to her best executive style, snapped, "Immediately."

"Like, 'essential' is when the sheriff gets back?"

"Myles?" Quill shook her head. "Now, that's what I mean by essential versus nonessential, Doreen. Myles is a person who's nonessential to our investigation. The discovery of the bolt that clears John, that's essential to the investigation."

"Got it," said Doreen.

Quill began to recover her increasingly elusive sense of being in charge. She'd tackle Tom Peterson first; the prayer breakfast would be breaking up in a few minutes, and she could ask him to stay behind for an extra cup of coffee. Then the Hemlock Diner and Marge and Betty Hall. Then on to the Marriott, where Baumer had presumably settled after his expressed displeasure with the comforts offered by the Inn, and finally, Baumer himself.

She, John, and Doreen would have the case wrapped up and solved in no time.

On the way back to the prayer breakfast, Quill ventured a whistle. It stopped in mid-trill at the sight of a familiar broad back in trooper gray at the front desk. So *that's* who Doreen had seen out the window.

"Myles?"

He turned, frowning.

"Sarah."

"Sarah" was not good. The last time Myles had called her Sarah was early on in their relationship when he'd been contacted by the SoHo precinct station about a misunderstanding over a large number of parking tickets she'd forgotten to pay when she left Manhattan to move to Hemlock Falls. She had lent her car for a few weeks to a fellow artist who was down on his uppers, and between explaining that no, they weren't involved any longer and yes, it was pretty typical of Simon to pull stuff like that, it took a few days before she went back to being Quill.

"Your note said you wouldn't be back until tomorrow."

"I got lucky. Forensics owed me a favor or two, and the autopsy on Mavis was done early this morning. I was on my way back to the station when Davey radioed the complaint to me. What's going on, Quill?"

"Complaint?" Quill craned her neck around Myles's height and pulled a face at Dina, who rolled her eyes expressively.

Myles flipped his notepad open—just for effect, since she'd never known him to forget a thing. "Christian terrorism?"

"That Baumer! Dina! I thought he checked out."

"Nope. Sorry, Quill. He made a lot of phone calls, though."

Quill groaned.

"What's been going on?"

Quill explained, downplaying the chest-pounding to a few brotherly taps.

"I'm going to see him. I've got a couple of questions for him myself. I'll be a half-hour or so. Will you be here? I want to talk to you."

"I want to talk to you, too," Quill said glibly, "but I have a few things to do today in the village. Can we meet for an early dinner?"

"Let me rephrase my request," said Myles cordially. "I will see you here in half an hour. Consider it a date, Sarah. The official kind."

"Oh." Quill pulled her lower lip. "Does this mean you won't tell me the results of the autopsy on Mavis?"

"Sure, I'll tell you the results of the autopsy on Mavis. The media already has the results of the autopsy on Mavis because some damn fool at the morgue leaked the results. So you can hear it from me, or you can wait for the six o'clock news. Take your pick."

"I'd rather hear even the weather report from you than some boring old reporter," said Quill earnestly, "or even the price of hogs, or arrivals and departures at La Guardia. The sound of your voice alone sends . . ."

"You do want to drive me to an early grave," said Myles. Quill wondered if the noise he was making really came from grinding his teeth, as she thought it might. "Mavis had ingested a large amount of alcohol an hour or two before her death. But the amount of alcohol wasn't sufficient to cause a blackout; she also took ten milligrams of Valium about eight o'clock that morning. The Valium and the alcohol weren't sufficient to cause unconsciousness, either."

Quill wondered for a wild moment if the Scotch Bonnet pepper had made her pass out.

"She had either taken—or someone had given her—five grains of Seconal, probably in a drink twenty minutes or so before she went on as Clarissa Martin. There was so much junk in her system, it's hard for me to believe that she didn't drown in the ducking pool.

"Seconal," said Myles, "means we can prove premeditation." He looked at her grimly. "You stay here. I'll be back after I talk to Baumer."

Baumer had been drinking with Mavis just before she went on. Quill caught her breath. "Why don't I come up with you?" said Quill. "We can give him the old one-two."

"No."

"Won't you need a witness?" asked Quill. "You know, in case Baumer tells you one thing in private and then lies to you later?"

"No."

"But, Myles, Baumer was with Mavis the whole morning before the play. He ate breakfast with her. He showed up at the play with her."

"And Baumer came down to the station at noon to put up bail for his wife," said Myles. "He was at the station until well after two-thirty. He left to walk down to the Pavilion—a twenty-minute walk from the station, Quill—and I saw him leave."

"But he could have gotten a lift and gotten there early."

"Mavis hadn't had any beer; four or five mint juleps, judging from the stomach contents, and only beer is served at History Days. You know the ordinance. She must have gotten them from a private source, or a bar. Baumer wasn't carrying a Thermos when he left the station."

So Nate would know who she'd been drinking with.

"So Nate will know who she'd been drinking with, since the Croh Bar sure as hell doesn't make mint juleps. Quill, you are *not* to question Nate. Do you understand me? I love you. I will also put you in jail for obstruction of a criminal investigation."

" 'Oh God of love, and God of reason sa-a-a-y,' " sang Quill, " 'which of you twain shall my poor heart obey?' "

Myles grinned. A reluctant, very small grin, but a grin nonetheless. "Stick to the contralto roles. Your voice cracks on the B flat. Gilbert, not to say Sullivan, would spin in his grave."

Quill bobbed a mock curtsy. She watched Myles jog upstairs to beard Baumer in his den, then went into her office to place a call to Nate.

"Nope, sorry, boss," he said. "Bar was busy at one, but I remember the damn mint juleps. I didn't make any on Sunday."

"Was Kathleen waiting tables? She sometimes makes up orders when we're busy."

"Nope. Two of the kids from Cornell were on the early shift. And I don't let them behind my bar."

Quill hung up the phone and pulled out a pad of paper.

She wrote: "Bolt. Must find."

Then she wrote: "Seconal: Who has?"

Followed by: "Follow the money!"

Then: "More matchbooks?"

And last: "Mint juleps: Who can make?"
Then she drew a chart.

DUCK POND

	OPPORTUNITY	MOTIVE
Marge	Yes, if she and Mavis were together	Set up beforehand to get Mavis?
Tom Peterson	Yes	Business/tainted meat?
Baumer	Yes	Mavis blackmailing him?

She scrawled John's name in pencil, so she could erase it, and listed Yes, for opportunity and motive.

She scribbled and drew little arrows under "Motive." She was certain that the duck pond murder had been aimed at Mavis, not Gil. She considered the possibility that Mavis had murdered Gil, and that Marge had murdered Mavis in revenge. The chart exercise began to resemble her note-taking as Chamber secretary. She got irritated, balled it up and threw it in the wastebasket. Mavis couldn't possibly have wanted to murder Gil, at least not until she'd gotten her hands on his car business.

A new chart would serve a more useful function.

THE PAVILION
MOTIVE (ALL HAD OPPORTUNITY)

Marge	Yes, if she stole $300,000; if Mavis was blackmailing her?
Baumer	Yes, if Mavis was blackmailing him?
Tom	Yes, if Mavis had leaned on him to give bigger cut of proceeds from car deal? Query: tainted meat?

Then again in pencil, for John, "Yes." She promptly erased it.

Quill perused her chart with a sense of accomplishment. She had a very satisfying list of suspects. It was becoming more and more clear to Quill that Mavis had drawn the unfortunate—although still revolting—Keith Baumer to the Inn the same week as she and Mrs. Hallenbeck had planned to stay. She was probably going to hit him up for an increase in the blackmail money. Stranger things had happened before, Quill mused. Far, far stranger things. If she could get Marge and Baumer to answer the right questions, she could solve this case.

The door to her office opened. Harvey Bozzel poked his head inside. "Hel-lo!" he said.

"Harvey? What are you doing here?"

The look (resignation mixed with hurt) on Harvey's face told Quill that this was probably his usual reception, and she hastily apologized.

"Yes. Our meeting was for ten o'clock, right?" Harvey edged into the office. He was carrying an oversized briefcase.

"Oh," said Quill, "The ad campaign for the Inn. I forgot . . . I mean, I'm delighted to see you."

"You'll be delighted to see *these*," said Harvey heartily. "Now, I never got a chance to properly pitch my first and, I believe, my best campaign for the Inn, Quill. If you could sit right here—" He grasped her by the shoulders and piloted her to the couch. Quill sat down. Harvey swept the top of her desk clear and set up an A-frame display. Next to it he placed a battery-operated tape recorder. "I have to show you the print ad first." Harvey flipped the A-frame open. A pen-and-ink sketch of the Inn, which, Quill admitted, wasn't half bad, covered the upper two-thirds of the display.

"What's that big wooden thing in front of the Inn?" Quill asked.

"I'll get to that," said Harvey. "What do you think of the copy?"

Quill leaned forward and read:

THE INN AT HEMLOCK FALLS!

* Four-Star Food (word of Edward Lancashire's intent must have gotten around.)

   * And splendid views (true, thought Quill)

   * Luxury rooms (absolutely)

   * Splendid yews (?)

"There's no yew here, Harvey," said Quill.

"I couldn't think of anything to rhyme with Hemlock," said Harvey, "and it's a mnemonic aid. You know what a mnemonic aid is, Quill?"

"Yes."

"It's a rhyme that helps your customers remember your product. Very important, mnemonic aids. Essential principle of good advertising. Now," said Harvey expansively, "here's the best part." He reached over and turned on the tape recorder. There were a few bars of jazzy music, then a bark, then a "shit" from someone who sounded like Harvey. "The dog," said Harvey apologetically. "I recorded this at home." He fast-forwarded the tape. "Here we go. I picked up one of those musical scores from a catalog. You know, where you can sing the lyrics along to the background music? Sounds pretty professional, if I do say so myself."

The tape played the intro to "Rock Around the Clock." A voice (Harvey's) sang the opening bars, with verve, if not with accurate pitch, and ending with *smash*! instead of the expected chord in A major.

"What's that smashing sound?" said Quill.

"The rocks! You know! On the barn door that squashes Clarissa. Wait-wait-wait. You gotta hear the verse after the intro."

Harvey's recorded voice finally reached twelve o'clock, assured his audience that there were "Rocks! Around! The! Park! Tonight!" and then attacked the verse:

> "When you walk on through that old Inn door
> You'll find gourmet food and historic lore
> And yeah! There's more. That old barn door
> That turned into a coffin floor . . ."

Quill reached over and turned the tape recorder off.

"See, what I figure is this—" said Harvey excitedly. "We get that barn door from the sheriff's office. You know that Tom Peterson would have burned that sucker if Myles hadn't gotten it away from him and held it for evidence? But the publicity, Quill! Think of it! It's the most fabulous PR campaign I've ever . . ."

"Stop," said Quill.

Harvey stopped.

Quill took a deliberate breath. "Now. Explain to me slowly. Myles has the barn door?"

"Evidence," said Harvey, knowledgeably.

"And Tom Peterson tried to burn it?"

"He was upset, he said. Want'd to get rid of the dang thing."

"Hmm," said Quill. "Now that is *very* interesting."

"Am I interrupting anything?" Myles eased in the door. "Hello, Harvey."

"Hi, Sheriff. Just presenting some new advertising ideas to Quill, here."

"And I'm thinking very hard about buying them, Harvey." Quill avoided Myles's penetrating eye. "Why don't I call you later this week, and we can discuss it further?"

Harvey shook hands with Quill and Myles, then gathered up his A-frame and his cassette recorder.

Myles waited until he was gone, then said bluntly, "What did you do last night?"

Taken aback, Quill found herself stuttering. "I went to bed."

"When did you last see John Raintree?"

Quill's face turned red. She could feel it.

Myles shuffled through the papers Harvey had shoved into an untidy pile. He picked up her charts. "Little sketchy," he said, "but not bad. The thing about a murder investigation, Quill, is just one thing. Facts. And more facts. You're right about the bolt and the Seconal." He read on. "I take it Nate didn't make any mint juleps yesterday. Who told you to 'follow the money'? John, I suppose. That's good advice, sometimes, but nothing's as direct and unambiguous as hard evidence." His eyes softened. "Sit down a minute, honey."

Quill sat.

"Doreen found two of the items on your list."

"The bolt? And the Seconal? So it *was* Baumer."

"She found them in John Raintree's room."

Quill sat upright, as though she'd been shot and didn't realize the extent of the damage. "That's impossible. I searched . . ." She stopped.

"I asked Davey to pick John up at a house on Maple about fifteen minutes ago."

Quill stared at Myles. He came and sat down beside her on the couch. "I'm going to place him under arrest on suspicion of murder, Quill. I wanted to be the one to tell you. I didn't want you to hear it over the grapevine. God knows there's enough gossip in this town." He put his arm around her and rested his chin on the top of her head. "I called Howie Murchison. He's going to represent John until we can get an expert in criminal law in from either Rochester or Syracuse. There's a guy named Sam Monfredo who's got an excellent reputation. We'll try and get him." His arm tightened. "Are you crying?"

"No!" said Quill. Myles handed her his handkerchief. She blew her nose. "This isn't right, Myles."

"I agree with you. It's too easy. It doesn't smell right. I swear to you, Quill, I'll do everything I can to keep the investigation open. But there's just too much evidence for me to ignore."

"I'd like to know when you had the time to get it," said Quill bitterly. "You've spent half the time in Ithaca. Have you got a spy here, or something?"

"I much prefer anger to tears," said Myles. "I'm glad it doesn't take you a long time to bounce back."

"You're evading the question. How did you know John was at that house on Maple? Don't try and tell me you put Davey on stakeout. He's on traffic patrol every single day of the week, and he has to count on his fingers to figure out if people are over or under the speed limit."

"No, it wasn't Davey."

"Who then?"

"We've been working with a private investigator from Long Island. Doggone Good Dogs hired him to tail Mavis. Apparently they were pretty convinced that she'd had the money—

they just haven't been able to find it. And they're pretty sure she's involved with something else."

"The tainted meat," said Quill. "You know about that?"

"Edward's been tracking her and Tom Peterson for several months. He alerted the office a few days before . . ."

"Edward Lancashire!"

"Uh, yeah."

"Edward Lancashire's a private eye?" Quill slumped back and closed her eyes. "Oh, my God. We thought he was from *L'Aperitif*. Myles, Meg's been feeding that guy like a king!"

"He's a pretty good guy. It won't hurt him."

"You knew all along," Quill accused, "and you let us think he was the . . . the . . ."

"It was harmless, Quill. And if either Eddie or I had told you the truth, you would have kept it to yourself, and six of your closest friends."

"That's not fair," Quill raged. "It's a chauvinist remark of the most insulting kind."

"I didn't tell Davey, either. He's as upset with me as you are. And only three people knew that John was back, right? Doreen, you. The widow. It's impossible for you to keep anything to yourself, Quill. Part of it's that you're too trusting, and the other part . . ."

Quill's voice was dangerous. "The other part?"

"That you're too trusting." He smiled again and kissed her. "We're going to do what we can for John. And I've got to go now." He eased himself off the couch. "Quill, do me a favor, please. Stop these amateur efforts at solving the crime, will you? Leave it to the experts."

"These are the experts that have John Raintree in jail for murder," said Quill, "based on what?—a bolt, some drugs, a prison term . . ." She trailed off.

As he left, Myles said, "That's the hell of it, Quill. There's always the chance that he did do it."

"Stubborn!" Quill shouted after him as he left. "That's the second thing, isn't it? Stubborn!"

CHAPTER 13

Quill's first impulse was to march down to the jail carrying a sign: FREE JOHN RAINTREE. Maximum effect would have been created by a subheading: "Another Wounded Knee? Police harassment MUST be stopped to preserve our freedoms!" but she doubted Myles's wholehearted support.

She looked out the window of her office; the parking lot was less than half full, which meant Dookie and the deacons had left, along with her chance to nail Tom Peterson.

Her second impulse was to see if Meg was over her prayer breakfast hissy fit. The sooner she knew about Edward Lancashire, the better.

Meg was humming "I Come to The Garden Alone" while chopping herbs. White beans soaking in a crock on the butcher's block, and several pounds of The Sausage gave Quill two clues to her sister's mood: hymn and cassoulet meant a return to the traditional.

"How's by you, Hawkshaw?" Meg scattered the herbs into the sausage and vigorously worked the meat.

"Fine," said Quill cautiously. "How's by you?"

"I felt a definite impulse for Basque, tonight," said Meg dreamily. "It's soothing. Satisfying. Besides, I'm getting tired thinking up new haute cuisine for Edward. It's time to give him the good straight stuff."

"The prayer breakfast buffet was terrific," said Quill. "You heard about the Rolling Moses?"

Meg grinned. "Anybody checked out yet?"

Quill hadn't thought of the effect of the Christian Terrorists on the rest of the guests. "I know Baumer hasn't. Do you think we'll lose people?"

Meg shrugged. "Probably. They've canceled History Days, right?"

"You seem pretty sanguine about this. I mean, between the practical joke about the cancellations and the murders, we're going to be hurtin' turkeys."

"Won't last," said Meg confidently. "I'm guaranteeing you a rave review in *L'Aperitif*. Edward thinks my cooking is fabulous."

This did not bode well for Myles's revelation. Quill weighed the relative merits of Meg's temper tantrum over Edward Lancashire's imposture—although to be fair, he'd never claimed to be anything at all, much less a food critic—against Meg's gradual realization that the *L'Aperitif* review wasn't going to appear. And of course, Quill thought optimistically, the magazine would have to review them sometime; they always checked on the progress of their starred restaurants. It was not at all cowardly, she decided, to neglect to mention Edward Lancashire's real occupation. Diplomacy was the province of successful innkeepers as well as long-lived kings.

"Myles is back early, Meg. The autopsy showed enough Seconal in Mavis' system to sink a tugboat. The stomach contents showed the Seconal was in the mint juleps she was drinking just before the play. He says this shows premeditation."

"Really?" said Meg. "That's interesting."

"There's something else." Quill told her of John's return and his suspicions about the embezzled three hundred thousand dollars.

"Jeez." Meg began stuffing the sausage meat into the casings. "Maybe you're right, after all."

"You think John's innocent, too?"

"I never thought he was guilty. All I said was that your reasoning was screwed up. The facts say John did it. But it doesn't seem to me that murder is a rational act—you know what I mean?" She waved a half-stuffed sausage aloft. "It's like recipes. People think they can learn to cook if they follow a recipe *exactly*. Remember the Armenian dentist?"

"Haaiganash? The one who thought she'd have a more profitable career as a pastry chef? Yeah. You threw her out of the kitchen."

"She didn't have any soul," said Meg. "She thought cooking was a science. She didn't understand the basic ambiguity of cooking. Something goes into the recipe you can't account for. Cooking isn't rational. Neither is murder."

Quill, who thought this was a somewhat dubious simile, ate some parsley.

Meg worked in silence for a moment. "You know what I think?"

"What?"

"You're exactly right about the mint juleps. Find out who made those mint juleps for Mavis, and you've got the murderer."

"I've already decided mint juleps are the essential clue," Quill said testily.

"There's one other thing." Meg took the colander of beans to the sink and rinsed them. "A recipe's a pattern of ingredients. Everything that goes into it reacts so that you get something else. The whole is greater than its parts."

This foray into Jungian theory impressed Quill not at all. "So?"

"So look at everything that's happened since Mavis got here. All of it resulted in murder."

"All right," said Quill irritably. Meg hadn't been out of the kitchen once the entire four days, except for the play, and here she was giving Quill advice about the investigation. "Mavis shows up. She falls off the balcony. Mrs. Hallenbeck says this is a little con game she cooked up, which, for all we know, she's been running for ages. John disappears. Gil drowns in the duck pond, presumably because somebody set a trap for Mavis. Mavis gets squashed under a barn door. John comes back. We learn that Mavis is a blackmailer who's probably been getting money from Keith Baumer and Marge Schmidt for years. We learn that Mavis very probably approached Tom Peterson with some scheme for buying the business, which Marge may have discovered . . . God! It's Marge. It has to be."

Meg looked at her. The water ran unheeded over the beans. There was a distant look in her eye. "Who called up our customers and told them the Inn was closed? Who called the Christian Terrorists to hold an exorcism at the Inn, which can only result in the worst possible publicity for us? Who poured the sulfuric acid around the balcony, which resulted in even worse publicity for us?"

"Marge?" said Quill doubtfully.

"She could have done stuff like that any time these years past," said Meg. "There's something odd going on, Quill. None of this fits. If it were a soufflé, it wouldn't rise more than an inch."

Quill glanced at the kitchen clock. "It's twelve-thirty. The lunch crowd will have left Marge's diner by the time I get there. It'll be a perfect time to talk."

"You're not going to eat there, are you?"

"Do you think she'll try to poison me?"

"Not on purpose," said Meg seriously. "Besides, it's too public."

Quill parked in the bank's lot, near the sign that said "For Hemlock Falls Savings and Loan Bank Customers Only! Violators will be towed," walked to the diner, and peered in the plate-glass window. Two of the Formica-covered tables were filled; the rest were littered with the small detritus of a busy restaurant after a herd of customers has left.

Marge slouched against the cash register, talking to Mark Anthony Jefferson. He smiled at Marge, teeth white in his dark face, and shook her hand with the enthusiasm of a banker happy with his deposits. Quill pushed the glass door open and went in.

"Hi, Mark, Marge."

"Hello, Quill." Mark offered her a prim smile and a genial nod. Quill wondered if bankers took affability courses. *The object of this course is smile wattage: the small depositor, or the cash-poor, should be greeted with the proper degree of reserve, say seventy-five watts.*

Mark shook hands with Marge a second time. "Drop by any time, Marge. Be happy to talk about that transfer. I'm sure I can get that extra point for you. Quill? I wonder if we could meet this week sometime to talk about who is going to take over from John. He's a great loss to the business, and we'll want to be sure that whoever replaces him has the same level of expertise."

Quill muttered, "It's a little soon, Mark," and both she and Marge watched him leave.

"Good fella," Marge said. "Knows his onions. What're you here for?"

"Lunch," said Quill.

"Yeah?" Marge eyed her with a certain degree of skepticism. "Betty!" she hollered suddenly. "You wanna bring out a couple of Blue Plates? Have a seat, Quill."

Quill sat down at one of the small tables. Marge swung a chair around backwards and straddled the seat, elbows on the back. She and Quill regarded each other in a silence that stretched on until Betty plunked a platter in front of each of them. The Monday Blue Plate was meatloaf and French fries smothered in gravy. A small dish of green peas accompanied the platter. Quill took a bite of the meatloaf. Her eyebrows went up.

"Marge, this is delicious."

Marge methodically cut both potatoes and meat into small squares, and just as methodically ate each fork-sized bite.

Quill tried a French fry. Both it and the gravy spooned over the contents of the plate were as delicious as the meat.

Marge swept her plate clean of gravy with a soft roll slathered in butter.

Quill started on the peas. "These aren't canned," she said in surprise. "They're fresh."

Marge burped. She held up a pat of butter; its significance was momentarily lost on Quill. "Good food is good business," she said, "but if you want to know somethin', leave this out of it."

"I'm not buttering you up, Marge. I mean it." Quill hesitated, then said, "I'll bring Meg up here, if you don't mind. She never lies about food. And you'll believe her, if you won't believe me. It's wonderful."

"Huh!" said Marge. Her cheeks turned pink. She grinned and shouted over her shoulder, "Hear that, Betty? Miss Fancy Food here likes the grub!"

"I more than like it," said Quill honestly. "I love it."

"Not everything has to be goormay," Marge drawled.

"It doesn't. Marge, can we talk a little bit about what's been happening over the last couple of days?"

"If you want. Been good for business, I'll say that for it. Everybody comes in here to talk. And when they talk, they eat. Good for Chris Croh, too. Gossip and drink are a good mix."

"How well did you know Mavis? Well enough to know her personal tastes? What she liked to eat, what she liked to drink?"

"What she liked to eat and drink?" Marge, for once, seemed at a loss for words. "I dunno. She didn't much like that French gunk you serve up there at the Inn."

Quill put this down to Marge's automatic rejection of Meg's cooking, and waited.

"And drink? Hell, I don't know that either." Her heavy brow creased in thought. "I know she asked for some damn fool thing at the Croh Bar Saturday night. Chris had to look it up in the bar book, which always pisses him off, and then he couldn't make it because he didn't have lemon or peppermint or something."

"So you've never made a drink for Mavis?"

"Served her beer," said Marge. "What the hell is this about, anyways?"

"Did Mavis take prescription drugs? Or ever ask you for prescription drugs?"

"I don't know what you're gettin' at, missy, but I can tell you one thing right now. I take aspirin. That's it. You ask Doc Bishop, you think I'm lying. I," said Marge proudly, "barf up most anything that ain't natural. Penicillin, and that. Barf it up right away." She patted her ample stomach. "I'm that delicate, Gil used to say to me."

"Did you—correspond with Mavis on a regular basis, say once a month?"

Enlightenment spread over Marge's face like the sun coming up over the gorge. "You mean you wanna know if she was blackmailing me as well as John?"

"You knew about that?"

"Not till she came here. But I had my suspicions. I was Northeast regional manager for Doggone Good Dogs for pretty near five years. Worked my way up from waitressin'. Heard a lot of gossip about Mavis, of course. Never could prove anything. And what the hell did it mean to me, anyways? She was a lot of fun when she came into the district to do the personnel stuff. We'd go out, have a few pops—Mave knew how to have a good time.

"I decided to come back here and open my own business. Didn't much like having to run things other people's way, wanted to do it on my own; I grew up here"—Quill caught the unspoken message: unlike you and your sister, who moved in and tried to take over—"and this is the natural place for me. 'Sides, Betty and I'd been best friends in high school, and you can't run a place like this all by yourself.

"Anyhow, Mavis came to see me just before I quit the company. Said the home office wanted to keep me, and she offered me a raise and all that. I said no thanks.

"Didn't hear much from her a-tall until she hove into town with that Mrs. Hallenbeck. You know what it's like seein' somebody from way back. You may not have been all that good buddies, but there's some stuff to talk about. That's about it."

"Did you know John well?"

"He was after my time at the company. Heard about it, of course. Not every day the company has an employee what turns out to be a murderer. He come in here on his way back from Attica, as a matter of fact." She eyed Quill sharply. "You know about that?"

"Yes," Quill said.

"Headin' on out to Syracuse to look for a job there. We got to talkin'. Don' matter to me a guy that's been in the joint, so we cleared that up right away. We swapped a couple stories about the company. Things changed quite a bit after Armour bought us out, and ol' John got a couple of laughs out of it. I needed someone to do the books once a month; not enough for a full-time job, and Gil, bless his soul, needed somebody, too, and he always liked John and felt he had to make up for his sister bein' a vegetable and all. The two of us offered him wages for a couple of hours a month work. Then you placed that ad in the paper for a business manager, and he just settled in."

"And you know about Mavis being a blackmailer?"

"Do you know that old girl wanted me to come in on it?" Marge's astonishment was genuine. "We got to swapping stories Saturday about how we each was doin', and she said she was on to a good thing. Wanted me to cut a separate deal with Tom if the old lady coughed up the investment, as kind of, what'd she call it, a fee for brokering the deal. Then we'd split it." Marge shook her head. "Mavis couldn't spit straight, much less do a good honest deal. Just wasn't in her nature."

"John said she insisted the letters with his money be addressed to Scarlett O'Hara. Some Southern belle."

"You mean like that movie, *Gone With the Wind*?"

"Yes. Marge? What happened when you refused?"

Marge shrugged. "Guess she talked to Tom herself. I tolt her to pound salt. I wasn't so hot on Gil gettin' out after that. I mean"—Marge colored painfully—"I wanted the old biddy to cough up the cash for the dealership. We had this idea, Gil and me. He'd get enough cash together to pay off that Nadine and he'd come into the business with Betty and me." She cleared her throat with an attempt at carelessness. "Said he'd always wanted a wife who'd help him, you know. Rather than being a drag. Didn't matter I was no beauty queen, he said; I had something better than that. I had some sense." Marge crumpled a paper napkin in her fist and blew her nose. "Said our kids would have some sense, too."

Quill bent her head and concentrated on the meatloaf. She waited a few minutes, then said, "I thought maybe you killed them, Marge."

"Me!" As she'd hoped, Marge's outrage doused the tears as effectively as a candle snuffer. "You gotta be kidding!"

"Well, it seemed logical," Quill apologized. "I mean, all this weird stuff's been going on at the Inn, and Meg and I thought you might want us out of business, and then Mavis shows up and you two are connected in what appears to be a shady deal over tainted meat and . . ."

"Tainted meat?" Marge demanded.

Quill, alarmed, not trusting Marge, stammered, "And I thought maybe *you* thought John would be a good scapegoat, because of what you knew about him."

"Jee-sus Kee-rist and eight hands around," said Marge, appearing to drop the tainted meat issue. "What the hell do you think I'm made of?"

"I didn't know," Quill said frankly. "Any more than I knew what kind of cook Betty is. She's good, Marge. I should have been down to your diner before. It's my fault that I never made the effort. But I will from now on. And so will Meg."

"Good," said Marge flatly.

Quill extended her hand cautiously. "I apologize, Marge."

Marge shook it. Her hands were callused. "Don' mention it."

Quill swallowed the last of the peas, then leaned forward and said, "I've been doing a bit of a . . . well . . . an investigation into this."

"Do tell," said Marge sarcastically. "Myles know anything about this?"

"Yes," said Quill, which was the literal truth. "Actually, he doesn't approve, but Marge, this stuff can't keep up. I mean it can't be good publicity for the town, no matter what Harvey Bozzel says."

"That boy's a bozo." Marge rubbed her second chin with one massive hand. "So now that I ain't a suspect, who is?"

"Keith Baumer."

"That one!" Marge appeared to consider this. "He's an asshole, that's for sure."

"Do you think Mavis could have been blackmailing him?"

"Hell, yes. Wouldn't put it past her. And that jerk's done enough in this life to be ripe for it."

"You remember him from Doggone Good Dogs?"

"What female there didn't!" Marge scowled. "Went after two of my girls in the region. I would have been next, excepting he finally got his ass canned. I'll tell you something, though, never met anyone with as good a taste buds. Good nose, too. Could sniff one twenty-pound pack of froze hamburg meat and tell you what kinda cow it come from."

"John told me three hundred thousand dollars had been embezzled from the company just before the acquisition. He also said you had one of the best heads for business of anyone he'd ever met. Do you know of any way we could find out if Baumer had that money?"

Marge, preening at the compliment to her business acumen, was by now as chatty as Kathleen Kiddermeister's mother, who'd been known to talk to telephone solicitors for hours at a time. "Lemme think on it. To tell you the truth, I don't know what the hell happened to Baumer after the company canned his ass. If John wasn't in the slammer, he and I could probably figure it out. Be best if we knew where Baumer came from, and who he's working for, though."

"He's with some sales convention at the Marriott," Quill said. "His booking got messed up and that's why he landed on us. I'm going over there and see if I can find out a few facts."

"He use a credit card to pay for the room?"

"Traveler's checks," said Quill regretfully. "And Peter deposited them in the bank Friday afternoon, so we can't trace him through the registered numbers. But if I can find his boss at the Marriott, I'll bet I can get a little more information."

"Maybe I'll truck on down to the bank. See if Mark'll let me on to the computer," said Marge. "If the two of us put our heads together, we can figure out somethin'."

"Then you don't think John did it, either?" said Quill.

"Hell, no." Marge reconsidered this. "At least, if he did, he musta had a damn good reason."

"I can't think of any reason that would force John into premeditated murder," said Quill. "I understand—at least I think I understand—the reasons that drove him to the defense of his sister. But this is different."

"It's all different," said Marge obscurely. "And it's all the same."

Quill left the diner with hope burgeoning, if not exactly springing, in her breast. Marge maybe was innocent of involvement with Peterson's scam. Quill would bet a year's income from the Inn that Marge was innocent of murder.

The Marriott lay twelve miles south of town on Route 15, and served both Ithaca and the surrounding small towns. Traffic was light, and it took Quill less than twenty minutes to pull into the hotel parking lot. She knew the manager from meetings of the local Hotel and Motel Association meetings. A big, tall, open-faced man in his thirties—and single. Completely charmed by him after they met, Quill had bullied Meg into attending the next Association meeting with her, only to discover that Sean was quite happily gay. The three of them made a point of getting together for lunch at least once a month.

She asked for Sean at the reservations desk, and the ubiquitous Cornell student trotted cheerfully away to find him. The hotel business would certainly suffer if Cornell ever decided to move to, say, Seneca Falls or Waterloo.

"It's Sarah Quilliam!" Sean greeted her with a smile.

"So it is." She raised herself on tiptoe and kissed him. "How's the hotel biz?"

"Fine. Fine." He looked at her sidelong. "I understand you're making a killing."

"Yes. It's why I'm here."

"Serious discussion? Come into my office, said the spider to the fly." She followed him into the manager's quarters, impressed as usual by the array of computers, the NYNEX phone system, and the middle-class expensiveness of the furniture and carpeting.

"Can I get you some juice? Coffee?" he asked, as they settled into comfortable chairs.

"Not now, thanks. What you can do for me is give me some information about a guest. Or rather, a non-guest."

"Can't do it, Quill." He shook his head, "HQ would send small fierce people down with large weapons to kill me."

Quill pulled her lip. "You've got a sales convention here?"

"It's listed right outside on the welcome board. AmaTex Textiles, out of Buffalo . . ."

"Do you have a list of convention attendees?"

"As a matter of fact, I do. You can pick one up in any of the meeting rooms they're using, and I just stuck one in my file. Hang on a second." He reached one long arm out to a filing cabinet, and within a few seconds, pulled a manila folder out of the drawer. "Here it is."

The names were listed alphabetically. Quill scanned the *B*'s. There was no Keith Baumer listed.

"Are all the convention-goers listed, Sean, including the ones that don't have rooms here?"

"I believe so. But we were able to accommodate everyone that came in from out of town."

"Are you at capacity?"

"About seventy-five per cent. Good for us this time of year."

The address and phone number of AmaTex headquarters was listed at the top of the page. "Can I use your phone to make a call to AmaTex?"

"Of course." He eased himself out of his chair. "Tell you what, I'll go get us some Coke."

Quill waited until his office door swung silently shut behind him. She dialed the 716 area code for Buffalo, hesitated briefly, then the rest of the number.

"AmaTex Textiles," said a young voice.

"Could I speak to Personnel, please?"

"Human Resources, Compensation and Benefits, Pension Funding, or Training Department?" the voice asked.

"Um. I'm checking out a résumé. I wanted to confirm a prospective employee's background."

"One moment, please." Canned music blared onto the line: Tom Jones singing "The Green Green Grass of Home." Quill held the phone away from her ear.

"Department of Human Resources. This is Miss Shirley, may I help you?"

"Miss Shirley, this is Sarah Quilliam. I have an application for employment from a gentleman who lists AmaTex Textiles as a reference." Quill felt a modicum of remorse. If word circulated among Baumer's employers that he was job hunting, he'd probably lose his current job for certain.

"And?" said the insistent voice of Miss Shirley.

"I'm sorry. His name is Keith Baumer. I asked him for a résumé." Quill said hastily, "I wouldn't want you to think he was actively job hunting or anything."

"How do you spell that last name?"

Quill spelled it, waited the requested one moment for Miss Shirley to come back on the line, and smiled at Sean as he came back into the room bearing a tray.

"We have no record of a Mr. Keith Baumer ever being employed by AmaTex Textiles," said Miss Shirley.

"Are you certain?" said Quill. "How far back do your records go?"

Miss Shirley chose to take Quill's question as an affront to the efficiency of AmaTex Textiles' record-keeping. "Our files go back fifteen years. They're computerized. And who is this calling again?"

Quill apologized for the inconvenience, thanked her, and hung up. She turned to Sean. "Have you had any other sales conventions here in the past couple of weeks?"

"Nope. Not a one. What's up?"

"I don't know, Sean. This just doesn't make any sense."

CHAPTER 14

Driving back into town, Quill tried to make sense of Baumer's lie, and couldn't. Had Mavis summoned him to Hemlock Falls to increase the blackmail payment? Was the sales convention a cover for involvement in the spoiled-meat scam? Were he and Mavis partners? Quill worked through this possibility. Baumer and Mavis could have made a practice of bilking inns and hotels of insurance monies. Quill got dizzy at the prospect of a litigious Baumer. She grasped the steering wheel firmly, and forged ahead. If so, there was likely to be a record through the cross-index maintained by insurance companies to track fraud. The person who would know about that would be Edward Lancashire.

If Baumer had made phone calls canceling the Inn business, it was out of malice. Assuming that Baumer and Mavis were partners, why would Baumer murder her? Could Baumer have found out about Mavis' separate deal with Tom and murdered her to keep Mavis from running off with the loot collected from the insurance scams?

This, Quill thought to herself, was pure supposition. Myles was right. What she needed were facts. Who placed the bolt and the Seconal in John's room? Who fed Mavis those mint juleps?

She parked at the Inn's back door, and went to find one of the people who could give her the answers.

Edward Lancashire was sitting at a table in the bar, feet propped up on a neighboring chair, contemplating a painting she'd finished shortly after the Inn had opened. It was an iris, a miniature Dutch variety spread across the canvas in a tidal wave of purple and sun-yellow.

"A lot of relief in that," he said as she sat down. "Retirement must have seemed good to you, then."

Quill blushed. "I didn't realize private eyes were art critics, too."

"I looked at the signature and date before I sat down," he said. "Not too hard to figure out."

Quill laughed. Nate brought her an iced tea and refilled Edward's coffee. "I quit because I peaked," she said frankly. "There weren't any more edges for me to push."

"There was a nice article in *Art Review* about the abrupt truncation of a promising career." He smiled at Quill's surprise. "Private eyes read *Art Review*, too. I don't know much about art . . ."

"But I know what I like," Quill finished for him. "I could feel it, the fact that the work wasn't growing. To stick with it and repeat myself"—she shuddered—"kind of a little death."

His eyes wandered back to the painting. "You may have been wrong."

"I had an idea for the heart of a hybrid tea rose yesterday," she admitted. "A Chrysler Imperial. It's a dumb name for an artificial organism. It was to have been a painting awash with irony and the angst of modern life."

He raised an eyebrow. "Do you miss it?"

Quill nodded. "The thing that's important about the rose is that I'm starting to think in concepts again."

"So it's a hiatus. Not a total break."

"You're right," said Quill surprised. "Although I hadn't thought of it that way. Somehow, that's a very reassuring idea. Thanks."

"You're a nice woman, Quill."

Quill, momentarily tongue-tied, finally said, "Well, you are definitely not a nice guy. How could you trick my poor sister?"

"So Myles told you I'm not the food critic for *L'Aperitif*, incognito."

"Yes."

"I take it you haven't told her yet. My food is still ipecac-free. I'd appreciate it if you wouldn't, at least until this is all over."

"What is it, exactly, that's going to be all over?"

"You mean the investigation?" He sighed, straightened up in his chair, and put his feet on the floor. "I uncover corporate crime. Stolen product. Embezzlement. Industrial espionage. When Armour went through the discovery process to purchase the Hallenbeck Franchise, the auditors discovered a total of three hundred thousand dollars had been drained away from the corporate coffers over a period of time. That's not a lot of money, and normally, in a deal the size of this one, Armour wouldn't have brought someone like me in . . ."

So that's why he can afford the Armani suits, Quill thought.

" . . . but the search for the funds led to something a little bigger than that." He stopped and looked into his coffee cup.

Quill didn't move, afraid that he wouldn't tell her.

"The origin of the three hundred thousand was interesting. Eventually, we discovered that two managers in the meat division had been diverting meat that didn't pass USDA or Hallenbeck's inspection to third-world countries."

"Contaminated meat?"

"Yeah."

"Any idea who's behind it?"

"Maybe."

Edward needed a nudge. "Baumer!" said Quill. "That weasel."

"Keith Baumer?" Edward grinned. "You really have it in for that guy, don't you? I haven't ruled out Baumer. But the scam occurred both before and after his short career at the company. Mavis, on the other hand, knew all about it. We also know that the three hundred thousand passed through her hands, but it disappeared about a year ago. I haven't been able to track it."

"Do you think you're close?"

"To finding the money? My client's not all that concerned about recovering the cash, although it'd help pay my fees."

The Armanis, thought Quill, must be his knock-around clothes. She'd love to see what he wore when he had to dress for the occasion. She examined him through narrowed eyes. Edward, she decided, was not to be forgiven his deception. His client was going to be *very* impressed when she and John turned up with the photographic evidence of Peterson's involvement.

"We haven't enough to convict the people responsible for sending the contaminated food overseas." He paused. "A number of children died after eating the meat. Believe it or not, my client's got a conscience. Not all that usual with big business. It's a bit of a pleasure, working for them. They aren't as concerned with the money as they are with nailing the people responsible for the shipments. And we were all pretty sure that Mavis knew who they were. That's why I came here. I was going to offer her a deal; the company wouldn't prosecute for the embezzlement if she'd give us some names."

"And did she?"

"Somebody took care of her before I could get to her. I tried to set up a meeting with her Sunday morning, but it was hard to find Mavis alone."

"Do you think these people are in Hemlock Falls?" said Quill cleverly.

"I'm pretty close to finding out. But Mavis got herself murdered for another set of reasons entirely. At least, that's what Myles and I think."

"So you've talked to Myles about this. You don't think John was responsible, do you?"

"I don't know," said Edward. "There's a lot of physical evidence against him, Quill. And he had a pretty compelling reason."

"What! The two hundred dollars a month he sent to that miserable Mavis?"

"No. How much did he tell you about the death of his brother-in-law?"

"That guy Jackie?" Quill settled back in her chair, trying to remember. "He said that he found his sister in the kitchen. . . ."

"How did he know she was in the kitchen?"

"He got a phone call."

"Did he ever find out who?"

"He didn't say that he did." Quill, utterly bewildered, pulled her lower lip.

Edward took her hand and held it. "John was the one who initially reported his suspicions of the tainted meat scandal to company headquarters."

It took Quill a minute. She felt her face pale, and withdrew her hand from his. "You mean he was set up?"

"There's a strong suggestion that these people waited for an opportune moment."

"Oh, God," said Quill. "Poor John."

"I have an idea that John suspected it, too. He had quite a bit of time to think about it, in prison."

"And Mavis was the logical informant."

"That's occurred to both Myles and to me."

Quill shook her head. "I refuse to believe it."

"Myles said you were stubborn."

"*Excuse* me!" an outraged voice demanded.

Quill jumped.

Mrs. Hallenbeck stood in front of them. The Glare was in full force. "We had an appointment, Sarah. At five o'clock, for tea. It is now five-fifteen. You have kept me waiting." The old lady's face was pink with outrage. "I went to the kitchen, and waited there, thinking perhaps you were wasting your time with that sister of yours. You weren't there. I searched the entire dining room and the lobby, and I find you here, with this man. Do you have an explanation?"

"I'm sorry, Mrs. Hallenbeck," said Quill. "It's been a long day, and it slipped my mind."

"It slipped your mind! I've mentioned before that I'm considering offering you Mavis' job. Do you really want to jeopardize that offer?" Her eyes filled with sudden tears. "I have something to report on the progress of our investigation."

Quill, whose temper had been rising in a way quite unbecoming to an innkeeper of principle, was disarmed by this last statement. She smiled a little ruefully at Edward, then got to her feet. "Why don't we go into the kitchen to have our tea?"

"The kitchen?"

"None of the guests are allowed there," said Quill comfortingly. "Just our special friends. We'll have Meg make us something delicious. And then we can pool our information."

Meg had been out jogging, and her face was flushed and sweaty. "I just stopped to make sure everybody was here and the breads were rising properly," she said as Quill steered Mrs. Hallenbeck into the kitchen. "I'm going up to take a shower."

"Would you have time to make us some tea?" said Quill. She sent a pleading glance to her sister over Mrs. Hallenbeck's head.

Mrs. Hallenbeck settled herself into the rocker by the fireplace. "We are going to discuss the progress of our investigation," she said complacently. "I will have hot water only. Out of the tap. With a little lemon."

"Oh, okay. I could use a cup of coffee." Meg filled the electric teakettle, then her own espresso machine with spring water, and cut three slices of seedcake. "So, how'd it go with Marge?"

"You wouldn't believe that food, Meg. It's great."

"It is?"

Quill nodded emphatically.

"You're not serious. Jeez!" She bit her forefinger. "How great?"

"Oh, it's quite good," Mrs. Hallenbeck assured her. "Perhaps you could get a job there after the Inn closes."

"The Inn is not going to close," said Meg, astonished. "What are you talking about?"

"Well, that's what I have to report." Mrs. Hallenbeck opened her purse and withdrew her little notebook. "I made notes every half hour. My memory," she admitted, in a rare moment of humility, "is not quite what it was." She cleared her throat. "I sat on the leather couch in the lobby. From there, you can see people going to all parts of the Inn. I thought it would be a good observation post."

"Yay, Miss Marple!" said Meg, by now fascinated.

"As I sat there, precisely fifteen people checked out of the Inn early. They were alarmed by the presence of what one party referred to as 'Devil worshippers.' "

"Oh, no!" said Quill, dismayed.

"You see my concern for the Inn," said Mrs. Hallenbeck. "I did not record the times of those departures. There were," she said frankly, "too many.

"You, Sarah, left the breakfast table at eight twenty-two. You stated you were headed for the prayer breakfast, and I had no reason to assume you were lying."

"Thank you, ma'am," said Quill. The sisters exchanged grins.

"I finished my breakfast and went to the, er, ladies room." Mrs. Hallenbeck flushed slightly. "When you drink as much hot water as I do, it is convenient to be near a WC. It is very good for the kidneys, however. I took up my post at nine-ten. At nine-eleven, three thugs came out of the lounge, followed by you, Quill, and Peter Williams. You didn't notice me, which led me to conclude that my choice of observation post was correct."

"Willy Max and the Jerks for Jesus," said Quill.

"The guests will be back," said Meg. "Just wait for the review from *L'Aperitif*."

"You came back three and a half minutes later. You went into your office. Forty-five seconds after that, Keith Baumer crossed the landing upstairs and went down the hall. I got up to look to see who it was. He returned two and one-half minutes later. Seven minutes later, Doreen Muxworthy went into your office. Eleven minutes later, she left and went upstairs. Then, a young man named Harvey Bozzel knocked on your door and went in."

Meg rolled her eyes at Quill and poured herself a cup of coffee.

Mrs. Hallenbeck primly took a sip of hot water, replaced the cup in the saucer, and took a delicate bite of seedcake. "How am I doing so far?" She twinkled at Quill.

"Go on," said Quill. "I think you may have something here."

"Four minutes later Doreen came downstairs, carrying something in a plastic bag. She went out the front door. About five and one-half minutes after that, the sheriff came in the front door and went upstairs. He was upstairs for about ten minutes. Then he came down and went into your office."

"The bolt!" Meg cried, and took a triumphant gulp of coffee.

Quill yelled, "The pills. Baumer planted the pills in John's room! We have proof!"

Meg howled, "Jeez!" and spat the coffee into the sink.

"Good heavens!" said Mrs. Hallenbeck disapprovingly.

"What?" said Quill.

"Something miserable's in that damn coffee. Darn! I swallowed a slug of it, too. Yuck!"

"Sit down, Meg." Quill pushed her sister anxiously onto a stool. "I'm calling Andy Bishop."

"Why?" Meg demanded.

"Why? There's that damn Baumer wandering around the Inn putting God knows what into things, that's why. He knows we're on to him, Meg. Do you feel all right?" Quill, dialing Andy's number on the kitchen phone, looked worriedly over her shoulder.

"I feel fine," said Meg. She went to the espresso maker and looked critically at the coffee grounds. She held them to her nose and sniffed them, then poked them experimentally with one finger.

"Don't do that!" said Quill. "You're messing with evidence."

"Quill, if it'd been poison or something, I would have been dead by now, and I feel perfectly fine. Don't fuss!" She picked up the jug of spring water she used to make the coffee, unscrewed it, and sniffed the contents. "I can't smell anything. Whatever it was, I didn't get enough of it to matter."

A nurse-like voice put Quill on hold for several long minutes. Suddenly, Meg yawned.

"Andy?" said Quill into the phone. "Could you get the ambulance over here? I think Meg's swallowed something. What? I don't know. Just a minute."

Meg sat down on the stool. Her eyelids drooped. She yawned again, prodigiously.

Quill set the phone receiver on the counter and put her finger into the coffee grounds, then tasted them. She picked up the phone. "Very alkaline. Very bitter. What?"

She heard the sound of a body falling. She whirled and shouted into the phone. "Andy! Get here right away! She's passed out!"

CHAPTER 15

Hair flatter than Quill had ever seen it, Meg lay prone in the hospital bed.

"I'm fine!" she insisted. "I am just bloody *fine* and I want to get out of here!" Her voice was hoarse from the esophageal tube that had been stuck down her throat. An IV drip ran into her left forearm. Quill was convinced that as soon as Myles, Andy, and the nurse were out of the room, Meg would detach the IV and escape out the hospital window. The Hemlock Falls Community Hospital was small, a single-story building tucked modestly behind the high school. The sounds of an evening baseball game came through the open window; to get back to the Inn, Meg would have to cross the field. Quill had taken Meg's jogging clothes and put them in the car, doubting even her sister would have the nerve to stalk across the diamond in an open-backed hospital gown. But she wasn't absolutely sure.

"Just for observation. One night. That's all. Then you can bounce out of here in the morning," said Andy Bishop.

"I didn't swallow enough of that stuff to kill a cat, much less an adult human being," said Meg angrily.

"The mineral water had a four-grain solution of Seconal dissolved in it," said Andy patiently. "You don't weigh much more than one hundred pounds, Meg, and you were dehydrated from running. That's why you passed out, and a patient who's been unconscious has to stay twenty-four hours for observation. Them's the rules." He hung her chart at the foot of her bed. "Why don't you settle down and go to sleep? We'll be right outside, in the hall."

"So you can discuss who dunnit without me? Not on your life." She sat up in bed. Quill folded one of the pillows in half and stuck it behind her back.

"You did not," Meg informed her, "save my life."

"No," Quill said. "But I thought I did at the time."

Meg squeezed her hand. "Were you scared?"

"I was scared." Quill squeezed back. "Not on your account. The paramedics were, guess who?"

"Not Maureen and Doyle?"

"Who else? Maureen's tickled pink. Guaranteed this woman will never ever eat in our dining room, but this is the most attention the Department of Health has paid her in years. She loves us. Oliver kept making noises about how this call interrupted him and his girl friend and giving me hopeful looks as we passed the Croh Bar."

"It was the volunteer firemen you sent to the Croh Bar," said Meg. "You gave the volunteer ambulance a straight donation." She yawned. Quill glanced at Andy, who smiled reassuringly. "Quill, Myles. You know the thing that strikes me about these murders?"

"What?" Myles sat calmly in a green plastic chair near the open window, his arms folded across his chest.

"That they were so inept."

"Yes. There'd be no guarantee that the front loader would actually kill Mavis. The Pavilion was jammed with four hundred people, any one of whom could have noticed a live body on the sledge before the barn door was lowered on to her."

"And the balcony."

"Yes. If Mavis had gone over, she would have landed in five feet of water. Enough to break her fall, not enough to drown her."

"So you agree with me." Meg yawned again, hugely. "And as for me, that Seconal wasn't enough to stun a pig, much less Mad Margaret." Her eyelids drooped.

Myles smiled a little at Quill. "Mad Margaret?"

"We were Gilbert and Sullivan fans as kids. You know Mad Margaret."

He nodded. "From *Ruddigore*."

"Myles?" Meg forced her eyes open. "I'm not going to sleep until you tell me I was right. About who dunnit."

"You were right, Meg." Myles got up and drew the pillow from behind her back.

"Meg was right!" demanded Quill. "What do you mean? Who is it? I thought that I was doing the investigation!"

Meg slid down flat on the bed. She smiled seraphically at Quill. "Mrs. Hallenbeck, stupid." She closed her eyes and was almost instantly asleep.

"Mrs. Hallenbeck?" said Quill stupidly. "You said that just so she'd shut up and get some rest, didn't you?"

"Let's go out in the hall," said Andy.

They left the hospital room and went into the corridor. Quill could see the front lobby from where they stood. Mrs. Hallenbeck, who'd insisted on calling a taxi and accompanying Quill to the hospital, sat upright in one of the green plastic chairs. She was reading a magazine. From this distance, Quill couldn't tell what it was.

Myles leaned against the wall and regarded the elegant figure. "Meg's right."

"You're telling me that an eighty-three-year-old widow who's richer than all of us put together killed Gil and Mavis Collinwood?"

"She's got it right on the third try," said Myles. "And she's not richer than all of us put together. She's living on the three hundred thousand dollars she took from Mavis, who basically stole it from her in the first place."

"You mean because she was part owner of Doggone Good Dogs?"

"No. Because Mrs. Hallenbeck was ripping the company off by selling inferior quality meat to third-world countries. Mavis started her blackmail routine with the couriers, first Jack Peterson, and then, when he was killed, Tom Peterson; she had no idea what she was up against. When the couriers reported Mavis' attempts at blackmail to our lethal widow, Mavis didn't have a chance. Mrs. Hallenbeck swooped in, took the money, and convinced her she'd be jailed for blackmail. The two of them had a brief career bilking various hostelries across the country of insurance monies. That was confirmed this afternoon, too."

"I don't get it," said Quill. "What about the money from the black market sales?"

"Leslie Hallenbeck made restitution before he killed himself. Eddie thinks he knew his wife was involved, and so do I. We talked to John this afternoon, and he helped us confirm it. Hallenbeck didn't have much of an alternative. He couldn't turn his wife of sixty years into the police. But he could give their personal fortune to the parents and relatives of the people who died after eating that meat. And he could take his own life. Which he did."

"But none of this is a reason for her to kill Mavis. They're all reasons for her to keep Mavis alive," said Quill.

"Oh, she needed Mavis to take care of her. But she found a replacement. And when Mrs. Hallenbeck wanted something, she didn't let much stand in her way."

"Oh, no. No, Myles. No."

"Let's go into this examining room," said Andy. He craned his neck; the elderly figure was still there. "She'll wait for you."

Quill walked blindly into the examining room, Andy and Myles behind her.

Myles leaned against the wall with a sigh.

"There were three things that stood in Mrs. Hallenbeck's way to having you substitute for Mavis. Mavis herself, the Inn, and the two people you most cared for, John and Meg. That first night, she summoned Tom Peterson to her room. We don't know what they discussed, but we can guess that it had something to do with the shipments. Peterson left the matchbook there. It's funny about nervous habits. At any rate, after he left, Mrs. Hallenbeck made her first attempt at murder. I had my suspicions then."

"You didn't say anything to me," Quill said indignantly.

"You noticed the scratches on Mrs. Hallenbeck's cheek? She sent Mavis down to find sulfuric acid in the storeroom. John saw her near the kitchen, remember? Mavis poured it around the wrought-iron balustrade. But when the time came to stage the accident, Mrs. Hallenbeck pushed her. Eighty-three's pretty frail, and that ended the first unsuccessful attempt."

"But why didn't Mavis *say* something?" Quill demanded.

"Because Mrs. Hallenbeck could send her to jail. She knew all about Mavis' blackmail schemes. And Mrs. Hallenbeck was right, you know. Mavis was a stupid woman.

"The second attempt you know about. Motive's the most important thing in a murder investigation, Quill—even more than the facts. You were right again—Baumer, Tom Peterson, and Marge all had the opportunity to remove that bolt from the front loader, but their motives were nowhere near strong enough. Mavis was a petty thief, and a small-time blackmail-er. Mrs. Hallenbeck herself would have been a more likely candidate for murder. Baumer denies Mavis was blackmailing him—but I have a strong hunch she summoned him here, just like she contacted John. Baumer makes enough mon-ey so that the two or three hundred dollars a month Mavis demanded wouldn't have proven a strong enough motive to kill. And Marge is just plain too smart to have made an attempt that wasn't one hundred per cent sure. Now, if Marge decided to commit murder, I wouldn't bet on my being able to prove it, but I'd bet a lot on the surety of the victim's demise.

"Mrs. Hallenbeck did get Mavis, of course. The day of the play, Mavis walked from the Inn to the Pavilion with Mrs. Hallenbeck. They'd been in their room drinking mint juleps. Mavis', of course, were laced with the Seconal Mrs. Hallenbeck takes to sleep."

"She said she never takes drugs," said Quill.

"She's a pretty good liar. Consistent, and with an excellent memory," said Myles.

"I checked the prescription register," said Andy. "She's had a refillable prescription for years."

"The barn door. Why did Tom Peterson try to burn the barn door? When Harvey told me that, I was *sure* . . ."

"Edward planted that idea, when the four of you were walking back to the Inn the day of the murder. Guilt's an odd thing, Quill. There could be all sorts of logical explanations about why a shred of clothing was caught on a splinter. But Mrs. Hallenbeck wanted no clues. So she ordered Peterson to burn it.

"So Mavis' death took care of obstacle number one," Myles continued. "Obstacle two was the Inn itself. You leave your guest register out for everyone to see far too often, Quill. She noticed it the morning they checked in. She always gets up early to walk every day. Saturday morning, she got up, took the register, and had time to make enough phone calls to clear the Inn's business for the rest of the summer."

"But a man claiming he was John Raintree made those calls," said Quill.

"You didn't listen carefully to what Dina said, or question your agents closely. Each of the guests who received the call got a message from someone calling on *behalf* of John Raintree. I checked with several of them, and each confirmed it'd been an elderly woman."

"I thought it was Baumer. I was *sure.*"

"Nope. Although you'd given him enough reasons to do it by that time. Then Doreen's latest craze provided another opportunity to wreck the business; Mrs. Hallenbeck got a note shoved under her door, too, of course. All the guests did. And each of the notes listed the 1-800-PRAY toll-free line. Mrs. Hallenbeck called that one right from the Inn. You'll find it in the telephone records."

"And John?"

"She planted the bolt and the Seconal in his room, once you explained to her that this was the evidence the police needed."

"Ouch," said Quill.

"And of course, she knew about Meg's private stock of coffee. While she was waiting in the kitchen for you to show up for tea, she dosed the spring water."

"And Meg figured it out?"

"It was Meg who pointed out that Mrs. Hallenbeck had fixated on you," said Andy Bishop. "And she, of course, found the attempts at destruction both clumsy and ineffectual. The work not only of a rank amateur, but of the kind of pathology that may come with great age."

"You can't tell me that she's senile. Or has Alzheimer's," said Quill.

"No," said Andy. "We don't really understand what age does to the individual, Quill. But there's sufficient research to establish that in some kinds of personalities, age strips away the normal inhibitors to sociopathic behaviors. Mrs. Hallenbeck was undoubtedly as autocratic and self-focused in her youth as she is now; she just doesn't have the barriers to acting out that she had while young."

Quill took a moment to absorb this. "What's going to happen?"

"Eighty-three's pretty old for a trial," said Myles. "And our hard evidence is slim to nonexistent. We have the bolt, which has been wiped clean of fingerprints, but the chain of evidence has been broken. We can't establish for certain that it was in her possession, or even that she was at the park. We have a better chance with the Seconal; she's refilled the prescription a sufficient number of times to have the quantities on hand needed to drug Mavis and Meg's jug of spring water. Again, a good defense attorney would make mincemeat out of the evidence chain. It's all circumstantial."

"The phone calls to the Inn's guests? The call to Willy Max? Those aren't crimes?"

"Malicious mischief," said Myles. "A misdemeanor."

"So what now?" Quill looked at the two men.

"Eddie's client is Mrs. Hallenbeck's son." Andy Bishop cleared his throat. "He's agreed to commit her to a very comfortable institution. She'll be taken care of, confined, of course, and I will see to it that a complete record of what's happened here is in the psychiatrist's file."

"Have you met him, the son?"

"Just talked to him on the phone." Myles's expression didn't change much, but Quill knew he'd found either the man or the conversation distasteful. "He's made the arrangements to have her picked up. Refused to come himself. There's a secure room here at the hospital. Andy's arranged to have her checked in. I'll have Davey at the door until the morning. Just as a precaution."

"Does she know?" asked Quill.

"We were hoping," said Myles, "that you would tell her." He put his arm around her. She leaned into him and closed her eyes.

Quill walked down the hall and sat in the chair opposite Mrs. Hallenbeck.

She set aside the magazine. *Vogue*, Quill saw.

"And how is your sister?"

"She'll be fine. She wants to go home now, but hospital rules say she has to stay. She's asleep."

"We'll go back to the Inn, then? I would like some dinner. It's late. But I suppose someone on the kitchen staff can be gotten up to make something."

"Dr. Bishop is a little concerned about you," said Quill carefully. "He's arranged for you to stay here tonight, too."

Mrs. Hallenbeck smiled. "Such a nice young man. I always find it easier to get along with men than with women, don't you?"

"No," said Quill truthfully. "I think it's about the same."

"I appreciate Dr. Bishop's concern for my welfare. I don't know how it is, but young physicians always seem to take the greatest care of me." She laughed girlishly. "I've been frequently complimented on my state of preservation, I suppose you'd call it. But I would prefer to go back to the Inn. You take such good care of me, my dear."

Quill took a long moment to reply. "The sheriff would like you to stay, as well. He called your son earlier this evening, and your son has made some very comfortable arrangements for you. The . . ." Quill stumbled, "hotel where you will be staying will send a limousine for you in the morning. He's concerned for your comfort now that Mavis isn't here to see to you."

Mrs. Hallenbeck's eyes clouded. Her lips trembled. The light from the lamp at her elbow strengthened the lines in her cheeks and forehead. She leaned forward and hissed, "You have no idea what it's like, being eighty-three. But it will happen to you, dear. Just like it's happened to me."

Once again Quill thought of her own mother, her loving spirit still strong in a body fine-honed by the years.

"No, it won't," she said.

CHAPTER 16

A July thunderstorm was brewing in the west when Quill brought Meg home from the hospital. It just goes to show you, Quill thought, the perversity of nature. After four days of hell, things were looking up. Doreen had seen to the discreet and tactful (she claimed) removal of Mrs. Hallenbeck's luggage and Mavis' effects. The American Association of Swamp Reclamation Engineers had called and fully booked the Inn for a week in August, which would help offset the fiscal consequences of yesterday's guest exodus. Best of all, Keith Baumer was checking out. Quill, heretofore neutral on the topic of religion, sent a prayer of thanks skyward, toward the thunderheads boiling over the top of the Falls, followed by a promise of a healthy donation to the American Association of Retired Persons, whose members had proved the exception to Mrs. Hallenbeck's homicidal tendencies, and who would undoubtedly be back, like the perennials, next spring.

"A trial would have been tough," she said to Meg as they sat in the kitchen watching the rain lash the windows.

"They came to get her while I was waiting for you in the hospital lobby." Meg poured white vinegar for the third time into her expresso machine in an effort to remove all traces of the Seconal. She was not, she'd informed Quill tartly, over her sister's protests, going to dispose of a perfectly good piece of equipment just because an inept murderer had used it in an attempt to kill her.

212

"Not so inept, with two deaths on her conscience. Did she seem . . ." Quill trailed off.

"Seem what? Remorseful? No. Upset? No. Tell me goodbye and thanks for the best meals she's ever had for free? No." The expresso machine hissed, and Meg fussed with it, not meeting Quill's gaze. "I'll tell you what you ought to do, though. Give Myles credit for calling in as many favors as he could to avoid prosecution and a trial. He knows how bad you feel, Quill. A trial would really do you in."

Quill rubbed the back of her neck. She'd dreamed, the night before, of Mrs. Hallenbeck soundlessly screaming her name, over and over again, and of long-nailed fingers shredding the canvas of the Chrysler Rose.

The back door slammed. Doreen stumped in wearing a yellow slicker. Water streamed off the hood. "Wetter'n hell out there," she grumbled.

"I thought this storm hit because you prayed for rain yesterday," said Meg.

"Thought they mighta pumped some of that sass out of you along with the dope."

"No," said Meg truthfully, "I think they added some."

"Wunnerful." Doreen hung up the slicker, tied her apron around her waist, and sat down at the butcher block. "Got time for coffee," she suggested. "Only one room is still occupied. Baumer."

"*Everybody* left yesterday?" said Quill.

"Pret' near. It was the ambl'ance comin' and goin' that done it, I think. When it come for that one"—she pointed an accusing finger at Meg—"lady in one-o-six said if they were tryin' to kill the cook now, it was time to leave."

Quill braced herself. For the past four days, Meg had met prophecies of financial disaster with the sunny confidence of a high-caliber chef cooking for the most influential of captive audiences: the food critic from *L'Aperitif*.

"John will think of something," said Meg. "If not, we can always purchase Harvey Bozzel's rewrite of "Rock Around the Park" and depend on advertising to bring the customers back."

"That's 'clock,' " said Doreen loftily.

"No, it's not," said Meg. "It's sung by the Chili Stompers on the Three Bean label. Quill sang it to me in the hospital. I told her I'd heard it before."

"Sass," grumbled Doreen.

"Wait a second," said Quill. "What about our four-star review in *L'Aperitif*?"

"Now that you know who Edward Lancashire really is," said Meg airily, "I don't have to keep up the charade anymore."

"You thought Edward was the food critic from the very beginning!" said Quill. "You cooked your brains out for that guy!"

"You've got to be kidding." Meg scowled. "I knew the second meal I created that he wasn't any gourmet critic. The man's a peasant. I was just keeping your spirits up by going along with your delusion."

"Admit it, Meg. He had you going."

There was a suspicious tinge of pink in Meg's cheek, but she said obstinately, "I knew all the time."

"You did not!"

"I did, too!"

"Good to be home," said John Raintree as he came through the dining room doors. Myles was with him. Both men were soaked. "Not as quiet as your jail though, Myles."

"Has it ever been?" Myles shook the water from his raincoat and hung it on the peg near the back door. He came up to Quill and stood close.

She looked up at him and touched his cheek. "You're soaked. Meg's got coffee on. You both should have something hot." Myles settled into the rocker, declined the expresso with a grimace, and accepted a cup of the Melitta drip.

John sat on the stool next to Doreen. "Quill, I'm not much good at thanks . . ."

"Neither is she," Meg said briskly. "What we want to know is how all this came down while I was getting my stomach pumped."

"Marge and Doreen," said Myles.

"Marge?" said Quill. "Doreen?"

He shot her an amused look. "What I'm about to tell you is not true. It's a guess. If it were true, I'd have to make a few arrests, for illegal hacking, unlawful entry into private data, and violation of several interstate banking laws." He stretched his long legs in front of him. "I gather that after your visit to the diner, something clicked in Marge's brain."

"It did?" said Quill. "I told her Mavis always referred to herself as a modern-day Scarlett O'Hara. Marge got this funny look in her eye."

"It would have helped Eddie a lot to know about Scarlett O'Hara," said Myles. "Even her son didn't know where Mrs. Hallenbeck hid her money, although he guessed that Mavis was concealing it for her. After you left, Marge hared off to solve the mystery of the missing three hundred thousand. She walked over to Mark Anthony Jefferson's bank. The two of them got on to the phone and into the computer, and they tracked down information that turned most of Eddie's guesses into evidence. Mavis Collinwood, as Scarlett O'Hara and with a fictitious social security number, had close to four hundred thousand dollars in a checking account in Atlanta. The only authorized signatory to the account was Amelia Hallenbeck. Incidentally, six payments averaging twenty thousand dollars each had been paid into the account by various hotel and motel insurance companies over the past eight months. This cross-checks with the information Eddie had from the Insurance Index about fraudulent claims the women had been making."

"So he knew Mrs. Hallenbeck was guilty!" said Quill. "He never said a word to me."

"He was pretty certain she was behind the tainted-meat scandal," said Myles. "And Quill, Eddie wasn't here to solve the murders. He worked for the son. His job was to stop the trafficking in the meat. And I don't blame him for keeping undercover. Confidentiality is the core of his business. Without it, he wouldn't get another assignment."

"Confidentiality," Meg said sarcastically. "Try *deceit*. Try ripping people off. Try *bogus*!"

"I *knew* you thought he was from *L'Aperitif*," said Quill. "Ha!"

Myles rapped the arm of the rocker for silence. "May I continue? Then Marge and Mark turned the computer on to Keith Baumer. They called the American Express Travelers

Cheque operations center in Salt Lake. Mark, in his capacity as bank vice-president, convinced the Fraud Unit there of the urgency of the situation. The Fraud Unit gave them Baumer's address, and the name of the bank where he'd bought his cheques. Marge thought there was a strong likelihood the cheques would have been purchased at the bank where he had a checking and savings account, and she was right."

"And?" said Quill. "Baumer was in on it. I knew it!"

Myles shrugged. "My guess is he's guilty of something. Just what that is, is anybody's guess. His savings account showed regular deposits of amounts varying from three to five thousand dollars, ever since he left Doggone Good Dogs. But I have no official knowledge of this. Baumer doesn't appear to have committed any crimes here. I don't have jurisdiction anyway, so there's no way for me to follow up. I did suggest to Eddie that he have breakfast at Marge's diner this morning. It may be that Baumer was a co-conspirator with Mrs. Hallenbeck—and that Eddie can prove it after he talks to Marge. But the money must have come from somewhere else."

"What do you think, Myles?" said Meg.

Myles hesitated. "I believe that Mavis was blackmailing Baumer, just as she was blackmailing John and Tom Peterson. I don't believe in coincidence. Baumer, Marge, John, and Tom were all connected through Mavis. There are some people who are natural catalysts. Mavis was a catalyst for disaster."

"You put dough into the oven, and heat turns it to brioche," said Quill. "Mrs. Hallenbeck was the heat. Mavis was the yeast."

"Come again?" said Myles.

"Meg." Quill gestured at her sister. "She said murder's like a recipe. The same set of ingredients don't guarantee the same dish. Everyone who came into contact with Mavis ended up with a motive to murder—but only one killed her."

"Thank you, Dr. Watson," said Meg.

"*You're* Watson," said Quill. "I'm Holmes. If I'd had a little more time . . ."

"But it was Doreen, there, who provided the hard evidence in the case," John interrupted loudly.

"You did?" said Quill. "Doreen, how clever of you!"

"That there Willy Max," grumbled Doreen. "*I* din't call him."

"She got Dina to call the phone company and check the outgoing calls," said Myles. "Tracked the call to Rolling Moses to Mrs. Hallenbeck's room."

"Old witch!" said Doreen. "Lied and made me out a fool. Searched her room proper. Found the makin's of them stupid drinks Mavis liked."

"The mint juleps?" said Quill. "Of course! She fed them to Mavis before they walked down to the Pavilion."

"Tied the glasses and the bottles up in a Baggie and turned them over to Davey," said Myles. "Andy Bishop had them tested for Seconal right there at the hospital. I sent the glasses on to the state lab for fingerprinting. I expect that both Mavis' and Mrs. Hallenbeck's will appear all over them."

"So that's the link to the murder in the Pavilion," said Meg.

"Only piece of hard evidence we have," admitted Myles, "and it's circumstantial. There was such confusion the day of the play that no one remembers seeing Mrs. Hallenbeck going around to the back of the shed, much less pulling the hood over Mavis' face."

"Did she confess?" asked Meg.

Quill winced. Myles reached up and covered her hand with his. "Yes. She did."

"What'd she say?" Meg persisted.

Quill answered the question in Myles's eyes with a reluctant nod.

"There's nothing wrong with her intellect. That sets her apart from most murderers I've known." He grimaced. "Almost all of them are borderline intelligence. Of course, my experience has been with street crime. But she shares one characteristic with them. She's proud of the result. Confessions are easier than the public thinks. Most killers can't wait to tell you, once they know we know."

"So she boasted about it?" said Doreen.

"She wouldn't talk to me with witnesses present and until she was sure I wasn't wired. When she knew, for certain, I couldn't do anything with the confession, she told me she'd decided to kill Mavis as soon as an opportunity presented itself—a decision she'd made before she met you, Quill.

"That first night, she and Mavis had planned an 'accident' on the balcony, and as we suspected, Mrs. Hallenbeck tried pushing Mavis over the edge. Mavis was a lot younger, and a lot tougher, and Mrs. Hallenbeck lost that round, as we know.

"After the rehearsal at the duck pond, she took a walk while the others were making plans for the dinner that evening, and removed the bolt from the front loader of Harland's tractor. 'No one really pays attention to the old,' she said. 'We're overlooked, ignored, discounted. I just took advantage of that.'

"She shrugged Gil's death off as an 'unfortunate circumstance.' She knew her next good opportunity would come at *The Trial of Goody Martin*. She poured doctored mint juleps into Mavis. When Harland came around to the front of the stage, she nipped around the back. Mavis was passed out on the sledge. She pulled the hood over her face, hid the dummy, and came around to the bandstand in the space of three minutes."

"It was so *chancey*," complained Meg.

"She said she'd try until she did it," said Myles.

"That ought to help you sleep better, Quill," said Meg. "Good grief."

"Pretty single-minded," said John. "But then, she always was."

Quill sipped at her coffee and said nothing.

"She did give me enough evidence to convict Tom Peterson on several counts of Federal violations." He looked at his watch. "Couple of the boys should be pulling up to that warehouse now."

"And Mrs. Hallenbeck?" said Quill. "Where is she now?"

"It's done," said Myles. "They picked her up this morning. She'll be there until she passes on to whatever justice there is."

"Wow," said Meg. "Now if I just had some people to eat what I cook, things would be back to normal."

"You just wait," said Quill optimistically. "We've never been sunk for long. You the gourmet chef, me the efficient manager . . ."

John cleared his throat. "I haven't had much of a chance to go over the accounts, Quill, but I understand that we've been pretty free with donations lately."

"Donations?" said Quill.

"He means the two checks to the volunteer ambulance fund, the free brandy and *crème brûlée* for the Chamber the night of the dress rehearsal, the full buffet breakfast on the house, for forty-two, Monday morning, the bar bill for the volunteer firemen, and not to mention the fact that we've got no hope of collecting from Mrs. Hallenbeck," said Meg. She grinned. "Maybe we can put a percentage of it on Baumer's bill. Sort of a P.I.A. surcharge."

"P.I.A.?" said Myles blankly.

"Pain-in-the-ass," explained Doreen. "We talk about it, but we ain't never done it, yet."

"Baumer's a P.I.A. candidate if there ever was one," said Quill, "except that he should be charging *us*. I let his wife into his room so she could sue him for adultery with Mavis. Meg poisoned him with various noxious substances, and he got exorcised by Willy Max and the two Creeps for Christ. I can't believe the guy stuck it out this long."

"Leastways Meg can still cook," said Doreen practically. "Long as the kitchen's open, we got people wantin' to eat."

"Well," said Quill, "it could be worse. I thought maybe Marge had made that phone call to the D.O.H., but she obviously didn't, since we haven't seen anything of them."

There was a double tap on the dining room doors. A thin, unhealthy-looking guy in a polyester suit pushed the doors open. He carried a clipboard and wore a New York State badge reading "Department of Health."

"Until now," said Quill, feebly.

"You!" said Meg, "get out of my kitchen." She ran her hands through her hair. It began to flatten ominously.

"Look, lady, I get a call, I gotta show up."

"I got rooms to clean," Doreen said, "Well, two, anyways." She trotted out of the kitchen.

"I'll give you a call later, Quill," said Myles hastily. He disappeared out the back door.

"Rats deserting the sinking ship," Quill yelled after them.

Meg advanced on the inspector, a wooden spatula in one

hand. "I've got the cleanest kitchen in Central New York," she said through gritted teeth. "I hire the best *sous* chef in six states. I use the finest ingredients you can buy!"

"Meg—" said Quill.

"GET YOUR CLIPBOARD OUT OF MY KITCHEN!"

"Excuse me, sir," said Quill.

She nodded to John. John took Meg by the right arm, Quill the left. They dragged her to the dining room. "Just keep quiet, Meg. Everything's going to be fine." Quill forced Meg into a chair at one of the tables and sat down next to her, keeping a firm grip on her arm.

Meg slumped over the table and groaned. "I can't believe that Marge did this! She's a fellow cook! She's a member of the clan! I'll wring her fat little neck."

"Maybe it wasn't Marge," said Quill. "It could have been Maureen, the paramedic. Or her pal, Doyle."

The guy from the D.O.H. poked his head around the door. He held up a small white card. "How often do you use this recipe for zabaglione?"

Meg threw the sugar bowl at him. The inspector ducked. The bowl shattered against the door frame and powdered the inspector with white snow.

"I gotta lot of questions," he said severely, and disappeared once again.

"I see you have company," said Keith Baumer.

Quill blinked at him. He looked different somehow. Cleaner. Less shabby. More . . . elegant. The baggy blue suit had been replaced by a beautifully cut double-breasted blazer and cream flannel trousers, the ash-covered ratty tie by a tasteful silk cravat. His weekender dangled from one shoulder.

"Just stopped in to say goodbye." Baumer extended his hand. Quill took it, reluctantly. Baumer clasped it and wiggled his middle finger suggestively against her palm. "Wanted to thank you for the interesting stay."

Quill, mindful of the courtesies incumbent on innkeepers who strove for professionalism (and of the fact that they were finally going to see the last of Baumer), shook her hand free, but said politely, "I sincerely apologize for the last few days, Mr. Baumer. I'm afraid you didn't find us at our best."

The kitchen door banged open. The man from the D.O.H.

came out with a second recipe card in his hand. "This recipe for mayonnaise . . ." he said. "Oh! Mr. Baumer! How are you, sir?"

"So *you* called them in," said Meg. "It figures."

"At least it wasn't Marge," Quill whispered. "Just keep your lip buttoned. After Baumer leaves we can explain all about him to this guy. Maybe he'll give us a break."

"And your name?" said Baumer to the man from the D.O.H., with a hearty "my man" attitude that set Quill's teeth on edge.

"Arnie Stankard."

"It's a pleasure, Arnie."

"The pleasure's *mine*, sir."

The two men shook hands.

"Stoolie," muttered Meg in disgust.

Baumer lit a cigarette and flicked the match on the floor. "Mayonnaise, zabaglione, and don't forget the Caesar salad, Arnie. Ladies? It's been an experience." He strolled out.

"Arnie," said Quill, as soon as Baumer was out of earshot. "I don't know where you met that man, but we need to explain him to you."

"You mean you know?" said Arnie. "I'm kinda surprised that you do. He always makes such a big deal of traveling incognito. Usually poses as a grungy salesman. Quite a boost for your restaurant, being visited by the food critic from *L'Aperitif*."

L'Aperitif, October issue

from the review column, "Fair's Fare"

Traveling through Central New York is normally a joy in summer. Red-painted barns nestle between neatly bisected fields of rye, and the streams and rivers of this glaciated country flow swift and clear. In past years, come traveling time, those in the culinary know headed straight through this delightful country for the Inn at Hemlock Falls.

L'Aperitif should have taken a detour.

Two years ago, on our first visit to the Inn, Master Chef Margaret Quilliam put on a bravura performance, delivering the Best of the Basque in the most unlikely of places, a rural farming community. Alas! Like the notorious California Chardonnays of '87, Quilliam's early promise has flowered into a disappointing maturity. Although the simplest of American fare—pancakes, omelettes, steaks—remain competently cooked, the complexities of the truly sophisticated chef have eluded the kitchen. The *Pot au Feu* is a trifle bland, the bread textures prey to the vagaries of a succession of beleaguered *sous* chefs, the sausage which made the Inn's reputation, overripe.

(The recent visit of the New York State Department of Health to Quilliam's kitchen is *not* germane.)

It is with regret that we remove our starred rating from the Inn at Hemlock Falls; it is with hope that our demotion is only temporary. We'll return next spring to this delightful part of New York State, to see if Ms. Quilliam has regained her genius for food in the *L'Aperitif* tradition.

The Inn At Hemlock Falls
4 Hemlock Avenue
Hemlock Falls, New York
Fare Score: 0

NEWSWEEK, November issue

Sentenced, for bribery: **Keith Baumer**, 56, food critic for the gourmet magazine *L'Aperitif*. Convicted of accepting a $5,000 bribe in exchange for a favorable review of the trendy restaurant Chien Cous-Cous, Baumer received a suspended 10-day sentence, pending restitution.

TV GUIDE, November issue

60 Minutes—Mike Wallace interviews super PI Edward Lancashire on Doggone Good Dogs and gourmet mag scandal.

ZABAGLIONE
À LA QUILLIAM

Per serving:
one tsp. superfine sugar per egg yolk
one tsp. marsala per egg yolk

1. Beat egg yolks into a thick, even consistency, adding a stream of sugar and wine.
2. Place custard over boiling water; beat it until it foams and thickens. AVOID CURDLING!
3. Serve warm over chilled berries or as is; if creating at tableside pour into crystal sherbet glasses that have been kept at room temperature.

Equipment: copper bowl; wire whisk